MURDER IN THE FOLLY

An addictive crime mystery full of twists

ROY LEWIS

Arnold Landon Mysteries Book 10

Originally published as
A Short-lived Ghost

JOFFE BOOKS

Revised edition 2021
Joffe Books, London
www.joffebooks.com

First published in Great Britain in 1995
as *A Short-lived Ghost*

ISBN: 978-1-78931-983-5

NOTE TO THE READER

Please note this book is set in the 1990s in England, a time before mobile phones and ubiquitous CCTV, and when social attitudes were very different.

Q. What is Man?
A. A short-lived ghost.
—*Roman school text*

CHAPTER ONE

1

They met for dinner in Blagrove's House on the Bank.

Most of the buildings in Barnard Castle dated from the eighteenth century, lining up in Thorngate, Newgate and the lower end of the Bank to present their prosperous, three-storey facades to the steep street above the woollen mills that had been established on the river banks below. Blagrove's House was older than its surroundings, with its worn stone facings and Cromwellian connections, but like all the houses on the Bank it was dominated by the towering, crumbling magnificence of the twelfth-century castle built by Bernard de Baliol, who had lent his name to the town itself.

The Romans had settled here, using a ford upstream from the present narrow bridge which had been erected in 1597, but tourists now came to admire the octagonal Butter Market built in 1747, or the George Hotel for its Dickens connections, before visiting the French chateau-styled Bowes Museum on the outskirts of the town, or the ruins of Egglestone Abbey, founded in the twelfth century for a colony of Premonstratensian canons.

Fred Brierley had not come as a tourist, though his wife had forced him to spend the day on a round of the tourist attractions. She had relatives in Teesdale, and when she heard he needed to travel north she had persuaded him to use Barnard Castle as a base. But this evening was business, and she was staying at her mother's house in Middleton in Teesdale, while he entertained Alan Crickley at Blagrove's.

'Well, I've eaten in worse restaurants,' Crickley remarked with a smile when he saw the menu. 'Good food, sixteenth-century building, a claim that Cromwell stayed here — I don't usually get invitations to such surroundings.'

'From another journalist, you mean,' Brierley replied. 'Well, it seemed the least I could do. I would have been quite prepared to come up to Newcastle—'

'That's all right. It suited me to get away from the office for the day — I had some items to chase up in Durham today and I'm off to Ripon tomorrow, so it's no great problem to drive across to Barney to meet you.'

'I'm grateful, nevertheless,' Brierley said, nodding. 'How long have you been with the *Journal?*'

Crickley shrugged. 'Seven years or more, now. And you're heading for retirement, I gather?'

'It's been a long haul. I'll keep on writing items, of course, as a freelance — I've plenty of connections in the business. And I plan to write a few books. Anyway, the waitress is hovering. We'd better check the menu and decide what we're eating.' He caught Crickley's eye. 'And drinking, of course.'

He made his own mind up quickly, and was given a brief opportunity to study the man sitting opposite him in the first-floor dining room at Blagrove's. Alan Crickley was about thirty-five years of age, slight in stature with sandy, thinning hair worn long at the back. His features were narrow, marked with a certain foxiness, and his thin lips were down turned, as though soured by a life that had not turned out as well as expected. His eyes were a pale grey and quick-moving: he seemed to be alert to danger, habitually edgy, wary in a search for real and imagined slights. There was an angry, sore mark on his chin, as though he had been scratching at it in nervous irritation for some time. He was a quick-tempered, unfulfilled man, Brierley guessed.

Yet Fred Brierley had read some of Crickley's work: it was competent, sometimes sharp and occasionally very sound . . . He was left with the feeling that he would need to tread carefully with Crickley, not least because his task was a delicate one.

When they had placed their orders, Alan Crickley leaned back in his chair with a gin and tonic in his hand and raised his eyebrows questioningly. 'So, Mr Brierley, what's this all about?'

He was clearly not much given to small talk. Brierley toyed with his own brandy and soda for a moment before replying. He shifted his heavy bulk in his chair and stared wistfully at the dark brown skin splotches on the back of his hand. 'As I said, nearing retirement, there are some books I intend writing. The first of them, I'm at proof stage with, but it recently came to my attention that there were aspects of my . . . ah . . . subject's life that hadn't really been covered.'

'Your subject?'

'James Thornton.'

'It was a very public life,' Crickley remarked, with a touch of frost in his tone.

'James Thornton was a very public man.'

'He was that.' Crickley threw his head back and stared at the ceiling for a moment. 'Son of a merchant banker, Oundle, Cambridge, the Brigade of Guards, distinguished war record, Queen's Counsel and head of chambers, CBE . . . very public. But you know all that.'

'There are other aspects of his life that . . . puzzle me.'

'And you are looking for dirt.'

'I didn't say that.'

'No, you didn't.'

'Was there?'

'What?'

'Dirt.'

Crickley shrugged and sipped his drink. He put his glass down as the waitress placed their first orders before them. 'It depends what you mean, I suppose. Anyway, I doubt that I could help you with things like that.'

'Why?'

'Because I've had little interest in James Thornton for many years.'

'He raised you.'

'He adopted me, took me in when I was five. I left when I was sixteen.'

'I suppose that's why I asked to see you,' Brierley said gently, after a little while. 'All I've come across in the public record of Thornton's life is eulogistic: his outstanding career at university, his achievements as a major during the war, his glittering successes at the Bar — it's as though the man was spotless, a paragon, no vices whatsoever.'

'Maybe that's the way he was,' Crickley grunted evasively, and finished his drink.

'Yet you left home, and didn't keep in touch with him even though you both continued to live in the north-east. It's a puzzle. He had no natural children—' Brierley broke off. From the angry glance Crickley flashed at him, he could tell he'd touched a nerve. 'He and his wife adopted you, and then when she died . . . you'd have been about nine—'

'I was almost ten.'

'After her death he continued to look after you at Chester House—'

'Bloody mausoleum.' Crickley pushed his plate aside, the salad half finished. 'And a succession of housekeepers, followed by bloody boarding school. Yes, he looked after me.'

There was a short silence. Crickley's eyes were hard and bitter and he seemed to be thinking over the past, dredging up old wounds and hurts. Brierley waited. The wine arrived and he poured a glass of Chardonnay for his companion. Crickley sipped it, glanced at the bottle.

'Australian.'

'Hunter Valley.'

'You been there?'

'Twice.'

Almost resentfully, Crickley shook his head. 'Done no travelling, me. Stayed in the north-east, in spite of boarding school at Durham, or maybe because of it. You get . . . tied to an area . . . and a state of mind. Still . . .' He sipped his wine again and glanced at Brierley, better humour returning. 'If you're looking for dirt, I think you'll be disappointed. James Thornton was clean as a brass whistle — and just as bright and hard.'

Brierley shrugged. 'I wasn't really looking for dirt. There's nothing in the man's background which leads me to believe he had any dark secrets. But the odd thing is that while it's easy to get hold of the public side of Thornton — much of it is in the public domain anyway, and there's his books as well — I'm still left with the feeling that I haven't got hold of him, do you know what I mean?'

'I know exactly what you mean.' Despite himself, Crickley's fingers strayed to the mark on his chin; he rubbed at it, glaring at his wine glass.

'You said clean as a whistle, but bright and hard as well. What did you mean by that?'

Crickley shrugged. 'Just an observation.'

'He treated you harshly?'

Crickley hesitated; his mouth was stiff as he struggled with half-buried memories. He shook his head. 'I wouldn't say that. He took me in as a child. There was no birching, no beating, no harsh words.'

'So?'

Crickley shrugged unwillingly. 'There just weren't many words at all.'

Brierley waited patiently as his duck was served; when Crickley had helped himself to vegetables with the steak he had ordered, Brierley leaned forward and poured him a glass of the Semillon. 'How do you mean, there weren't many words?'

Crickley sipped at the red wine and rolled it around his palate. He nodded approval. 'James Thornton always liked good wine.' The thought seemed to brighten him somewhat. Cynically, he grinned at his host. 'All right, Fred — may I call you Fred?'

'Of course.'

'Just tell me how the old man comes out with you — the later years of his life.'

'James Thornton . . .' Brierley hesitated, then nodded. 'I think his character comes out fairly clearly. He was a committed, caring person, aware of the wrongs that were heaped upon individuals, careful about the dangers of an overweening power in the State and the Judiciary, concerned to right wrongs where he found them — in short, a man of heart, and feeling, and compassion.'

'And where do you get these views from?' Crickley asked, almost jeeringly.

'From his record. After a successful career at the Bar in civil suits he chose to move sideways and in a sense downwards; he represented a number of defendants on serious charges in criminal cases and discovered a flawed system. Thereafter, he left his practice as such and began a series of campaigns, to right perceived wrongs.'

'He became a media man.'

'I suppose one could say that. He gained a deal of publicity for his views, attacking mistakes made by the judges, exposing the idiocies of successive home secretaries, insisting on rehearings and appeals for several men who had spent years in jail, unjustly. And finally, he seized upon a whole succession of forensic mistakes perpetrated by Dr Steven O'Connor, and after five years campaigning he succeeded in having a number of convictions overturned. And he was still campaigning against injustice when he died.'

'Ah yes, the knight on a white charger.' Crickley was silent for a while as he cut into his steak and sipped his wine. Brierley sensed it was a moment to keep quiet, as Crickley's mind churned and his eyes sparkled with a confusing resentment. At last, he spoke.

'You're all the same,' he said, wagging his table knife in Brierley's direction. 'You look at what he did but don't see it in the round: you're dazzled by the flair and ignore the hollow foundations. Let's take the O'Connor thing, for instance. Tell me what you know about it.'

Brierley shrugged. 'O'Connor was a respected pathologist; he'd worked closely with the police for years in the Midlands and no questions had been raised. And then Thornton defended a young man called Cunliffe, and cast considerable doubt on the forensic evidence that was used by the prosecution. Cunliffe went inside — and that was when Thornton started his campaign. Not just for Cunliffe; there was Weaver, the Midland arson case, the Annette Wentbridge killing—'

'Ah yes,' Crickley sighed, 'tell me about that.'

Brierley sipped his wine and eyed Crickley.

Resentment and bitterness was building up in the man, and it puzzled Brierley. 'It was a well-reported case.'

'A fourteen-year-old schoolgirl who was raped and murdered.'

'That's right. A man called Simon Ford, a teacher at the school she attended, was arrested and convicted of the murder. He had a rough time in prison—'

'Like all rapists.'

'Or *alleged* rapists. Thornton interviewed him in prison and became convinced that he was innocent.'

'And started his own investigation.'

'Correct. He started investigating the whole thing, found Dr O'Connor was involved, and spent five years digging away, pushing, threatening, raising public awareness of the problem, until finally there was an inquiry.'

'Not just into the Simon Ford case,' Crickley sneered. 'No, but into a number of convictions where Dr O'Connor had been used to produce forensic evidence. And it finally came to light. The police themselves had not been blameless—'

'I know, the usual thing, a certain amount of withholding of evidence, using doubtful confessions and so on . . .'

'Yes, but the main problem was that O'Connor had come to see himself as some sort of avenging angel. He had listened to the police when they arrested a suspect and talked to them about the possible guilt of the man they'd fixed on. He had then convinced himself that it lay in his hands alone, when the case was weak, to bring the guilty to justice. He began to manufacture evidence, cook reports, perjure himself in the evidence he gave as an expert witness. He suffered a breakdown in the end. And Thornton was shown to have been justified in his campaign. Pardons were issued. Simon Ford went free after five brutal years in prison . . . convicted rapists and child-murderers need protection within the prison system . . . the convictions in which Dr O'Connor had been involved in giving evidence were deemed to have been wrong. Or "unsafe" as the back-pedalling Appeal Court described them.'

There was a thin line of perspiration on Brierley's brow. He was aware of Crickley's cool amusement at his impassioned statement and he felt a mild anger at himself as he brushed his fingers across his forehead.

'That's fine,' Crickley remarked. 'The Appeal Court backpedals. And James Thornton comes out as a hero.'

'Some would say that. It was his last campaign, of course, because shortly after that he experienced a stroke, and was incapacitated for two years before he died: Brierley hesitated. 'Did you go to see him in that period?'

'Why should I?' Crickley demanded, bridling.

'You were his adopted son.'

'Son!' Crickley snorted. 'That's a laugh!' He leaned back in his chair and stared at Brierley contemptuously. 'You know, when you talk to me about Thornton it's as though you were talking about a stranger, as far as I'm concerned. You all do. All this public face: the good deeds, the upright man, the seeker for justice, the champion of the underdog, the righter of wrongs. Yes, maybe the old man was all of those things. But there was another side to it all, you know.'

'How do you mean?'

'James Thornton — he had a problem, you see. He looked out at the wide world, gazed above the parapets of Chester House and saw all the evils writhing in that world, the corruption in the courts, the covering up of errors by the Establishment, and he rode out to do battle.'

'So?'

'What he never did was to look behind him, below the parapet, *inside* Chester House.'

'What do you mean?'

Crickley stared at him owlishly for a moment, as though uncertain whether he should continue. He shrugged. 'Oh, I know there were people out there in the prisons who deserved his help — here, what have you got in your briefcase?'

Confused, Brierley said, 'Draft proofs, some photographs for the book, additional items—'

'OK, let's have a quick look at them. The photographs.'

Crickley pushed aside his half-eaten steak and cleared a space for the photographs that Brierley produced. 'Right — now who's this?'

'It's Weaver — after his release from prison.'

'And this one will be the Midlands arson group.'

'That's right.'

Crickley shuffled through the photographs. He picked out one of a young girl, freckled face, smiling crookedly, a school photograph. 'This one will be Annette Wentbridge.'

'That's right.'

'And this?'

Brierley squinted at it. 'Simon Ford, when he was still teaching. Two years before he was accused of the Wentbridge murder. I couldn't get one of him after his release from prison. He was granted a degree of privacy at his request: the authorities were embarrassed enough to go along with that after Thornton's exposure of them.'

Crickley grunted. 'No doubt he'd have changed after five years inside. Perhaps the compensation will have cheered him up, on the other hand. Ford . . .' He stared moodily at the photograph. 'OK. Now let me ask you this. Thornton helped all these people, guys like this character Ford, but why is it he couldn't look inward to his own home, his own family and give help there?'

'I don't understand.' Brierley replied quietly.

'You asked me if there was any dirt. No, there wasn't,' Crickley said bitterly. 'But there was disregard, lack of thought, no recognition that there were problems closer to home that he could have solved. He stretched out a hand of friendship to all these people, but chose not to see there was a need in Chester House. He worked his guts out for strangers and wouldn't lift a finger for those whom he ostensibly loved and lived with. I'll make no bones about it, Fred — it was a cold house.'

'I wasn't aware of that.'

'Who was?' Crickley sneered. 'Everyone was wrapped up in the warm glow of the public image. But let me make this clear to you. James Thornton's wife — the woman who adopted me — died of loneliness. She shrivelled up inside, over the years. They were blank times, when you could hardly hear the whisper of her feet in the house, when she barely saw him, when he rarely spoke to her more than once a week. He paid no more attention to her over the years than to a door-mat. She died in loneliness, not having experienced warmth or affection for most of her marriage. And when she died, there was no longer anyone to give a ten-year-old boy any love, affection . . . or even time.' Crickley gritted his teeth in sudden anger. 'That's what I resented most of all. The time.'

'His campaigns—'

'Took up all his life.' Crickley took a hefty swallow of wine and poured himself another glass without asking Brierley's permission. 'It left him nothing to give at home.'

'It couldn't *always* have been like that,' Brierley protested. Crickley pulled a face at him over the glass, and shrugged. 'I can't really remember what it was like the first few years after they took me in — except that my memories of my adopted mother are that she gave me warmth and affection. But also there was a great sadness. I remember nothing of James Thornton himself — he was hazy . . . there, but not there, if you know what I mean. And later, as I grew older, I realized he really lived a separate life from us.'

'He resided at Chester House.'

'Oh, yes, he lived there. But when he was in the house I never saw him.'

'But he adopted you as his son—'

'I've thought often about that. I think it was, maybe, convenient.' Crickley smiled cynically. 'He had worlds to conquer, battles to win. A child in the house could keep his wife occupied. No need to impinge much on his time. And it would give her something to occupy herself with — give him more freedom to pursue the things that really interested him.'

Brierley was silent. Crickley was finishing the bottle of wine.

'And remember, I was eight when my adoptive mother died, and suddenly what security that had come to me was shaky again. I had no one to turn to for support at a traumatic time. No friends in that bloody mausoleum . . . '

'But at school—'

'I was sent to a good school, naturally. Part of the image. And at school, when I got into trouble, oh, it was all sorted — discreetly, of course. There was a case of theft—' Crickley grinned, but there was a hard edge of cynicism to his mouth. 'The social workers these days would say I was probably stealing love, wouldn't they? But it was all sorted, brushed over between Thornton and my housemaster. I mean, we can't have scandals in the Thornton family, can we? But, you know, he never even said a word to me about it, damn it. It was as though it had never happened. But it was part of the pattern — I just never *saw* him!'

'That's why you left Chester House at sixteen?' Brierley asked softly.

'That's exactly why. And I never went back. Never even saw him again.'

'You were named as his son in earlier editions of *Who's Who*. Later—'

'I was deleted. I let him down, you see — never mind the fact that he let me down, when I was vulnerable, plagued with teenage problems, adrift emotionally. I'd let him down, embarrassed him by leaving, going my own way, so he simply . . . expunged me, is perhaps the best way to put it. Wiped me from his life. But that was all right with me. We grow up quickly, and we all build a carapace in adulthood, don't we, Fred?'

'It's sometimes necessary,' Brierley agreed gently. Crickley grunted. 'I built mine. But he didn't care for my independence, so he simply removed me from his life. Deleted me from *Who's Who* — as if it was important! And, incidentally, made no mention of me in his will.'

'I wondered about that,' Brierley said. 'I thought maybe there had been some other private provision.'

'Forget it.' Crickley shook his head in frustration, angry that he had allowed emotion to spill out from him when he had controlled it over the years. 'Let's put it like this, Fred. Get on with your book. Write about the great man. But don't put me in it. I was never a part of his life when I was alive, and there's no reason why I should enter it now, in your book. The past is dead and gone—'

'There's a record to be put straight.'

'The hell with that. How important is it, anyway? He was a righteous man, a do-gooder who was always right. Always damned right. Why spoil that image now? Why blot the perfect copybook? Just leave it, Fred, leave it.'

'I—'

'Bloody good wine, this,' Crickley interrupted, raising the glass to observe the rich red colour. 'Maybe I ought to get a few bottles of it in, to use when I'm interviewing awkward customers, the way you've been doing. Certainly gets a man talking, doesn't it?' He grinned, mirthlessly. 'It gets a man to produce all sorts of emotional crap!'

'That wasn't my intention—'

Crickley laughed unpleasantly. 'But you'll use it in your book, won't you? — in spite of what I say. That's the journalist in you. But there's the ink of malice in my veins too, Fred, you know that? Years in the game, it gets to ooze into you without you knowing it. You think I'm resentful about Thornton? About the big image, and the hollow reality? About the man who befriended the underdogs, and who made dogs of his own family? Damn *right* I am!'

He glared at the empty glass in his hands. 'But it's not just resentment. It's the thought that he couldn't always have been right — not always. And one day, maybe, I'll put my finger on something that'll show the world there were times when James Thornton was a hollow man — a man of no substance. A man who could make a bad mistake.'

'He did many good things,' Brierley replied, defensively.

'Don't deny it. But was never wrong?' Crickley shook his head. 'Against nature. One day, maybe I'll find something—'

'And then?'

There was an unpleasant twist to Crickley's mouth. 'What else is there to do? You learn it, as you know, in the hard world of journalism. James Thornton is nothing to me. And if I ever do come across something that'll dent his reputation — I'll do it. Like the best of the press guttersnipes, I'll go for the jugular.' He scratched nervously at the mark on his chin and contemplated his empty wine glass. 'So, as they say, watch this space.'

Brierley ordered another bottle of Semillon.

2

Karen Stannard was beautiful.

She came into the conference room with a swinging, elegant stride, just three paces behind Simon Brent-Ellis, the director of the Department of Museums and Antiquities, and she took her seat to his left and slightly behind him, at the table on the raised dais. While Brent-Ellis shuffled the papers in front of him she crossed her legs smoothly and viewed the group in the conference room with a half-smile, confident, poised and at ease.

'Pity about her,' Jerry Picton muttered.

'How do you mean?' Arnold Landon asked.

'You'll find out.'

As Brent-Ellis shuffled his papers irritably, seeking the agenda for the meeting, Arnold, in common with most of the men and all of the women in the room, studied the new arrival. She was tall — about five feet eight, he guessed and slender in build. Her hair was a russet colour, probably natural, and the shaft of sunlight from the window behind her caught stray gleams of gold, backlighting her with a halo effect. Her skin was tanned, her features perfectly formed, high cheekbones, wide, red mouth, slightly slanting eyes whose colour challenged description.

She sat very erect with her head up and shoulders back, emphasizing the line of her breasts, and her glance swept the room; below the tabletop the audience caught a glimpse of thigh where her short skirt had ridden up, and could see that her legs were long and slim and bare. She was dressed in a dark grey suit, beautifully cut, and a white blouse caught at the throat with a discreet cameo brooch. She was confident, cool, aware of the impact she was making — and impossibly beautiful.

Brent-Ellis grunted in satisfaction.

'Got it,' he said and glowered around the room as though it was the fault of the departmental gathering that he had mislaid the order of his papers. Then he glanced at Karen, and his mood changed. He smiled, meltingly. Arnold had never seen Brent-Ellis melt before.

Arnold wondered what Mrs Brent-Ellis would have thought about that look: over the years she had kept a tight rein on appointments to the department, making sure dragons rather than sylphs remained the order of the day: her husband's gauleiter-like secretary was a case in point. But Mrs Brent-Ellis seemed to have slipped up on this one, even if she was Chair of the Appointments Committee.

'He's hooked,' Jerry Picton whispered. 'Poor, misguided bastard.'

'I've called this meeting today,' Brent-Ellis began, stroking his moustache self-consciously, 'as a sort of getting-to-know you meeting. As you'll all be aware, a great many changes have occurred during the last few months. The capping of government grants, the recession, the changes in function for the Education Department, among others, the new roles that local authorities are called upon to undertake, all this has meant a reorganization of the staffing throughout County Hall.'

He paused and glanced about him vaguely. He was dressed as flamboyantly as ever, in his cream suit, bright red flowered tie, patterned waistcoat and blue shoes, but there was nothing flamboyant about Brent-Ellis's personality. He disliked meeting people except on the golf course, and gatherings of this kind would not be to his liking. He seemed lost now, wishing he was anywhere but here, but then Karen Stannard uncrossed her legs. The sibilant whisper of her skirt drew his attention and someone at the back of the room sighed. Brent-Ellis stared, and smiled again, nervously, hurried his glance away from Karen Stannard's thighs and went on.

'This reorganization has meant a considerable movement of staff into this department. We are retaining our name for the sake of simplicity — but our functions are somewhat widened with the closing of the Leisure Department. Some of the staff affected have opted for early retirement, of course, but since the authority is unwilling to adopt a redundancy policy, except where absolutely necessary, it has been decided that this department — Museums and Antiquities should be expanded. To all those — and there are twelve people in all — who have now joined us by transfer, I offer a warm welcome.'

He shuffled the papers in front of him with shaky fingers as he turned and nodded to the goddess on his left.

'And in particular, I extend a welcome to Karen Stannard. She will be known to some of you because in her professional work at the university she has come into contact with activities in both the Education Department and the Antiquities area. With the expansion of the Museums and Antiquities' responsibilities it was decided that it would be sensible to strengthen the senior management of the department.'

He glanced up from his notes and surveyed his kingdom. 'There is only so much one man can do,' he remarked and nodded his head, smiling in self-deprecation. He seemed unaware of the vast silent sea of indifference that greeted his admission.

'The post of deputy director of the department was advertised—'

'Should have been done by internal transfer,' Picton grumbled *sotto voce*.

'—and out of a strong — I may say, very strong — short-list, Karen was chosen.' Brent-Ellis peered at the papers on the table in front of him. 'She comes to us from a well-qualified background. A first degree at Nottingham University, a post-graduate programme at Cambridge, a lectureship at Newcastle, and authorship of several well-regarded papers on Mesolithic sites. She is a contributor to a number of archaeological magazines and has produced a book on *Chambered Cairns in the Northern Isles* — and all by the age of twenty-eight!'

Arnold glanced at Karen Stannard. She was looking at the director and smiling, but there was a certain edge to the smile suddenly. Arnold guessed she would already have summed up Brent-Ellis, maybe recognized him for the politically connected buffoon he was. It did not augur well for Brent-Ellis, he suspected: obviously charmed by Karen Stannard he had probably not yet realized he might have a tigress in his management team.

'So,' Arnold murmured to no one in particular, 'another historian in the department.'

Picton snickered. '*Herstorian,* you mean.'

Puzzled, Arnold glanced at him. Jerry Picton was one of the new arrivals in the department, a transfer from Education. A small, middle-aged man with a badly pitted skin and narrow, mean eyes, he was reputed to have a sharp tongue and a disinclination to work. Arnold had heard he was a mutterer in corners, a fomenter of discontent, and a man to be avoided in general. He had not chosen to sit next to him in the conference room.

'At this point, having introduced Miss Stannard,' Brent-Ellis was saying, 'it might be opportune to invite her to say a few words.'

Her smile was dazzling. She rose effortlessly in a swaying, elegant movement. Her voice was richly modulated, slightly throaty and low in register. It made Arnold think of dark, smooth chocolate.

'A very few words, indeed. I may say I look forward to working in the department. I am sure you will all bear with me in these early weeks. I have a great deal to learn — and I'm not afraid to admit it. I am confident, nevertheless, that I'll have your support in making my learning curve as short as possible. Mr Brent-Ellis has already put me on the . . . er . . . right track—' she flashed a demurely grateful glance in his direction and Brent-Ellis positively preened — 'but I am sure we will all work closely, and effectively, together.'

There was a rustling murmur among the men in the conference room: it had something to do with the use of the word 'closely'. Simon Brent-Ellis beamed, almost beside himself with pleasure and pride at having appointed such a devastating creature.

'Fine. I'm sure all will be . . . sweetness and light, hey?' He giggled, an embarrassingly middle-aged man making a fool of himself before his colleagues. 'Now then, preliminaries over, there are some announcements to make. With the advent of new people into the department it has become necessary to make some changes in duties. I have discussed these with K — Miss Stannard, and we have reached agreement on redispositions.' He hesitated and glanced at her uncertainly. 'Perhaps you'd like to take over at this point?'

Karen Stannard nodded and favoured him with a flash of her white teeth. She rose again, and all eyes fixed upon her. 'I have a list here of departmental staff and their duties. Since I am new here, and can't yet put faces to names, it would be of great assistance to me if, when I call out your name, you would stand.' There was a rustling among the seats again, a murmuring of surprised discontent.

'Like being at bloody school,' Picton whispered.

Karen Stannard raised a perfectly arched eyebrow and smiled. 'Mr Coulson,' she called in her chocolate voice.

Alan Coulson, an elderly man employed in the Records Section, stood up reluctantly. She smiled at him and a faint touch of colour came to his face. 'Thank you,' she said, seeming to mean it personally. 'You are one whose duties remain as they are . . .'

The names were called, the men and women stood up.

Brent-Ellis seemed bored and his glance wandered to the windows, only to flicker back from time to time to Karen Stannard's legs. Arnold was left with the impression that his habitual concentration upon his golfing achievements was being eroded by her presence.

'Mr Kirkby.'

The man seated in front of Arnold rose to his feet. Arnold did not recognize him, but there were several newcomers he had not yet had an opportunity to meet. Kirkby was of medium height, slimly built, with narrow shoulders and a bald patch at the crown of his head. The hair he had retained was starting to grey and the man was slightly hunched, nervous and defensive in his stance as he faced the woman on the platform.

'Ah, Mr Kirkby — you're one of the newcomers,' Karen Stannard said, eyeing him shrewdly.

Kirkby shuffled nervously. 'That's right. I've been working in the Education Department.'

'How long were you there?'

'Last two years.'

Arnold was surprised. He had heard that recent entrants to the Education Department had been shuffled off as the first response to financial cuts. Kirkby must have been one of the lucky ones.

Karen Stannard was looking at her notes. 'Ah, yes. Cutbacks on Schools Section administrative staff with the opting out arrangements. You didn't take the option of redundancy.'

'No,' Kirkby said shortly.

'Most who were offered the chance decided to take the money and run, since it was regarded as a generous package,' Karen Stannard commented, and smiled. Kirkby made no response. The smile tightened on her lips.

'And your background . . . ?'

'A general degree in English, History and French. Bristol. A few years' teaching. Then administration.'

'I see. Well, Mr Kirkby, there are still some concerns, shared by Mr Brent-Ellis and myself, about exactly where you'll fit in at Museums and Antiquities, but be assured we'll be looking constructively at the situation. Meanwhile . . . Mr Landon . . . ?'

As Kirkby re-seated himself Arnold rose hurriedly to his feet. The chair he had been sitting on turned over with a crash. He bent over to retrieve it, and cannoned into Kirkby's chair, pushing him forward. Red-faced, Arnold apologized, set his own chair upright again and someone in the conference room laughed. He looked up towards the dais and Karen Stannard was regarding him coolly.

'All right now, Mr Landon?'

Arnold was not alone in catching the tinge of amused contempt in her tone. There was a sniggering sound at the back of the room. Arnold nodded. 'Yes, thank you.'

Her glance held his for several seconds. She stared at him, almost as though she was weighing him up in her mind. The glance was almost competitive, containing a hint of antagonism, and Arnold was puzzled. Then her glance dropped,' she consulted the papers in her hand. 'Your assignments are currently rather . . . widespread.'

Blame the director, Arnold thought: if there's a problem to be faced, he hands it over to Arnold Landon.

'Some of these responsibilities would seem properly to belong to the . . . er . . . senior executive area,' Karen Stannard commented. Her eyes fixed on his challengingly. 'Is that how you would see them?'

Arnold shrugged. 'I haven't thought about it. I deal with those files that are handed to me.'

Brent-Ellis shifted in his seat; for a moment he seemed vaguely uncomfortable.

Karen Stannard smiled thinly. 'Some changes will be necessary, I think. Both the director and I are of the same mind. I propose to take over some of these activities myself.'

Good for you, Arnold thought warmly. He glanced at Brent-Ellis: the director was nodding agreement, his brow furrowed in a pretence of deep consideration. He seemed not to realize the implied criticisms that lay behind the situation.

'That means,' Karen Stannard continued, 'you will be able to concentrate on other matters. There is one in particular which is arising, in relation to the Viking Research Trust and Ridgeway Manor — are you familiar with it, Mr Landon?'

'Not entirely. Some of the newspaper publicity—'

'Quite. But one shouldn't believe all one reads in the newspapers.' She glittered her teeth at him, almost wolfishly. 'Perhaps you would make an appointment to see me to discuss it . . . Unless, Director, you wish to deal with this one yourself . . . ?'

Brent-Ellis started in his chair, kicking one foot forward in a surprised reaction. 'No, no, carry on.' He waved his hand airily, not even aware of the issue she was talking about. 'You're the deputy, after all.' He glanced proudly around at his audience for approval, as though he had made a telling point.

Her eyelids fluttered. 'Thank you, Director.'

Chocolate coated with ice.

'Bitch,' Jerry Picton muttered and Arnold took his seat again.

* * *

It was several days before Arnold was able to confirm an appointment with Karen Stannard. He had some work to do cataloguing some recently discovered Roman artefacts with the assistance of the site curator of the dig at Ogle and it kept him out of the office for three days. When he got back, he found that the deputy's diary was full for most of the following week: there had been a constant stream of colleagues to her door. Arnold gained the impression some of the visits were due to curiosity, and occasionally lust, but what was significant was the attitude of those men who had been to see her. Invariably they returned somewhat chastened, though silent about their individual experiences. They did not seem to want to discuss the meetings.

'So you've not managed to get in there yet?' Jerry Picton leered, as he leaned against the doorjamb of Arnold's room.

'Where?'

'Come on! Into a headlock with our luscious deputy director! Keeping you at arm's length, is she? I thought she displayed a certain warmth towards you at the departmental meeting the other day.'

'I'm booked to see her Tuesday.'

Picton grinned. 'Well, don't let the old hormones run riot until then. It will be a waste of time.'

'I don't understand.'

Picton's mean mouth twisted unpleasantly. 'You're an innocent abroad, man. Haven't you seen how she's already emasculated the department in just these last few days?' He hesitated, peering at Arnold as though he was puzzled. 'Don't you even know how she got the job?'

'I've heard nothing about it. As a historian, she's well qualified—'

'I told you — she's a *herstorian.*'

'I don't follow—'

'My God, haven't you heard about her? She's so damned politically correct it's unbelievable.' He giggled squeakily. 'When I was in the Education Department the story was that she'd caused a row in the university over the word menstruation — she insisted it had to be described as *misstruation.*'

'You can't be serious—'

'It's what I heard, I'm telling you,' Picton protested, mockingly. 'But you mark my words, there'll be a clamp-down in the DMA over what language is politically correct and what isn't. She had quite a reputation for it at the university. Leader of the women's movement for equality in education — that sort of thing. She started like that, and then it got out of hand, apparently. The vice chancellor was not displeased when she applied for the deputy's job here. And she's got a spine made of ice. She can cut a man down to size just by freezing him with a look. That's how she got the job.'

'I don't follow—'

'She's a raving lesbian, man!'

Impatiently, Arnold slammed shut the minute book he had been reading. 'I don't see that comments like that—'

'Landon, you make me almost sorry for you,' Picton sneered. 'Our revered director — we all know what an idiot he is. We all know that he got his job through political chicanery. His wife is a powerful woman — but she's also a careful one. I've heard all about how she makes use of her position as a councillor to make appointments to this department. And I've also heard that she keeps an eagle eye on her old man. So, do you really believe she would allow a beautiful woman to act as deputy to her husband, allow a close working relationship of that kind, unless she was absolutely sure there'd be no problems?'

Arnold's mouth set in disapproval; yet he knew there was something in what Picton was suggesting. 'I don't see it's any of my business how she got the job,' he remarked.

'A job that should have gone internally?'

Arnold shrugged. 'It was a council decision.'

'If it had been internal it could have gone to you.'

'I've never seen myself in the running for promotion.'

'Others have. You've been doing most of Brent-Ellis's dirty work, as far as I hear. And now, you don't even get niggled about being passed over without interview, when they decide to appoint a number two?'

'I don't see it that way. I never regarded myself as being a candidate for that kind of job.' Arnold hesitated. 'In fact, I wasn't even aware the job was being created.'

'There you are! Exactly the point I was making! The whole thing was rushed through without discussion within the department!' Picton grunted contemptuously. 'I suppose you didn't even pick up the challenge in Stannard's tone when she said at the conference that you seemed to be doing Brent-Ellis's job? Work she was now taking away from you?'

'She's welcome to it.'

Picton shook his head mournfully. 'I worry about you, Landon. She'll eat you alive. You're a threat to her.'

'I can't see why.'

'Ah, man, it's power politics, don't you understand? The eternal struggle between the sexes.'

'That's nonsense—'

'She might have been nice to you to start, but really she resents the fact that you've carved out a niche of responsibility for yourself—'

'I haven't—'

'You've been doing work she describes as senior executive tasks, troubleshooting — it's a challenge to her in her new role. She doesn't lack confidence — she knows she's tougher than any man she's met and she's out to prove it. And you'll be one of the guys she'll trample, to make sure the point is made.' Picton straightened and, hands in pockets, sauntered away from the door. His voice drifted back from the corridor. 'But you'll see, man, you'll soon see . . .'

* * *

Rumour certainly had it in the office that there were a number of men displeased with the attitude shown by the new deputy director — though they said little about it publicly, preferring to nurse their emotional bruises in private. But there were women who were displeased also, and one of them was the director's secretary and personal assistant, Miss Sansom. Grizzled at forty, muscularly mannish in her dress, dark-visaged and constitutionally surly, she had been one of Mrs Brent-Ellis's safer appointments. She adored the director and protected him like a savage watchdog, guarding his door with a fierce eye and snarling gap-toothed at the merest hint of criticism when he was not in his room. No matter that he was off cavorting on some Northumberland golf course. On the other hand, Mrs Brent-Ellis knew her physical characteristics were not of the kind likely to generate affection in Simon Brent-Ellis's breast.

Miss Sansom had not been pleased by the appointment of the deputy, however, and she made it clear to all who crossed her path. It could have been due to the fact she was now serving a master and a mistress — she was responsible for both offices for the time being — but her fury was more likely rooted in the physical appearance of Karen Stannard, the shell shock she had seen in Brent-Ellis's eyes over the last few days, and the coolness with which the deputy saw fit to communicate — at any time — directly with Brent-Ellis without the slightest reference to her.

As Arnold waited in the anteroom for his appointment with Karen Stannard, the Teutonic Miss Sansom glared at him as though he was personally responsible for this devastating change of affairs. He was tempted to disavow responsibility, but he had the feeling Miss Sansom would rend him verbally if he even as much as mentioned Karen Stannard's name. So he sat quietly until, after a few minutes, the door opened and another man slipped quietly into the room, to take a seat across from Arnold.

'Mr Kirkby?' Cerberus barked.

'That's right. An appointment with Miss Stannard.'

Miss Sansom snapped her jaw shut, clearly wishing it was clamping on to the deputy director's smooth thigh. Arnold glanced at Kirkby.

'We're in together, looks like.'

'Yes?'

'We've not really had the chance to meet properly. My name's Arnold Landon.'

'Yes, I know. You've been pointed out to me.'

'Can't imagine why.'

'You've a certain . . . reputation.' He hesitated, frowning slightly, and made an odd clucking sound behind his teeth. 'I'm . . . I'm Syl Kirkby . . . You know what this is about?'

Arnold observed the man facing him. The bald patch had misled him: Kirkby was not as old as Arnold had expected. He had certainly not reached forty years of age, but his skin was sallow and unhealthy looking, deep lines were marked around his mouth and there was a defeated, almost hunted look about his eyes as he asked the question. Arnold shrugged. 'It'll be the reallocation of duties, for me, I guess. Have you had your own job sorted out yet?'

Kirkby shook his head. 'Not yet. I've been sitting around twiddling my thumbs, really. I've been given a few files to read — when people thought I shouldn't get paid for doing absolutely nothing — but I've been given no real idea what is lined up for me. Maybe today's the day.'

Miss Sansom humphed, glared at them both as though unwilling to countenance further discussion in her office, and then started hammering away with a fierce zeal at the word processor in front of her. A buzzer sounded on her desk. She glared at it in exasperation and fury, then flicked a switch. Karen Stannard's clear voice came across the phone.

'You can send in Mr Kirkby and Mr Landon now.'

Miss Sansom said nothing. She flicked the switch again, and raised black eyebrows at the two men. Like sheep urged by a menacing sheepdog they rose as one, and headed for the door leading to the office of the deputy director of the Department of Museums and Antiquities.

3

The day was bright, and the sunshine that gleamed through the car window was warm as it touched Arnold's face, but there was a cold wind outside and since the site they would be visiting was an exposed one on the north side, Arnold had taken the precaution of bringing a wax jacket with him. He'd warned Syl Kirkby that it could be cold up on the fellside, and Kirkby had brought an expensively cut dark overcoat with him. It would probably look somewhat incongruous on the fell, but that was his business. Arnold glanced back towards the man as he sat quietly in the back of Arnold's car.

'You want a look at the paper? I've got one here.'

'No thanks. You think she'll be much longer?'

'Who knows?' Arnold smiled. 'Deputy directors have to deal with important affairs of state. Or didn't you get that impression when we minions were skewered in her office the other day?'

'Like prawns on a stick. I've seen them do that in Hong Kong. Poor bastards are still alive. When you put them in the steaming water their legs curl. Did *your* legs curl, Landon?'

'I did experience certain sensations in my lower body,' Arnold admitted. 'But not as low as my legs.'

'I know exactly what you mean.' There was feeling in Syl Kirkby's voice.

It had not been an easy interview.

She had looked magnificent, leaning back easily in her leather chair behind the new, curved, mahogany-topped desk that had been acquired for her. Her hair had been caught up loosely at the back and she wore an open-necked cream silk shirt and a formal grey skirt. She had a pencil in her hands, rolling it between her fingers as she watched them settle into chairs, and then she tapped the pencil thoughtfully against her teeth, displaying their even whiteness behind the red of her lips. Her eyes were green, Arnold guessed.

Or maybe hazel.

But her tone was ice.

'So, Mr Kirkby, just what are we going to do with you?' Syl Kirkby sat upright in his chair, stiff-backed. He was surprisingly firm in his reply. 'That should be a management decision — as it was when I was told I would be transferred.'

Karen Stannard tilted her head to one side slightly. 'Hmmm. Perhaps I should tell you at the outset that I don't care for words which have irremediably sexist connotations -like *management.* Let's talk of executive decisions, shall we?'

'Mr Brent-Ellis—'

'And yes, let's mention Mr Brent-Ellis immediately, so there are no misunderstandings in that direction also. You'll be seeing very little of the director in future.'

We didn't see much of him in the past, Arnold thought.

'The director has given me responsibility for personnel planning in the department, and task scheduling, so there's little for him to deal with as far as you gentlemen are concerned. And, I should add, Mr Brent-Ellis and I have reached a certain understanding. He no longer sees me as a . . . woman, so much as a colleague he can rely upon. So decisions regarding you, Mr Kirkby, will be made in this office. So I ask again. What are we to do with you?'

Stubbornly, Kirkby replied, 'It's not for me to say. Managerial decisions—'

'Executive decisions, Mr Kirkby,' Karen Stannard put down her pencil and leaned forward. Arnold could see the line of her throat, the first swell of her breast. 'I'm going to be brutally frank with you. I'm at a loss to know what to do with you. I have no idea what strings you managed to pull in the Education Department to be treated differently from the others. They were shunted out on early retirement or so-called sick leave — but you were allowed to stay, and then you were transferred when it was clear there was no work there for you. But what did you really do there? What are you good for here? I'm at a loss, and I freely admit it. The clerical activities you undertook — counting toilet rolls or whatever — in your last department have no equivalence here. I don't see you as an intellectual giant—' her glance shifted briefly to Arnold, as she added sardonically — 'unlike Mr Landon here, and frankly, I think it would be best if you simply saved us a lot of embarrassment and left.'

Kirkby was shaking slightly, but there was a dogged defiance in him yet. 'I'm a member of this department, Miss Stannard, and I'll do what work the *management* call upon me to do.'

For a moment, Arnold thought her anger would get the better of her, but finally she smiled unpleasantly. 'I see . . . the worm can still wriggle, can it? All right — I suppose we'd better do the obvious, then. Send you back to school.'

'What's that supposed to mean?' Kirkby asked edgily, a note of alarm in his voice.

'You've no training for work in this department. You need training. So that's what we'll do with you. Make you a trainee. And the excellent Mr Landon here — he can take you under his sympathetic wing. I hear your wings may be described in that manner, Mr Landon?'

'I wouldn't know, Miss Stannard,' Arnold replied stiffly, somewhat disturbed by the treatment afforded to Kirkby.

'Deputy Director will do.' Her eyes seemed paler now; perhaps it was a trick of the light as she turned to face him more fully. The smooth chocolate sound was back as she said,

'I've heard quite a lot about you, in the department. It's said, you're a . . . nice man. Are you nice, Mr Landon?'

She made the word sound offensive. Arnold made no reply.

'I'm told you get into all sorts of trouble, from time to time. You were thrown out of the last department you worked in — you and Kirkby have that in common, anyway. On the other hand, I hear you're tough enough to go your own way when you think the issue deserves it. I like that: shows independence. But let me make myself clear: independence is a mistaken quality around me. I like to feel I can trust my colleagues . . . rely on them, if you know what I mean.'

'What you really mean is you want them to do what you tell them.'

'In a nutshell, yes,' she agreed, almost purring. 'Are you going to do what I tell you, Mr Landon?'

'Where it's a reasonable request.'

'You misunderstand me. It will be an order, not a request! And, moreover, choice of action was not something I was offering.' She observed him soberly for several seconds.' He held her glance, aware of the seemingly shifting colours of her eyes. He wondered whether deep down in those eyes there was a shade of insecurity.

'At least,' she said abruptly, 'it's fairly clear to me what work you need to be doing.'

'I'm pleased,' Arnold replied drily.

'Not the rather . . . aggrandized role you've been used to. But you will report directly to me on those tasks I assign to you. On the other hand, I'm a generous soul, aren't I? Your status within the department will actually be enhanced, since I've given you an acolyte in Mr Kirkby.'

'I'm sure Mr Kirkby and I will work well together.'

She took the bite in the remark and smiled in approval. She enjoyed adversarial relationships. 'Good. Well, we'll be starting as a team, in fact. The director has handed me the file on the Viking Research Trust, and I gather you've had experience of digs of this kind before. So you will begin, Mr Landon, by joining me on a visit to Ridgeway Manor, where we can have a look at the problem on the ground, so to speak. Friday will suit me: I'm sure it will suit you too.'

'I'm sure it will, Deputy Director,' Arnold replied demurely and was rewarded with a flash from her eyes. Then she turned on Kirkby.

'You'll be coming too.'

* * *

She slipped into the front seat of Arnold's car. He glanced at her: she wore a lightweight topcoat that extended to the top of her thighs. Arnold hesitated. 'There'll be a cold wind up at the site.'

'Don't patronize me, Landon,' she snapped.

'I was only saying—'

'Idiots in the office have delayed me. We're already late. I suggest we get moving.'

Arnold looked in the mirror and caught Kirkby's glance: the man raised his brows and rolled his eyes. Arnold pulled out of the car park and headed north-west.

They drove out of Morpeth and took the rising ground that would eventually bring them to the rolling valley of the South Tyne and the Roman settlement at Corbridge. Some ten miles out of the town, however, Arnold turned north, along a narrow road that wound through high banks that suggested to him it would have been a road of some antiquity. The pre-Roman farmers who had tilled these lands had caused their tracks to wind between ancient landholdings, rather than strike out in a direct line. It was similar farmers who had held these lands when the Northmen had come raging across the narrow seas in search of plunder. But where the early years had been dominated by the sacking of Lindisfarne, Iona and other religious settlements, there had come a time when the invaders sought land not gold, and the later Vikings had been settlers and farmers rather than raiders.

'You'll notice as we climb higher,' Arnold explained to Kirkby, 'how the names of the villages change in origin. Along the river valleys and the alluvial settlements the names of the hamlets tend to be Saxon; higher up on the fells the hamlet names are of Norse derivation — it's because when they arrived, the Vikings necessarily had to take the less fertile ground on the fellside. They'd been beaten to it, as far as river valleys were concerned.'

'I thought they'd have taken the land they wanted, with the sword,' Kirkby suggested.

'Not when they were coming in as settlers. If you're hoping to stay, you don't start by looting and raping. It's a time for negotiation — coming to terms with the families that already live there. You intermarry; you farm side by side — but you have to take the poorer land, on the fellside. The raiders were earlier and they concentrated on looting the religious settlements and rich farms. The men who settled these hill farms weren't bloodthirsty berserkers.'

'You're taking your job seriously then, Landon,' Karen Stannard commented.

'I beg your pardon?'

'Teaching your acolyte.'

She had clearly not recovered her temper. Arnold shrugged. 'Oh, I don't know that Mr Kirkby needs much teaching. He's had experiences far beyond mine. For instance, I've never been to Asia.' He glanced in the mirror at Kirkby in the back seat. 'You were saying earlier you'd visited Hong Kong.'

'Just a brief visit. Holiday. I did Southeast Asia, India and Nepal.'

Karen Stannard turned her head slightly. 'Private means, I imagine, Kirkby. I wouldn't have thought holidays of that kind were possible on the salary of an administrative assistant — or a humble teacher, for that matter.'

Kirkby made no reply.

After a while, Karen Stannard asked, 'Have you been to this site many times, Landon?'

'Not really. I visited about eighteen months ago but it's not really fallen into our bailiwick, in the sense it's a private trust and we've only been called in to help give some expert advice when some Viking artefacts were recovered recently.'

'You've seen the publicity in the last month or so. What do you think about it?'

'I haven't really made a considered judgement. I gather a bit of a storm has arisen over the land held by the trust, but I don't know the details. There's been press coverage suggesting there's opposition to the decision of the trustees to sell some of the land, but that's about all I know.'

Karen Stannard was silent for a little while. 'We'll be meeting Peter Gaul this morning. He's the Trust director—'

'I've met him,' Arnold said.

'—and the professional adviser to the trust. He's agreed to show us around. I don't think we should get drawn into any discussion of the controversy with him. It may well be he has an axe to grind. We're here today just to have a look at the dig itself.' She flashed a quick glance at Arnold. 'So let's keep our noses out of business that doesn't concern us, yes?'

Arnold made no reply, as they breasted the hill, drove across a barren, heather-strewn fell and then began to drop steeply down into a wooded valley. His companions were both silent during the descent. As they dropped into the shadow of the hill, the surrounding woodland seemed to take on an eerie quality, the road winding down for almost three miles, with trees cloaking the steep flanks of the slopes on either side. The road became stony, its surface rougher and pitted and for Arnold it was like going back into another, more ancient world. The sense of the past surrounding them grew stronger as they caught glimpses through the trees of broken-walled buildings entwined with brambles and choking undergrowth, collapsed stone walls and stagnant pools above the dark river that tumbled down from the fell, crashing into small waterfalls, and sliding blackly over stony weirs.

Then, suddenly, as they trundled around the bend, the trees seemed to fall back and a clearing opened out, with the vista of a green valley beyond. At the far end of the valley, where it curved against the dark hillside they could make out the stark, jutting crenellations of a half-built house, black against the skyline, dramatically sited above a craggy, scarp slope that plunged down to the black trees below. Arnold heard Kirkby murmur under his breath as he caught sight of it.

It was an astonishing apparition: a prodigious stone pile, Gothic in style, adorned with a broken tower and crowning a steep, tree-strewn bluff. Arnold had already inspected it some time ago, struggling up the unmade road to stare at the gables and buttresses and crumbled walls, bristling with gargoyles.

'What the hell is that?' Karen Stannard asked.

'It's not an old ruin in terms of antiquity,' Arnold explained. 'It's in a state of considerable decay, as you can see even from here, but it's really something of a tragedy. It was built in the early nineteenth century — or half-built, I should say. I've heard it described as just a gaunt, stone skeleton, the uncompleted realization of the vision of a man who died in 1890. After his death the work was abandoned and it's now lain neglected for almost a hundred years.'

'Fascinating,' he heard Kirkby murmur.

'You should see it in the moonlight,' Arnold replied enthusiastically. 'It's enough to make your skin tingle. Dark shadows, white light on the broken walls, the spread of the valley below — the atmosphere of the place is also heightened by the birds that nest there: you get jackdaws, kestrels and pigeons swooping in and out of those gaping windows and there's the inevitable colony of bats to startle the wits out of you if you enter through the broken doorways up there.'

'I'd like to take a closer look some time,' Kirkby said.

'It's just a folly,' Karen Stannard said coldly. 'The Victorians used to build houses just to look like that. Waste of time.'

They drove slowly down into the valley and in a few moments the view of the ruin was lost. They bounced and lurched along the track until it swung left, and the building they were heading for came into view, protected by a narrow copse of trees. It was a straggling stone structure that had once served as a chapel — Primitive Methodist, Arnold believed — but had at some time been converted for other use. Smoke ascended from the chimney at the far end of the building, which was now designated, according to the wooden signboard near its entrance, as the Ridgeway Field Centre.

'That's where we'll find Peter Gaul,' Arnold said and the gravel rasped under the car tyres as he pulled into the small car park that had been laid out to the left of the stone building.

* * *

Peter Gaul was short, stocky and black-browed. He was barrel-chested, with long, powerful arms that gave him an anthropoid appearance. His hair was thick and curly, with just a light frosting at the temples, his nose prominent, his jaw stubbornly prognathous and determined. He had dark eyes below a frowning brow, and he clearly took life very seriously. He wore a windcheater, open at the neck, and coarse black hair struggled upwards at the base of his throat. He stumped towards them in corduroy trousers and sturdy boots. His accent was Lancastrian, his tone bluff and direct. He spoke first to Arnold, who made the introductions, and he greeted Arnold's companions with a firm handshake, but no offer of hospitality by way of coffee or anything else.

'So what is it you want up here?' he asked directly, staring at Karen Stannard.

'Mr Landon's been here before, but I'd like to familiarize myself with the dig.'

'That's easily done — to start with, we've got it mapped out in here.' Gaul turned and led the way into the study centre. The main area of what had been the original chapel had been partitioned off into three sections, with a display hall, and two smaller rooms, leading off. 'We use them for seminar purposes, and briefings.' Gaul explained. 'My own office is upstairs.' He nodded towards a narrow staircase that wound up to a mezzanine floor above them, built as an addition to a raised pulpit extending from the end wall above the doorway. He walked towards the display case set under the window.

'What we've done here in the field centre,' he explained, 'is to construct a scale model of the dig, and above that, on the wall, you can see a sketch map of the area excavated. We get occasional school visits and some university history departments use us as well at weekends. Partly for the valley itself — it's a good area for wildlife and we also have some mock-Saxon constructions further down the valley — but mainly for the excavations we've been carrying out. As you'll see from the map here, the dig's a rough, elongated oval in shape. On the right-hand side — the eastern side — there's been some considerable erosion—'

'That's where the waterfall had eaten away into the site,' Arnold commented.

Gaul nodded. 'That's right. It really started the whole thing. There were some heavy rains a few years ago which caused the bank on the hillside to collapse and an underground flow burst out. The water gradually washed away the surface soil on the plateau below, and a few human bones were found. The police were called in, and messed the place about trampling and digging here and there but they backed off once the forensic boys realized the bones were ancient remains. That's when the Trust stepped in and controlled the dig — the early finds were a couple of iron rivets and a small circular lead button, which turned out to be a Viking lead bullion weight — not a bit of a modern car battery, as the police thought!'

He traced the line of the excavation on the wall map with a black-haired index finger. 'As you can see, here on the right of the dig there's a great deal of packing stone. As we move across to the western part of the site we see where our first intimation of a burial appeared.'

'What was it?' Karen Stannard asked.

'A whalebone plaque, just below the level of the packing stones. Moving further left again we found some bone comb fragments, a brooch which we think is Norwegian, dated to the ninth century AD, a sickle blade and some gaming objects.' Gaul leaned back and folded his arms, gazing thoughtfully at the map as the others inspected it more closely.

'You've got some markers identified.' Syl Kirkby said.

'We think the whole area was actually divided into compartments, with the west chamber being the burial compartment. We even found an ironing board made out of whalebone.' Gaul's eyes glinted with amusement as he glanced at Karen Stannard. 'Apparently whalebone ironing boards were often used as betrothal gifts by the Norsemen. They were carved by the young men to present to their chosen women as part of a marriage proposal. It's how they saw their women in those days — tied to the whalebone ironing board.'

From the grim set of Karen Stannard's mouth, Arnold could see the deputy director was unamused. Perhaps Gaul felt the coolness of the atmosphere, for he abruptly suggested they visit the site.

They spent the next hour walking around the dig itself.

While Gaul explained to the others the detailed layout of the site, Arnold walked around by himself. He was somewhat puzzled by Gaul's suggestion that the burial chamber probably lay in the western compartment. His inspection of the site map, and the location of the artefacts, led him to suspect the interpretation was too simple. He looked up as the others joined him.

'Where did you say the rivets were found originally?'

Peter Gaul wrinkled his nose. 'Just along there,' he replied, pointing. 'It's not an area we're concentrating on at the moment. We don't really have too many staff involved, and we're fixing our attention on the western section in the hope that we'll find a burial.'

'No clues from the bones previously found?' Karen Stannard asked.

Gaul shook his head. 'No. They were washed out and exposed for some time — then the police tramped all over the place with their hobnailed boots.'

'Packing stones would suggest something is being held down,' Arnold remarked. 'And rivets . . . well, isn't there a chance of a boat burial?'

Gaul shrugged. 'We have doubts. With the comb, the brooch, the gaming pieces — we think the burial, if there is one, will be along there.'

'What are the gaming pieces you found?'

'Small, bone pieces — twenty-two in all.'

'For playing *hnefatafl*.'

'What's that?' Kirkby asked.

Arnold smiled. 'When it was too dark and chilly for looting and pillaging the Vikings played at *hnefatafl* — the "King's Table". It was a game that combined the intellectual challenge of chess with the ethics of ice hockey. Red and white bone pieces, supposed to represent Danes and Muscovites. It was a capture game, and often ended in violence.'

Gaul squinted thoughtfully at Arnold. 'You know a bit about Viking society, then.'

'A little.'

Karen Stannard humphed impatiently. 'A little isn't enough. Who's leading your team?'

'Dr Rena Williams. She and her team aren't here right now. They'll be back at the weekend.'

Karen Stannard nodded in approval. 'I know her — and her work. Extremely sound.' She glanced almost triumphantly at Arnold. 'Things like this are best left to university experts like Dr Williams. If she thinks that the area over there is the one to look at, I wouldn't argue with her. She's got a fine track record. Anyway, Mr Gaul, I'm grateful for the tour. I'm only recently appointed to the department and I need to get to see a number of sites. But we have to make our way back to Morpeth now. Still, if there's any way we can assist you in your work, please don't hesitate to ask.'

Peter Gaul frowned. 'There's the Trust issue.'

Karen Stannard was silent for a moment, then she shrugged. 'I'm not sure—'

'They think the way we're operating is inefficient.' Gaul said in an angry tone. 'But I could make it a really commercial venture if I was given a free hand. We already have a shop at the far end of the valley, where there's easier access to the site from the south. If I was allowed to expand—'

'I'm not sure that's our business,' Karen Stannard said carefully.

'Well, someone needs to make it their business! This bloody site can be destroyed . . . ruined!' He paused, glaring at her angrily. 'Everyone washes their hands of it — leaving the trustees to ride roughshod over logic! Your department ought to have a say in it.'

'It's a private site.'

'Of national importance! You say you have to go back to your office?'

'I'm afraid so—'

'Let me drive you. I have to go to Morpeth today. I can take you. Come back in my car, and I'll fill you in on the whole picture regarding the Trust dispute. You know the annual general meeting of the Friends of the Trust is to be held at Denham Hall next week.'

'I didn't, but—'

'There's going to be trouble there. You ought to know about it and all the background. This is a site of considerable archaeological importance.'

'Yes, but—'

'Dr Williams understands what is needed. But we need support from other clinical minds.'

He had struck the right note.

Arnold saw that Karen Stannard was suddenly interested.

There was a short silence as she hesitated, flattered by the comment that linked her with the estimable Dr Rena Williams. At last she glanced at Arnold thoughtfully. 'I think . . . perhaps it might be useful to get the background on this matter, at least. I'll take up Mr Gaul's offer, Landon. I'll go back with him, and you can continue to give Kirkby the benefit of your knowledge and expertise without me having to listen to it. That all right with you?'

It was more than all right with Arnold.

Kirkby too seemed happy. He stood at Arnold's shoulder with a faint smile on his face as they watched Gaul drive off up the valley with the deputy director, ten minutes later.

Arnold turned and walked back along the length of the site, with Kirkby just behind him. 'Were you serious when you said you think this could be a boat burial?' Kirkby asked.

'It's quite possible. I wouldn't mind spending a few days up here helping with the dig. You see, it's quite possible the site comprises an outer compartment where grave goods would have been left, leading on down here to a burial chamber — a deeper excavation but on the east side, not the west.'

He pointed to the packing rocks. The earth bank to one side had been tunnelled where it sloped up under the hill. 'Has someone been digging there in the past? Part of the excavation?' Kirkby asked.

Arnold shook his head. 'No. Badgers. They could well have done some damage — but they're long gone now. Those are old, abandoned setts. On the other hand, they've given us a sort of borehole, haven't they?' He hesitated, then got down on his knees and examined the badger sett entrance. Carefully, he scraped away at some of the loose earth, then shook his head. 'Not sensible. We'd better not mess about here unless we get permission to do it properly.'

He stood up, dusting his knees and hands. He looked quizzically at Syl Kirkby. 'I think maybe we'll have a chat with the Trust directors sometime, rather than Peter Gaul. He's got rather . . . positive views. Meanwhile . . . you said you'd like to have a closer look at the building on the hill up there. What about now?'

'Why not?' Kirkby said.

'It's a bit of a climb, but worth it. We'll leave the car where it is.'

He led the way across the clearing and along a narrow stone roadway that wound its way up through the trees to the slope on their left. It soon narrowed, and gave way to a stony track overgrown by brambles and tall clumps of grass. The track was badly patched and crumbling as it twisted to cross a small burn several times; a narrow stone bridge enabled them to enter a glade where the tall trees thinned somewhat and then Arnold moved on into the undergrowth again, following the roadway towards the crags above.

'It would have been somewhat wider in the old days,' he suggested as they paused to regain their breath on a small plateau that gave them a view across the valley. 'They'll have carted the building materials up here. Once they stopped the building work up above, the undergrowth swallowed the track up again and now it's just the narrow path that's left.'

Kirkby was breathing hard, his narrow face beaded with sweat. He was clearly glad of the rest after the stiff slope they had climbed. He stared across the wooded valley and pointed to the roofs of a building nestling among the distant trees. 'What's that?'

'Ridgeway Manor. The ruin we're going to look at was started by a prosperous merchant from Liverpool. He had family money behind him, mainly gained from the eighteenth-century slave trade, though he himself was into cotton. He bought about two hundred acres here, which included a seventeenth-century manor house — Ridgeway Manor, the house you can see down there. I think he bought here partly because the old manor reflected his own name — he himself was called William Ridge — but he wasn't satisfied with the manor itself: he decided he wanted to build his own hall, up here on the crags.'

'Did he live in the manor?'

'Oh, yes. And there's Ridgeway Home Farm that also went with the estate: quite productive. But his passion was this house up above. He was an eccentric — a Catholic convert who had some grandiose vision about creating a religious community in the valley.'

'The Victorians had great self-confidence,' Kirkby murmured, almost to himself.

'It wasn't enough — when the money ran out. His business failed about 1860 and Ridge stayed on, in declining, disappointed health, at Ridgeway Manor. He died there. He never finished the house up above — which was to be called Ridge Hall. Come on, let's climb on.'

The track levelled for a short time as they moved from the hillock and then began to twist through the trees again until after a steep, breath-wrenching climb they finally emerged at the top of the crags and the scarp slope below them swept down into the valley in a vertiginous, rocky, tree-strewn scree.

Ridge Hall stood before them, perched almost on the edge of the crag.

It was built of a creamy, honey-coloured limestone that had been quarried in Gloucestershire, and transported north at considerable expense to the valley. The stone had been used not only for the outer walls and staircase, ceiling vaults and door surrounds, but also for fireplaces, drainage pipes and gutters. Arnold explained that the house had been designed with four great wings, enclosing a courtyard dominated by the tower and the tall carved chimneys of the extensive stone roof. As they walked into the inner courtyard Kirkby looked around him in amazement at the mediaeval quality of the stonework, the mullioned windows, the extravagant bosses and the gargoyles, the details carved in the clock tower constructed in the centre of the courtyard.

'You said this was started in the nineteenth century — but it looks mediaeval in structure!'

'I told you he was an eccentric,' Arnold explained, smiling. 'Ridge had the idea of living in a thoroughly mediaeval manner — in a building complete with all the usual appurtenances of a religious community of that period. You see — a chapel, a laundry . . . over there a bakery, which is designed like the structure at Fontevrault, on the Loire. Inside the main building you'll see a cheese room and a buttery and a brewery. It was all magnificently impractical — and it ruined him in the end, I guess.'

He led the way into the chapel and showed Kirkby the soaring carved arches; in the drawing room he pointed out the vaulted ceiling with its superbly executed bosses. The kitchen also was vaulted, but timbers exposed in the wall demonstrated how the work had slowed and finally come to a halt about a hundred years earlier.

'But it's not like a house at all,' Kirkby said quietly. 'It's more like . . . I don't know .. .'

'An Oxford college?' Arnold suggested. 'It has the monastic air Ridge wanted, and I have to admit it's a marvellous synthesis of Gothic and traditional architecture, and the stone is beautiful . . .'

He led the way again, wandering from room to room, his voice echoing hollowly as he commented on the stonework and the vaulted roof, the mullioned windows and the carvings, the way in which the building had remained untouched by pollution, only to become the habitat of wild birds, and pointing out where the house had been vandalized during the Second World War, when it had been used for storage purposes by American and Canadian troops based in the valley below.

'And now, it's just a crumbling ruin. Unused, unwanted, uneconomic.'

'No one ever comes up here?'

'I would guess we're the first in years.'

Kirkby moved away and stood in the unglazed window arch, staring down at the magnificent view across the valley, where a faint mist was stealing among the trees, hazing the greensward and blurring the outlines of the hills beyond. The valley softened under the mist and seemed to grow silent as the long grey smoky fingers whispered their way among the trees.

'Unwanted, maybe . . . but it's a place where a man could lose himself,' Kirkby said quietly, after a while.

There was a desolation in the man's tone that caught Arnold's attention. For a moment, he did not know how to respond. Then, awkwardly, he said, 'It's a magnificent folly, certainly, and it has a unique atmosphere. For me, there's also the workmanship that's gone into the place. Not wasted, because it's still here, craftsmanship of a high order. But unseen and unappreciated, for the most part.'

'*You* appreciate it, Landon.'

Arnold nodded. Kirkby turned slightly and stared at him, over his shoulder. Curiously, he asked, 'Where did you get your knowledge and feeling for these old buildings? I've heard you were never trained.'

Arnold laughed. 'At university, like Ms Stannard, you mean? No, that's right. It was my father, really . . .' He stared at Kirkby and in a slightly embarrassed tone he said, 'He taught me a great deal, you see.'

There was a short silence, and then almost involuntarily Arnold started talking about the past in a manner that was most unusual for him. He told Kirkby about his childhood, about the long walks his father had taken with him in the Yorkshire Dales, exploring not just the magnificent achievements of the monastery builders at Fountains Abbey and Ripon, but the humbler dwellings in the hamlets on the fells, the traditional cottages, the ancient stones that had been robbed by succeeding generations for use over and over again. He told Kirkby how his father had shown him Roman stone, and the markings that demonstrated a thirteenth- or fifteenth-century stone dressing; six-hundred-year-old timber beams and the marks of the men who had carved them; pre-Saxon cup chiselling and runes that had been carved in the days of the Vikings, built into a sheep pen high on the fells.

'These days they claim you need to go to university, to get the formal training, to appreciate all this,' Arnold mused, 'but for us it was different. He had learned on the ground and he taught me, gave me his love and understanding of stone and timber. He showed me how men worked it, how they split massive rocks by the natural action of frost; how men experimented with joints in timber constructions; how they used flexible materials like chicken bones to hold together massive stone roofs. But he gave me more than that too. He made me understand about the people who had undertaken these works. My father taught me things you don't find in textbooks. He told me who these ancients were, made me know what they had felt and he showed me, he made me touch and feel and understand—'

Arnold stopped, suddenly abashed. It was rarely he spoke of his father. Kirkby was staring at him with an oddly haunted expression in his eyes. His mouth was set in a grim line. 'You and your father were . . . close.'

'We had a good relationship.'

Kirkby turned away to stare out over the valley again. 'You were lucky. My father . . . he had no time for me . . . not in that way, at least. His attitudes were . . . very different.' He frowned, and in an oddly defiant tone, added, 'I barely remember him.'

There was something in his voice that made Arnold believe he was not telling the truth: rather than barely remembering his father, Arnold suspected there was a curdling resentment in Syl Kirkby that made him recall his father only too well. And the memories were not pleasant.

'Is he still alive?' Arnold asked after a short silence.

'He died years ago. But I hadn't seen him for ten years before that. Still . . . that's all in the past.' He hunched his shoulders and peered out at the mist that was beginning to swathe the folds of the valley. 'Yes, a man could lose himself up here . . .'

Or find himself, Arnold almost added.

CHAPTER TWO

1

Denham Hall was owned by the local authority, open to the public, often used for public meetings and was well known to Arnold. He had visited it several times for it was one of his favourite structures — one of the few Georgian mansions in the north-east. The east wing and side elevations had been built in the mid-eighteenth century, though the house's history was mediaeval, but Arnold was particularly fond of the pele tower and hall, both of which had been improved and extended in the sixteenth century.

He had arrived early for the meeting to be held under the auspices of the Ridgeway Viking Research Trust, eager to look around Denham Hall one more time, and Arnold took pleasure in showing Syl Kirkby the Georgian apartments together with the Oak Room, and drawing his attention to the interesting ribbed plaster ceiling in the Fretwork Room.

'And what we have here,' Kirkby exclaimed triumphantly, 'is Chinese hand-painted wallpaper, probably acquired about 1750.'

Arnold was admiring the intricately carved wooden chimney piece. He turned, in surprise, to stare at the wall Kirkby was indicating. 'I didn't know that.'

'Neither did I, till I read this notice here.' Kirkby laughed, pointing.

Arnold grinned. Jane Wilson had chided him often enough in the past. 'I guess when I get caught up in my enthusiasms, I do go on a bit.'

'Not at all. I enjoy hearing you talk. It brings a place like this to life. You're lucky that you've got the sort of job that gives you the chance to visit places like this — where you enjoy yourself so much.' Kirkby paused. 'So am I, for that matter.' A shadow crossed his brow, his mood changing swiftly from amusement to depression. He was often troubled with gloomy thoughts, Arnold had noticed. But the moment quickly passed and Kirkby went on, 'I would have thought Ms Stannard would have taken the opportunity to come, rather than send you and me.'

Arnold himself had been surprised.

Karen Stannard had called him into her office. She had appeared thoughtful when she waved him to a seat and fixed her glance on him. It was steely. Her eyes, he concluded, were smoky-grey.

'I had a long conversation with Peter Gaul on the way back to the office the other day,' she said.

'He gave you all the background to the dispute regarding the Ridgeway Trust?'

'That's right.' She paused, thoughtfully, her gaze unblinking. 'He feels very strongly about the issues involved.'

'I'd got that impression.'

Karen Stannard put the tips of her slim fingers together and inspected them. Her nails were unpainted, but carefully manicured. 'It's all a private matter, of course, since the dig is on Trust land — and that's the only area in which we have an interest really — but some of the issues as Gaul explains them could have . . . repercussions. I've taken the opportunity to talk this over with the director.' .

Brent-Ellis would have enjoyed that, Arnold guessed. Like a boil on his backside.

'He agrees with me.'

Arnold was not surprised.

'The department needs to be kept closely informed as to what's happening, but a close involvement would not be wise. There are legal and political issues arising . . . and If we were seen to be having, shall we say, senior representation, even on a watching brief basis, it could become embarrassing, to say the least.'

Arnold began to guess what was coming.

'The main thing is that we should not be seen to be giving any of the . . . er . . . parties to the dispute our particular support, you see. The director himself, of course, is well known to some of the people involved — the trustees in particular — and it would be unwise if he were to adopt a high profile here. It would be quite wrong, for instance, if his presence at any inquiry were to be interpreted as support for any of the individual trustees. Equally, since Peter Gaul has already had a long, private conversation with me I think it inadvisable that I should be seen taking a personal interest in the dispute. One has to be so careful,' she added, her eyelashes drooping over eyes that suddenly seemed grey-green and seductive. 'I mean, merely having listened sympathetically to Gaul might raise suggestions of bias, don't you agree?'

'I can see your point of view,' Arnold replied tactfully. 'On the other hand, the department mustn't be seen to be washing its hands of the whole business. We *do* have public responsibilities.'

'Of course.'

'And we *do* need to be kept informed. The dig is important.'

'It is.'

Her eyes widened, greening in decision. 'So we've decided the director and I, that a presence at the meeting at Denham Hall is advisable. A sort of watching brief. It was the director himself who suggested you.'

'I can't imagine why,' Arnold lied.

She observed him carefully, seeking signs of irony. 'You're not a member of the directorate, like me. You are no longer seen as holding senior responsibilities, Landon. You have no authority to speak for the department. You will not be seen as, nor held out as, a spokesman for the director.'

And there is a view in the department, Arnold thought, that if anyone can be set up as a fall guy, then it should be Arnold Landon.

'I understand perfectly,' he said.

'But I should make one thing absolutely clear,' she purred, 'because it's likely there will be members of the press present, in view of the newspaper campaign that's been waged of recent weeks. No commitments. No taking sides. Observer status only. No offers of assistance. Absolute impartiality. You understand?'

'Absolutely.'

'And you can take that little weasel Kirkby with you. Get him out of the office.' She shot a sharp glance in Arnold's direction. 'You and he seem to get on well enough. For me, there's something about him that makes me shiver . . . but that's me being a woman, isn't it?' she smiled thinly.

He was reminded more of a beautiful jungle cat, smooth and silken, but with claws that could rip out in a flash.

* * *

At about eleven o'clock the room that had been booked for the meeting began to fill up. Arnold and Kirkby took seats in the third row and by eleven-fifteen the room was almost full. Arnold glanced around him from time to time but there were few familiar faces. He caught sight of Peter Gaul, seated in the front row, dark-visaged and glowering: the man nodded to him but his eyes were cold. There was another face Arnold could not put a name to: a slight man with sandy hair worn long, and a restlessness of manner. Arnold had met him but could not recall his name. He tended to fidget in his seat, kept looking about him, and after a while he caught sight of Arnold. He hesitated, then rose and came along the line of seats to take up an empty place just in front of Syl Kirkby. He turned his narrow face towards Arnold. 'Landon, isn't it?'

Arnold nodded.

'You here to represent the department?'

'Not exactly represent,' Arnold replied quickly. 'We're holding a kind of watching brief. I'm sorry, but—'

The man smiled thinly. 'You don't remember me. I interviewed you for the northern press some while ago — about the *sudarium:* that ancient cloth you found. You remember? I work for the *Journal.* Alan Crickley.'

'Ah, yes, I remember now. My apologies — but I have a dreadful memory for names.'

'That's all right. You said you had a watching brief . . . you and . . . ?'

'This is my colleague, Syl Kirkby.'

'Pleased to meet you,' Crickley said and held out his hand.

Kirkby shook it without enthusiasm.

Crickley turned back to Arnold. 'So what exactly is the department's position in this whole business?'

Arnold shook his head. 'We're taking no position as such. I'm here just to keep up to date with what's going on. We have an interest in the dig, that's all — but it's on private land—'

'Trust land.'

'That's right, and so we have no locus standi, so to speak.'

'But there must be a departmental view,' Crickley insisted.

'Not really. We've not been involved. For that matter there's a certain vagueness about what the issues really are. And whether they are really anything to do with us at all.'

Crickley's foxy eyes held a glint of cynicism. 'I think they'll be well enough exposed today. One side has even issued a press release, so an ignorant reporter like me won't fail to understand exactly what is at stake. We should be having a lively time — you seen the agenda?'

'No.'

'Well, to start with, it seems that it's inaccurate, compared with the notice of meeting, and they'll be making some play over that. But we'll see soon enough . . .' He glanced back at Kirkby, grinning, but then a slight frown touched his brow 'Mr Kirkby . . . the name rings no bells with me, but I have a feeling we've met before. Did you ever work in the newspaper business?'

'No.'

'You been with the Museums Department long?'

'Recently joined.'

'I have a feeling our paths have crossed.'

'I don't think so.'

Crickley grimaced. 'I have a good memory for faces though I admit your name . . . You never worked in Exeter did you?'

Kirkby's face was stony. He leaned back in his chair and folded his arms, staring directly at Crickley. 'I'm quite certain we've *never* met, Mr Crickley.'

There was a clear finality in his tone. Either he didn't care for journalists, or he resented being questioned. Crickley raised an eyebrow, glanced at Arnold and shrugged, turning away. Arnold was puzzled: Kirkby was clearly discomfited by Crickley's questions, but they had seemed innocent enough.

The platform party was making its way into the room.

They took their seats on the raised dais facing the audience and shuffled papers amongst themselves, talking in low voices and smiling at each other. There were four of them, all men, prosperous-looking, well-dressed, middle-aged. The youngest of them — Arnold guessed he would be about forty-five years of age — appeared to be the chairman, for there was a certain deference shown to him as they whispered to each other. Arnold's guess was confirmed when the grey-suited man rose to his feet and addressed the audience.

'Well, I must say it's gratifying to see such a large audience gathered here this morning for this general meeting, at which I hope we will be able to resolve some outstanding issues. One is accustomed to the conduct of Trust business — particularly in such esoteric areas as archaeological investigations in relative obscurity. I suppose it says something for the power of the press that the gathering is so large today.'

He paused as a drift of sycophantic laughter came from the front row of the audience. The chairman smiled, looked around at his listeners, and smoothed his right hand over his lower chest in a slightly nervous gesture. He was tall, with a thick shock of dark hair, greying at the temples. He bore himself very upright, in a soldierly manner, and he had blue, piercing eyes that gave him an air of easy confidence. His features were regular, his skin tanned, and his mouth was firm and determined. Arnold guessed he would be a man with a successful track record who was used to getting what he wanted — and involvement in the Trust would suggest that he was a self-made man, or a local politician, who would have time to spare for good works.

'I suppose I should introduce myself to those who are attending a general meeting for the first time. My name is David Hall and I'm chairman of the Ridgeway Viking Research Trust . . . indeed, I've been chairman since the Trust was first established by Miss Ridge, when the Viking discoveries were originally made. You might say I've been in on this since the beginning. Not the actual Viking beginning, of course.' He waited again until the knowing laughter in the front row subsided and then he smiled, self-deprecatingly. 'And the privilege falls to me of introducing to you the other trustees here on the platform with me today. First of all, Sir John Hertford — known as Jock to his friends . . .'

The stocky, florid-faced man in a dark pinstripe suit, seated immediately beside Hall, rose and inclined his head briefly. He was almost bald, except for strips of dark hair above his ears, and his features were pudgy, and self-satisfied. He had a bad-tempered mouth, Arnold considered.

'I'm also grateful for the attendance of Sam Frimley today.' Hall continued. 'As many of you will know, Sam is a busy man, having recently masterminded the contract at Teesport — but he still finds time to work with the rest of us on the Trust.'

Frimley did not rise. He was narrow-shouldered, lean and hawk-faced; his mouth was half hidden by a flamboyant moustache that was oddly out of keeping with the reticence of his eyes. He looked like a civil servant who was trying to break out of the mould, but not succeeding. He managed a smile at his introduction, but it was a nervous effort.

'And finally — but not least — we have Bill Norman. His background will be well known to many of you who followed northern rugby—' there was some laughter as Norman, grinning, fingered his broken nose ostentatiously — 'though of recent years he has been active in other spheres, as a press officer with one of the electricity boards.'

Arnold had heard of him, and seen him on television a few times: a big, burly man with short-cropped, grey curly hair, a broken nose that had been given to him in an Australian touring match and a scarred brow that testified to torrid years in the North of England pack. He was known to have given as much as he got in the matter of physical violence on the rugby field and had long had a reputation as a hard man. The scarring caused his left eye to appear to droop slightly, but he had an easy manner and a quick smile. He was clearly gregarious, and enjoyed public attention.

'Good.' Hall beamed. 'I now propose, with introductions completed, that we should proceed to business. I declare open the general meeting, and I draw your attention to the agenda papers which were circulated prior to this meeting, with due notice, I understand. The first item—'

'Mr Hall.'

The deep voice boomed out from the back of the room. In front of Arnold, Crickley stiffened and turned his head swiftly. A cynical, expectant smile appeared on his lips. Arnold also looked back. In the last row a man was standing up: tall, about sixty years of age with craggy features and an air of determination; he bore himself with a dignity that was emphasized by the portliness of his bulk. He sported a floral waistcoat under his dark blue suit and his bow tie was a flamboyant red. .

David Hall knew him, and recognized him from the chalf.

'You wish to make a statement, Mr Harcourt-Fanshaw?' There was a note of edgy resignation in his tones.

Crickley caught Arnold's eye. 'Joe Harcourt-Fanshaw,' he hissed in an undertone. 'Local solicitor. He was a friend of Miss Ridge — you know, the old biddy who made the original bequests to the Ridgeway Trust. This should produce some sparks, if I know Joe.'

Arnold listened to the man at the back of the room.

'It's not so much a statement I want to make, Mr Hall, as ask a question.'

'I think it would be appropriate if you addressed me formally as Chairman,' David Hall said stiffly.

'But that touches upon the question I want to ask.' Harcourt-Fanshaw said in a cheerful voice. 'Chairman of what?'

'I don't follow.' Hall replied, frowning. 'I am chairman of the Ridgeway Viking Research Trust, and I don't understand the issue you're trying to raise.'

Harcourt-Fanshaw swivelled his hips slightly, looking around the room in a portentous manner. He was confident, almost teasing in his attitude, and clearly enjoying himself. 'I merely want to establish the status of this meeting, and indeed, the status of the people who have appeared on the platform to face the meeting.'

'Really, Mr Harcourt-Fanshaw, is this necessary? The papers that were sent out in the post to all members—'

'Members of *what,* Mr Hall?'

There was a short silence. Stiffly, David Hall replied, 'The papers are self -explanatory.'

'Well, that's right.' Harcourt-Fanshaw tucked the thumb of his left hand into his waistcoat pocket and with his right hand flourished the agenda paper that had been sent out. 'This is what you mean, I take it. May I draw your attention to the heading?'

'We all know—'

'The agenda paper is headed, and I quote: *Friends of the Viking Research Trust — Annual General Meeting*. I assume that is what we have all received in this room?'

'Of course.' Hall agreed sourly.

'In other words this is *not* a meeting of the trustees of the Ridgeway Viking Research Trust as such, but a meeting of the Friends.'

'The papers make that clear.' Hall announced shortly. 'Good. Now, there are several items on the agenda, some of which are trivial but one of which purports to deal with the matter that is closest to our hearts and, indeed, has caused some furore in the local newspapers of late.'

'Fomented by you, Harcourt-Fanshaw.' Sir Jock Hertford interrupted angrily. 'Can we get on, Chairman?'

Harcourt-Fanshaw held up an admonitory hand. His rich, booming voice was stem. 'I would counsel against haste in this matter. I believe there are points which require clarification. We have just established this is truly the annual general meeting of the Friends of the Viking Research Trust: that is understood by all, I believe.'

Wearily, David Hall nodded and there was a murmur of assent in the room.

'The Friends,' the solicitor continued, 'are, in law, an unincorporated association. That is to say, they do not hold the legal status of a corporate body.'

There was a brief silence. David Hall stared fixedly at Harcourt-Fanshaw. 'I take it you have a point to make?'

'Assuredly. Were the body I speak of a limited company, it would have a board of directors — officers who would be able to take decisions that were binding upon the company itself, though answerable at annual general meeting to the shareholders of the company. Again, were the Friends recognized by the Charity Commissioners as a registered charity, once again there would be trustees appointed to act on behalf of the Friends.' He paused, and waved a hand grandiloquently, taking in everyone in the room with the gesture. 'But the Friends are neither a charitable trust nor a limited company — and consequently have no board of directors or trustees who can purport to act on their behalf.'

'I'm sure we would all be greatly improved in mind by a lecture from you about legal niceties, Mr Harcourt-Fanshaw, but I fail to see—'

'Give me a moment—' the solicitor smiled contemptuously — 'and all will be revealed. The notice you sent out was for a meeting of the Friends: an unincorporated association which, as such, has no officers, no board of directors.'

'So?'

'I come to my question. You describe yourself as chairman of this meeting. But what really is your status in this room?'

David Hall hesitated, glancing sideways to his colleagues on the dais. 'I . . . we are here as trustees of the Ridgeway Trust and—'

'Exactly! You are trustees of the Ridgeway Trust. But as such, I would contend, you have no status as far as the Friends are concerned.'

'You're quibbling, sir.' David Hall snapped, his temper rising. 'We all have the same interests at heart—'

'That's doubtful!'

'—and in our capacity as trustees it's obvious we are the people who should lead—'

'Obvious?' Harcourt-Fanshaw challenged. 'It's not obvious to me!'

'But we've always conducted meetings of the Friends like this and there's been no complaint on previous occasions.' Hall snapped hotly.

'That signifies nothing. Previous agendae did not hold important issues as this one does! I explain again, in case the legal issue has slipped past you, Mr Hall.' the solicitor added scornfully. 'This is a meeting of an unincorporated association. You and the others, as trustees of the Ridgeway Trust, may well be interested parties and staunch members of the Friends — but you have *not* been elected to hold any office in the Friends. This is a body separate from the Trust. You cannot simply arrogate to yourselves the status of a board of directors — this is not a limited company; you cannot simply take over the role of officers in the association — since you have not been elected. Your status and position as trustees is one thing — but it has nothing to do with the control and operation of a meeting of the Friends of the Viking Research Trust!'

Bill Norman rose slowly, his heavy bulk hunched and menacing as he faced the solicitor at the back of the room. Arnold could imagine him standing up to the muscular antipodeans in the gold jerseys on mud-raked northern rugby fields. 'For the last few years we've been running meetings to discuss matters of interest to the Friends, breaking our necks to get messages across—'

'We're not discussing your physical wellbeing, Mr Norman.' Harcourt-Fanshaw announced ponderously, 'we're discussing your right to sit up there pontificating as leaders of the Friends when you have assumed that position merely by virtue of being trustees of the Ridgeway Trust. I agree entirely that the interests of the Friends are closely bound up with the Trust, but that does not mean the trustees have the automatic right to organize and run the Friends. I repeat — you gentlemen are not elected officers, and therefore have no status up there on the platform. Not as far as this meeting is concerned.'

'Ah, I see the drift now.' Hall sneered. 'This is really a takeover bid, is it?'

With a studied equanimity, Harcourt-Fanshaw hooked both thumbs in his waistcoat pockets. 'That's not the way I would put it, Mr Hall. Let me just say that in the absence of elected officers in a meeting of an unincorporated association, it is open to the paid-up members of the association to elect a chairman for their meetings. There is no need or requirement for a platform party made up of persons who have no status in the meeting other than ordinary members of the Friends — if they are even that, for I understand that Mr Sam Frimley, at least, has not paid his dues this year.'

As Frimley looked around him in alarm, someone snorted with laughter and Harcourt-Fanshaw went on, 'So now that we have settled the legalities of the matter, namely, that you have no right to take the chair, Mr Hall, merely because you're a trustee, we can proceed properly.'

'And what in your legalistic view.' Hall replied icily, 'would be the proper way to proceed?'

The portly solicitor spread his hands wide, innocently. 'Why, in proceeding to the election of a chairman for this meeting, of course. And I will immediately put forward a candidate.' He paused, and in the hush looked slowly around the room, savouring the moment. 'I would like to propose that we dispense with this platform party that has been assembled, and invite Mr Phil Martin to take the chair at this annual general meeting of the Friends of the Viking Research Trust.'

The slight man sitting beside Harcourt-Fanshaw hurriedly rose to his feet. 'I second that motion.'

Immediately, pandemonium broke out.

Sir Jock Hertford was on his feet bawling that he had no intention of being treated in such a cavalier fashion after all the work he had put into the Trust. Someone yelled that the proposed chairman, Phil Martin, had a personal stake in the issues involved. Sam Frimley began an argument with a bald septuagenarian in the front row who, it seemed, was treasurer of the Friends and denied ever having received Frimley's subscription for that year. Bill Norman's face was flushed and his big hands were balled in fists as he seemed about ready to stride down among the audience and produce his own form of controlled mayhem. Chairs crashed over as numerous people surged to their feet, shouting at each other, supporters on the one hand of Harcourt-Fanshaw's proposal, and adherents on the other of David Hall and the Ridgeway trustees. There were catcalls, suggesting Hall was trying to rig the meeting; someone at the back broke a chair and yelled out he was ready to take on Bill Norman any time he wanted to, because of the way he'd played in 1963. David Hall was hammering on the table with a gavel and few were paying any attention to him.

'What the hell is going on?' Kirkby asked Arnold in wonderment.

‘I think we’re seeing the culmination of a long-standing feud,’ Arnold replied.

Alan Crickley’s face was flushed with malicious happiness. ‘Damn right we are. I was warned in the press release that old Joe was going to pull out all the stops. There was no way he was going to allow the trustees to smooth their way through this meeting — use it as a rubber stamp for awkward decisions they’re about to make.’

‘Well, I can’t see much sense arising out of all this!’ Arnold suggested.

David Hall took the matter in hand. His vigorous gavelling had produced no effect; he grabbed Jock Hertford and Bill Norman by the arm and spoke to them hastily. Norman reached forward and took hold of Sam Frimley by the collar, still arguing with the empurpled treasurer. Then, grimly, all four men marched off the platform and out through the side door, Hall angrily gesticulating at Harcourt-Fanshaw to join them. The floral-waistcoated solicitor smiled almost benignly upon the near-riot surging around him and then moved in a ponderous, measured stride towards the back of the room.

‘He’s going to join them in the anteroom,’ Crickley gasped. ‘I want to get in on this.’ He struggled out of his row and half-ran to the back of the room. Arnold glanced at Syl Kirkby.

‘Are archaeological meetings always like this?’ Kirkby asked.

Arnold smiled. ‘No. Sometimes they get exciting.’

A man with a red-veined nose was on his feet extolling the merits of Phil Martin, the proposed chairman; a man in a heavy sweater was shouting that putting Martin in the chair was a fix. Feelings were clearly running high as a middle-aged woman stood up with her hat askew and in a shrill Roedean voice denounced the whole proceedings, her voice piercing the cacophonous din.

‘I have been a member of the Friends since we began and I came here today in all innocence, expecting a sober, controlled meeting. I was unaware of any controversy though

I have read the papers recently — that was to be aired at this meeting. I thought I would be attending the usual, quiet, gentlemanly annual general meeting and I had not been expecting to be involved in a beer garden!'

The meeting was collectively unimpressed. The noise continued for another ten minutes. Arnold found the whole situation almost bizarre with normally controlled elderly people standing up and mouthing insults and obscenities at each other. There were proposals and counterproposals. None of them were properly put, because there was no chairman to put them to; a squabble began between an Egyptologist and a papyrologist which had nothing to do with the points at issue; voices grew hoarse and gradually the tumult subsided, occasional murmurings rising to simmering point and falling away again, small knots of people gathering in like-minded groups, and a general air of resentment and anger percolating throughout the whole room.

Crickley slipped back in, and took his seat in front of Kirkby. He seemed disappointed, his sly lips downturned. 'Couldn't get near them,' he explained. 'They were in a huddle, but old Joe was sticking to his guns, and David Hall and Bill Norman were just about doing their nuts! But I think they're coming back in.'

The re-emergence of the platform party, together with Harcourt-Fanshaw, had a calming effect. Arnold noted that Hertford, Norman and Frimley hung back, not stepping up on the dais, so that only Hall and Harcourt-Fanshaw stood there. David Hall raised his hands, placatingly, and the noise slowly died away. An expectant hush fell on the room.

'It is clear that feelings are running high among the Friends.' Hall began. 'I am the last to wish to see a breakdown in trust and communication. I have had a frank discussion with Mr Harcourt-Fanshaw and he now has a proposal to put to you. The proposal is one, I may add, which has the support of the trustees.'

Joe Harcourt-Fanshaw stepped forward, urbane, controlled, opening his jacket slightly so that the full glory of his waistcoat was visible to all. He appeared very satisfied with himself, and a smug smile played about his full lips.

'It will not have escaped the notice of the Friends in this room that if one looks at the agenda items for our meeting there are some that are completely normal and noncontentious. There is one item, however the proposed sale of Trust land, which is of a different category. There are many in this room who hold very strong views about this matter — indeed, it has been the subject of a newspaper campaign of recent weeks.' He paused, and swept a confident glance around the room. 'My proposal, therefore, is this. We should continue with our general meeting and deal with the noncontentious items. In that respect, although I have made a recommendation to the chair, I am happy to withdraw that recommendation, and indeed propose that our friend Mr Hall continue in that capacity.'

'Sell out!' There were hissing sounds from the back of the room.

Harcourt-Fanshaw held up his pudgy hand. 'This would be the . . . right gesture to make, I feel, in view of the agreement I have reached with the trustees. That agreement is as follows. The contentious issue should be set aside and be the subject of discussions outside this room, among a small committee. The group would comprise the trustees, Mr Phil Martin and myself . . . we are numerically inferior,' he smiled, 'but I feel sure you will agree that we can hold our own with the trustees.'

Someone at the back shouted, 'You go for them, Joe!'

There was a stirring to Arnold's left.

'I think it appropriate that I also should be a member of the committee.'

Arnold glanced across: it was Peter Gaul. He appeared to be very angry, his dark brows contracted, possibly upset because he had not automatically been included in the discussion group. Harcourt-Fanshaw looked at him soberly for a long moment. 'I do not think that would be at all appropriate.'

'But—'

'You are an *employee.*' Harcourt-Fanshaw interrupted dismissively. 'As the director of the Field Centre, you have an interest to protect.'

'Don't you?' Gaul flashed angrily.

'Not a personal one, like yours. No, I don't think having you party to the discussions would be . . . profitable.' There was an odd bite to Harcourt-Fanshaw's words. He turned away and looked around. 'If we can have general agreement to this proposal, I think we needn't do it formally — just a show of hands . . .'

There was a rustling of murmurs, and then a lifting of hands. Everyone was tired of the tumult: it seemed a sensible way forward.

David Hall sighed and stepped up beside Harcourt-Fanshaw. 'I'll be happy to continue with the meeting along the lines suggested. There does remain one matter to be resolved, however: we need a chairman for the discussion group.'

'Phil Martin!'

'No, no.' Hall shook his head. 'We are agreed it should be someone who, shall we say, has no axe to grind, someone who has no personal interest in the issues, someone who can be relied upon to be knowledgeable, and impartial. Can I have some suggestions?'

There was a short silence then, to Arnold's surprise, Alan Crickley stood up. 'I would think, Mr Hall, that anyone in this room, who is a member of the Friends, would already have taken a stance on the issue of the Trust land sale. As a Friend, it would be almost inevitable. So, if you want an impartial disinterested chairman, I think you'd have to go outside the circle of the Friends themselves. I offer the suggestion as an outsider myself.'

'Have a non-member as chairman, you mean?' Hall asked. Harcourt-Fanshaw frowned thoughtfully, and peered at the journalist. 'Do you have anyone in mind, Mr Crickley?'

'As a matter of fact, I do. He's seated here, just behind me, impartial uninvolved, taking no sides, but well known in northern archaeological circles.' Crickley turned his head and grinned at Arnold. 'I would suggest you invite Mr Landon to chair the meetings.'

2

'How could you possibly allow yourself to be put into that position?' Karen Stannard stormed.

Sunlight streamed through the window of the director's office and Simon Brent-Ellis was seated behind his desk, staring out at the distant hills, stroking his moustache and clearly wishing he was somewhere up there in the soft sunshine. Arnold stood facing the irate deputy director: her eyes were blazing at him, dark-flecked now and her fury was barely controlled.

'I didn't exactly have much choice,' he replied defensively.

'Choice?' she snapped. 'It was I who'd given you *no* choice, as I recall our conversation in my office! I told you quite distinctly that you were to go to that meeting as an observer only, that you held no authority, no brief for the department, and that you were not to get involved in the affairs of the Viking Research Trust!'

Brent-Ellis stirred uncomfortably in his chair. He glanced at Arnold and furrowed his brow. 'You *did* have instructions, Landon.'

'The instructions were not to get involved,' Arnold said stubbornly. 'But the department is *not* involved. The call at the meeting was for a chairman who had no axe to grind, an independent chairman whose only function would be to keep the warring factions apart and bring the dispute to a reasonable solution. When I was invited I found myself in an impossible position—'

'One that appealed to your ego, you mean!' Karen Stannard flashed at him.

'The only appeal,' Arnold replied stiffly, 'was to common sense. The atmosphere in that room was rather heated — you can confirm that with Kirkby—'

'Kirkby!' The anger in Karen Stannard's voice was tinged with open contempt.

'He would be able to tell you that once Alan Crickley proposed me as chairman I protested that I was there only as an observer and that I desired to play no part ill the proceedings. I stressed that I could not act for the department—'

'Too damn right!'

'—but the argument was turned around against me. Harcourt-Fanshaw made it clear to me and to the rest of the meeting that I was being invited to chair the working group not as a member of the department, but in a personal capacity.'

'Because of the sterling work you've done, and the high-flown reputation you've achieved in archaeological research, I suppose?' Karen Stannard sneered.

Nettled, Arnold stared at her levelly; her eyes were dark and cold. 'Something like that,' he replied quietly.

'Well, I think, Director, that we simply cannot allow this situation to continue,' Karen Stannard snapped. 'If Landon acts as chairman of this group it's inevitable that the department will get dragged into the controversy, and we'll be forced to take sides. From what I understand, things could get difficult, and this man Harcourt-Fanshaw is dangerous. He's out to damage the trustees because of some idea he has that they haven't properly followed the wishes of the deceased Miss Ridge. He was a friend of hers, it seems, and is somewhat miffed that he wasn't given control of the trust properties when she died, and—'.

'You seem to have taken a stand in the situation already, Miss Stannard,' Arnold interrupted.

She glared at him. 'It's clear to me—'

'From what Peter Gaul told you privately?'

There was a short silence. The deputy director stood with one hand on the back of Brent-Ellis's chair and her body was still as she stared at Arnold. Her features were expressionless, but she knew that he had caught her. She did not enjoy the knowledge and Arnold was aware of the coiled venom in her stance as she stared at him.

'Peter Gaul gave me his private views,' she said at last, in a cold tone. 'I certainly haven't taken them on board. And I have made no departmental commitment to him or anyone else involved in the whole business. I certainly have not been indiscreet. But the facts—'

'The facts are, apparently, in dispute,' Arnold said firmly. 'Gaul has a view. So does the solicitor Harcourt-Fanshaw. And then there's David Hall, and the other trustees. They all have views. Which need to be reconciled. I was asked to help, in a *private* capacity. And there's no need for the department to take sides at all. It's nothing to do with the department.'

His tone was icy but the blood was pounding in his veins. Arnold was angry. He had not wanted to be made chairman of the working group; he had protested loudly, resisted at the meeting. Moreover, he had regretted his final acceptance, and he had come away with the vague hope that the department would later rule that he should not take the chairmanship. But that had been before he saw the venom in Karen Stannard's eyes. Now, because of her anger and aggressiveness, he had changed his mind. He still didn't want the job, but he was not going to be bullied out of it simply because Miss Stannard had a view about the matter. They glared at each other, neither prepared to give way.

It was not a situation that the director enjoyed. Brent-Ellis coughed nervously, stroked his luxuriant moustache and swivelled in his chair. Karen Stannard removed her hand from the chairback, reluctantly, as Brent-Ellis swung and swivelled. 'A private thing you say, Landon? No departmental involvement?'

Arnold nodded. 'I agreed to accept it only on those terms. I stated I would be acting as an individual and none of my actions should be seen as binding upon the department. Moreover, I stipulated that the meetings would have to be scheduled outside my working hours so that they were not seen as part of my job. So to that extent, Director, I don't see that the department is in any way compromised: it simply won't be involved.'

'There are some on the working group who will see involvement,' Karen Stannard said in a gritty tone. 'They could make assumptions. The department could be embarrassed.'

'Not so. Decisions will be taken by the group and presented to the Friends of the Trust. I am merely there to act as a referee: I shall make no decisions. Neither on the department's part, nor my own.'

'That at least should be right up your street,' Karen Stannard said bitingly. Taking no decisions is your forte, I think.'

'Only last week you suggested I took too *many* decisions,' Arnold snapped back.

Brent-Ellis kicked his legs under the table. Things were getting out of hand. He was aware of a spreading dampness under his armpits as his anxiety increased. 'You . . . er . . . say this work is private, Landon, and to be done in your own time. In the circumstances, I can't exactly *prevent* you from doing this work . . . can I, Karen?'

After a short silence, she replied, 'No, you can't *forbid* Mr Landon.'

Brent-Ellis was relieved, and his moustache twitched involuntarily, but he felt it necessary to maintain a facade of displeasure. He frowned. 'That's it then. We can't stop you, Landon. We don't approve, that's clear. But if this is in a private capacity, and in your own time, we can't stop you. But we've made our feelings clear, hey?'

'Very clear.'

Simon Brent-Ellis smacked the palms of his hands on the desk in front of him, conscious of having asserted his authority. He lurched to his feet, glanced nervously at his deputy and then flashed his teeth at Arnold in a mirthless grimace.

'Right. Well, there's no more to be said, then.'

When Arnold looked at Karen Stannard that was hardly the message in her cold, grey-green eyes.

* * *

As they left the room and marched past the dark-browed, glowering Miss Sansom, Karen Stannard smiled at Arnold: it had a feline, false sweetness about it. 'Perhaps we could have a quick word in my office, Landon?'

'Certainly.'

She led the way and closed the door behind them carefully, before she sat down behind her desk. She did not offer Arnold a seat: he stood stiffly in front of her. She observed him for a little while, a wry, cynical smile on her lips. 'I've underestimated you, Landon.'

'Really?'

She nodded. 'There are those in the department who think you're a man who likes a quiet life; like stirring no ripples. I went along with that at first. For instance, when I relieved you of certain tasks, I thought you'd be happy to give up the responsibility. I was told that Brent-Ellis landed executive tasks on you because he wanted rid of them. Now I realize the situation was more complex than that.'

'I don't understand you.'

'Oh, come on, I think you do.' She stared at him coolly. 'You've been playing the director like a gasping fish — pretending reluctance when he offloads jobs on you, but grasping every opportunity for self-advancement . . .'

Arnold stared woodenly at her. He was aware of what was happening. She was crediting Arnold with the kind of motivation that drove her — and the kind of tactics she was accustomed to use. Arnold remained silent as she went on.

'. . . I'm sure Brent-Ellis gave you tasks you wanted, really. You've been committed to a power play in this department, ever since you got thrown out of the last job you had here in County Hall. I know your record. You didn't "fit" in the Planning Department so you got yourself moved; you've already seen off one departmental director — I really must do some probing to work out how you managed that. And you've been working on Brent-Ellis ever since he was appointed. But now . . . you'll have been really miffed that I came in here above your head. You wanted this job, didn't you, Landon?'

She was so wrong it was almost ludicrous. 'I didn't even know the job was contemplated. And if I had—'

'Yes, I see,' she interrupted reflectively. 'You'd have been angry . . . and you're a clever man. I really have underestimated you — and normally I can sniff out competition in ten minutes. And *snuff* it out, too.' She smiled thinly. 'But I've been slow off the mark this time. Still, better late than never. I can tell you, though, your tactics . . . they won't work, Landon.'

'Tactics?'

'Undermining my authority.'

'You're so far from the truth—' Arnold began.

'It's what you tried to do there this morning, with the director. And, I admit, to a certain extent you succeeded. Don't think I can't see through you, Landon. This chairmanship thing — you took it because I'd told you not to get involved — it was a way of undermining me. It's all just a deliberate ploy to weaken my position. But don't you realize it just won't work? I can handle that buffoon in there, like I can handle all the men in this department. And I can handle you too, Landon — even you.'

'That's what management is about,' Arnold replied. His coolness annoyed her.

'That's right. And you'll soon find out just how I'll *manage* you.' She hesitated for a moment, a frown of frustration scarring her brow, and then almost involuntarily she delved in her desk drawer and came out with a cigarette and lighter. She lit the cigarette and drew on it slowly, her eyes still watching Arnold through the wreathing smoke. 'This is only a small skirmish you've won, Landon. Don't think you can go on to bigger and better things. If there's a war to be fought, I can promise you, I'll win it.'

'Deputy Director, I'm sure you believe everything you say.' He was suddenly tired of this ridiculous, self-centred conversation, which buttressed her own suspicions and fears. 'Is there anything else?'

She tapped the end of her cigarette with a thoughtful finger. 'Not at the moment, Mr Landon. But I hope you'll recall all I've said in this private conversation. Tread carefully, my friend. I'll be watching you.'

She was utterly beautiful, but there were tiny lines of displeasure around her finely chiselled lips.

* * *

After Landon had gone Karen Stannard finished her cigarette nervily, conscious of the vein beating in her forehead, a sure sign that she was disturbed. She had not shown him how upset she really was — but she was angry with herself for grabbing a cigarette — it was a sure sign that she was losing self-control.

But the man annoyed her — made her feel uncomfortable, out of her depth. She couldn't really understand Landon, in spite of what she had said to him. He had shown defiance, but in a quiet, subdued manner, almost as though he didn't know what she was talking about. She had been quick enough to recognize the surprise in his eyes when she had challenged him about his ambitions, but that could have been because he thought he was a good dissembler. And yet she could not be sure. She was left with the feeling she had not yet weighed up exactly what made Arnold Landon tick, nor determined where his real ambitions lay.

But she had to be careful.

She was a woman in a man's harsh world, and she had learned how to use her appearance as well as her wits to fight her way through to success. She was better than any man she knew. There was no way that Landon would beat her, in the long run — but she needed to keep a careful eye on him.

She stubbed out the cigarette angrily, frustrated that she had been unable to come to grips with the man.

The buzzer sounded.

'Yes?'

It was the old battleaxe in the outer office.

'Your next appointment is here, Miss Stannard.'

'Thank you, Miss Sansom. Send him straight in.'

A few moments later the door opened and Alan Crickley sauntered in, sandy hair untidy, foxy eyes flickering casually around the room and sour mouth upturned in a sneer. He sniffed at the air, glanced at the cigarette still smouldering in the ashtray. 'Seeking solace, Miss Stannard, or soothing frayed nerves?'

'Mr Crickley, of the *Journal*, I believe?' she said, ignoring the jibe.

'Put Livingstonely, to be sure. Alan Crickley, one and the same. I'm pleased to meet you, Miss Stannard.' He extended his hand. 'I've heard a great deal about you.'

'And I've heard *nothing* about you.'

He wasn't fooled by the bantering tone or the insincere smile. 'That's the way it should be,' he countered. 'You're the subject — me, I'm just the scribe.'

'You want to interview me.'

'That's the size of it.'

'And your objective?'

'To find out all about you,' he leered, 'and find out how you've made it to where you are.'

'I'm sure there'll be plenty of stories about that already.'

'I'm not a man who listens to gossip — unless it has a basis in truth.'

'Maybe that's why you haven't got on in the newspaper business.'

His eyes narrowed. 'I've managed well enough. Though not a shooting star like you. What do you put your undoubted success down to, Miss Stannard?'

'Talent. And intelligence.'

'And application, I would guess,' he said, taking a seat.

'I think you could say that.' She hesitated, damping down the dislike she already felt for the man and his arrogant attitude. She had started the interview badly — it was the unsettling meeting she'd had with Landon that had caused her to be uncharacteristically sharp with this man. She liked weighing up people before she unsheathed her claws: find weak spots so that her strike could be the more effective. 'Shall we have some coffee, Mr Crickley? And then we can discuss what you want to know.'

He was mollified, if not fooled. She rang the unwilling dragon for coffee and then chatted inconsequentially with Crickley, allowing him to lead the conversation into her personal history in a gradual way, explaining to him about her life at university, her book, the work she'd done at Newcastle and Durham, and the challenges she saw herself facing in this new job with the Department of Museums and Antiquities.

Miss Sansom eventually entered with two cups of coffee and a grim mouth. After she'd gone, Crickley glanced back at the door and grinned. 'Doesn't look as though *everyone* is pleased by your arrival.'

She smiled confidentially. 'Mr Crickley, I would imagine there are very few who are pleased by my appearance here. But that's all right with me: I can handle unpopularity. It's a consequence of success.'

He wrinkled his brow. 'You sound like a tough lady.'

'*You* sound surprised.'

He breathed deeply and ducked his head. 'Well, if you don't mind me saying so, when a woman is as beautiful as you—'

'You're on dangerous ground, Mr Crickley,' she said, lighting another cigarette.

He laughed. 'I'm sure I am. So you're unpopular in the department?'

'What boss isn't?'

'And there'll be men who don't like being run by a woman.'

'More than a few.'

'Anyone in particular?'

She shook her head. 'You can hardly expect me to tell a newspaperman that. On the other hand . . .'

'Yes?'

'Why did you propose Arnold Landon as the chairman of the Trust working group?'

Alan Crickley set down his empty coffee cup and leaned back in his chair. He watched her carefully for several seconds before he replied. 'There was quite a shindig at that meeting. It was clear that the people in the hall would never have elected a chairman in a month of Sundays — unless they were given an independent chairman. The thought came to me — Arnold Landon. He's harmless enough.'

'Harmless? Is that how you see him?'

Crickley scratched at a sore spot on his chin and eyed her foxily. 'Clearly, you don't. Landon . . . let's say he's an interesting man. Self-made, no background of learning, and yet he's acknowledged by many people in the north-east and elsewhere, I understand — to be an expert in a field usually dominated by professional historians and archaeologists. But he doesn't shout about his talents and skills — he keeps a fairly low profile, in fact—'

'And yet his name keeps coming up. I wonder how he *does* that?'

'I would have said it was circumstance . . . but you think it's deliberate.'

'I think he's a clever man,' Karen Stannard said noncommittally.

Crickley was silent for a little while, staring at her almost abstractedly. 'So you're bothered about his taking the chair with the Trust,' he said at last.

'Bothered? Oh, I wouldn't say that. You overstate the issue. It's a matter of little consequence to me personally. But he's a member of this department. I wouldn't want to see the department embarrassed by any . . . indiscreet action that Mr Landon might take.'

'He stressed he was taking the task in a personal capacity,' Crickley said.

'So I understand. But the Landons of this world . . .' She let the words trail away into silence. She had stubbed out the cigarette; it lay smouldering in the ashtray. Crickley stared at it, thoughtfully.

'You don't like Arnold Landon.'

'I don't *understand* him . . . and I'm wary of people I don't understand.'

'You're being very frank with me.'

'You I *do* understand,' she replied coldly.

His eyes met hers and there was a genuine pleasure in his glance, albeit tinged with malice. 'I have a feeling I might be able to help you.'

'And I have a feeling that if you do help me, it won't be gratuitous.'

'All things have a cost — and if you will dance with the devil—'

'I've never been burned in my life.'

Alan Crickley sighed. 'Well, let me put it like this. I believe in casting bread upon the waters. If I can help someone, that's OK. There may be a time, later, when a favour could be returned.'

'Or not.'

'That's a risk a generous person like me is always prepared to take,' he replied, unconvincingly.

'So how do you think you can help me?' Karen Stannard asked.

Crickley shrugged. 'You say you don't understand Landon. Maybe you feel he's some kind of threat to you. I don't know,' he said quickly as she opened her mouth to contradict him, 'and I don't want to know. But in this matter of the Trust chairmanship, I could . . . ah . . . keep you informed about what's going on.'

'I'll get reports from Landon.'

'*His* version of events.'

'You could get me a different viewpoint?'

Crickley nodded. 'So that if you felt at any time that the department might be, as you put it, embarrassed, you could take early action to rein in your friend.'

There was a calculating gleam in Karen Stannard's grey-green eyes. She smiled thinly. 'You don't have a seat on that working group, Mr Crickley.'

'Who needs a seat?' He smiled wolfishly. 'You've got to remember — everyone wants something. Life's all about scratching backs. Take Mr Harcourt-Fanshaw, for instance. Now there's a man with a mission. He wants to right a wrong — after he's found out exactly what the wrong is. And so he is not averse to talking to me, asking me to ferret out what I can, that sort of thing. And he uses me from time to time — tells me when something interesting is likely to blow. He feels that through me he can orchestrate press coverage to his advantage.' Crickley paused. 'Then, on the other hand, when I want to know something . . .'

'Like just what's really going on in the Trust committee . . .'

'Exactly.'

Karen Stannard made no attempt to stifle a pointed yawn. 'This is all rather trivial. I'm not certain there's much point in this conversation. I'm not really bothered about what Landon gets up to.'

Crickley was not fooled. Casually, he said, 'But you wouldn't be averse to hearing snippets from time to time.'

She shrugged. 'If you think it would be of interest to the department.'

Alan Crickley rose to his feet. 'I think we can work along on that basis.'

She looked up at him carefully. 'I've no intention of seeing this as a cost to me. There's no quid pro quo here, Mr Crickley.'

He grinned unpleasantly. 'Who's talked of payment? Take it as a gift. On the other hand, sometime in the future, who knows how you might be able to help me?'

'No guarantees.'

'As you say.'

She stared at him coldly. He bowed mockingly to her. 'Thanks for the information anyway — and the coffee. There'll be a small write-up in the *Journal* for your personal scrapbook — young whizzwoman heads for the heights sort of thing.'

'Brilliant.'

He ignored her sarcasm. At the door he paused, as though a thought had struck him. 'I'll be in touch with you about Landon. And, as you said, no payment, or guarantee, but . . .'

'Yes?' she asked coldly.

'It does occur to me, there is something you could help me on right now. It's not terribly important . . .'

'What is it?'

He shrugged, frowning. 'There's a man in your department . . . I have a feeling I've met him before. He denied it — rather too forcibly, it seemed to me. I just wonder about him, his background, where he came from, that sort of thing.'

'Has he been here long?'

'No.'

'I don't think I can help,' she said shortly.

'Oh, I don't know. You have departmental files. A quick look,' he said airily. 'And it's no big deal. I'm just curious about him . . . can't place the face sort of thing.' Reluctantly, she asked, 'What's his name?'

'Kirkby.'

Syl Kirkby. That weasel. There was something about the man — Landon's acolyte — that disturbed Karen Stannard. She kept her features expressionless as she stared at the newspaperman, but his eyes were keen. Perhaps he had caught a vibration of dislike from her at the mention of Kirkby's name. Or perhaps she was being fanciful. But she was left with the impression that Crickley could see into her soul, and knew her rather better than she would have wished. It was not a thought that pleased her. Nevertheless . . .

'I might be able to have a look,' she said diffidently.

'Now that's what I call friendly,' Crickley said, grinning. 'I'll be in touch.' He waved his hand in farewell, and left the room.

She stared at the cigarette butts in the ashtray. Now that Alan Crickley had left the room she was vaguely aware of a nasty taste in her mouth.

3

M Harcourt-Fanshaw was clearly a man of considerable personal wealth. Arnold discovered that Fanshaw Hall was an old building which, he guessed, had started life as a monastic house. There were the ruins of a church close by, in the fields that ran down towards the meandering river, and the life of monastic houses typically centred around a church. But it was the layout of the house itself which gave Arnold the clues: the courtyard, the traces of the crucial waterway which would have served for sewage disposal, and a layout which pointed to a cellarage in the western range of the house, a cloister and a dormitory beyond a small chapter house.

The property had been converted into a private house at least two hundred and fifty years ago and it now served as a magnificent, well-maintained hall — a long, two-storeyed building which held a day stair in one corner of the main hall and a night stair contrived out of the thickness of what would have been the transept wall.

Arnold was waiting for his host in the library, which had been formed out of what he guessed would have been the monks' refectory. A tall window — clearly a later addition had been let into the wall to afford a long vista down across the water meadows to the rising Northumberland hills beyond. They seemed blue in the later afternoon haze, and there was a golden tinge to the sky beyond as the sun began to drop behind the quiet crags in the distance.

'You'll forgive me for keeping you waiting,' an affable voice boomed behind him.

Arnold turned. It was Harcourt-Fanshaw, a welcoming smile creasing his craggy features, the thumb of his left hand tucked into the floral waistcoat gaping on his portly frame. He was clearly fond of patterned waistcoats, an affectation that gave him an other-world appearance.

'Not at all. I've been musing about your house.'

'Magnificent, isn't it? Been in the family of my late wife for something like five generations. Goes way back, I believe — but you'll know more about these things than I do . . . As I say, sorry to keep you waiting, but I had some matters to discuss with my friends here. You'll have met Phil Martin, of course.'

'Not exactly met,' Arnold replied. 'I did see Mr Martin at the Friends' meeting the other day.'

'When you were elevated to the chairmanship of the working group, and a fine time was had by all.' Martin said, grinning, and held out his hand. His grasp was firm, the skin of his hand rough and calloused. He was a big man, broad-shouldered and deep-chested, with fair, tightly curled hair greying at the temples, and a dark-skinned, closed face that gave little away. He was demonstrating geniality at the moment, but Arnold suspected that in the negotiations he would be forced to conduct in his building business there would be times when his mouth would become iron, and his eyes granite. He would be a man who would not suffer fools gladly, and who would despise weakness in an opponent. Competition would be his life blood, and a fight — perhaps like the Friends' Trust meeting — would stir his blood pleasurably. But he would never enjoy being on the losing side.

'Phil came along to discuss tactics prior to the meeting.'

Harcourt-Fanshaw announced easily. 'Would you care for a drink, Landon? No? The usual for you, I guess, Phil.' He walked across to the far wall and opened the door of the drinks cabinet built into the bookcase. He poured out two whiskies, checked with Arnold that he had not changed his mind, and then came back, gesturing both men to take seats in the deep leather armchairs that stood near the long window.

'How did they take your chairmanship in the department?' Harcourt-Fanshaw asked.

Arnold shrugged. 'I stressed it was in a personal capacity.'

'I think Alan Crickley was being a little naughty, there . . . but I'm sure we've taken a wise step.'

'I'll do all I can to help — but I stress I'll try to retain a balanced view. I'm not sure, for instance, that it's wise to have a private conversation with you here. It could be misunderstood.'

Harcourt-Fanshaw eyed him carefully for a moment, then sighed theatrically. 'You'll have gathered already, Landon, that we have a battle on our hands. That much would have been obvious from the furore you witnessed the other day at the meeting. But my guess is that you'll know very little about the background to the whole thing. So, I thought it would be useful if we had a short discussion before we all proceed along the road to the arranged meeting — it's only a fifteen-minute drive to Ridgeway Manor — and I would then be able to fill you in so you're up to speed before the meeting itself begins.'

Arnold nodded. 'At the risk of sounding pompous, Mr Harcourt-Fanshaw, although I agreed to this meeting with you I'd better make it clear that you shouldn't see it as an opportunity to . . . shall we say, influence me to take sides.'

Harcourt-Fanshaw's flushed face broke into a wide smile. 'My dear boy, far from it. I'm aware of what you said at the last meeting: an independent chairman. That's what was required — that's what we got. No, no, I don't seek to influence you, but I still think it's useful to explain a few things.'

Arnold glanced at Phil Martin. The builder's features were impassive. He sat back in his chair, staring out unseeingly at the view, glass in hand, relaxed.

'I suppose I should start with my friendship with Miss Ridge.' Harcourt- Fanshaw began with a sigh. 'A nice old lady — I say that, though she was only about ten years older than me. Never married, you know, lived alone, apart from the servants at Ridgeway Manor, last in the line as far as the family was concerned.'

'She was a descendant of William Ridge, the man who built what was to be Ridge Hall?' Arnold asked.

'That folly up on the hill? You know it, then? Yes, that's right. I think at one stage she had it in mind to try to complete the building, but that was a youthful, romantic dream. It was uneconomic as a proposition. She was wealthy, of course. Investments since the Second World War mainly, but pouring money into that old ruin would soon have bankrupted her, in my view. Anyway, that's another story.'

He sipped his drink and savoured the taste of the malt whisky. He murmured in satisfaction. 'Well then, you should know that I first came into contact with Miss Ridge when I married and moved here to this house. Second marriage — I was called Harcourt in those days and had to take the Fanshaw bit as part of the marriage settlement, you know. Miss Ridge, she was friendly with my wife, and she soon handed over all her legal affairs to me. Not a lot to do, really: leases, administration of a trust which I finally advised her to end since she was the only beneficiary, that sort of thing. She was my wife's friend rather than mine, but I liked the old girl, and, well, I feel now that I let her down somewhat.'

'Let her down? In what way?' Arnold asked.

Harcourt-Fanshaw shrugged. 'Not being around when I was needed. You see, after my wife died I felt it necessary to get away for a while. Did an extended tour of the Far East: took my mind off things. But it was a critical time for Miss Ridge. First of all, there was a burglary, as a result of which she had a series of heart attacks — more frightening, really, than critical. And secondly, it was just about the time that the stream burst through at the hill on her property and they discovered the old bones. You know, the ones they realized later were probably Viking.'

Martin stirred in his chair, as though about to say something, but then remained silent.

'So, it was then she made the decision. Intimations of mortality, the thought that the find should be properly protected, the idea maybe that this would be one way of letting her name live on after her — I suppose there was a whole raft of reasons. Anyway, she took action — she set up the Viking Research Trust and appointed a group of people to administer the Trust. But, possibly because she was upset that I wasn't around at this critical juncture, she didn't make me one of the trustees.'

'Were you expecting to be one up to then?' Arnold asked.

'But naturally. I was her legal adviser. And a friend. But by the time I got back, it was too late. She'd set up the Trust, appointed the trustees, and the whole thing was set in motion. I went to see her and we talked about it. She was a bit cool to me, but she gradually came around and I think she had decided to add me to the list of trustees, after all. While she was alive, she still held that power for herself under the deed.'

'But she never did it?'

Harcourt-Fanshaw shook his head. 'Never got the chance. She had another coronary. It killed her. So that was that. Except . . .'

There was an odd gleam in his eyes. He sipped his whisky and leaned closer to Arnold, his tone confidential. 'I always felt . . . uneasy about the Trust.'

'Why?'

'Nothing I could put my finger on. But, well, the people involved. There's Jock Hertford, to start with — good old Sir Jock was well known to Miss Ridge, not that she had much time for him at one stage. But of recent years he'd inveigled himself into her affairs — became her confidant while I was absent. I wouldn't trust Jock further than I could throw him.' He frowned at his whisky. 'Then there was the setting up of the Trust. Hertford recommended a legal firm in Morpeth. Then the trustees — Hertford pulled them together, but they were all Johnny Come Latelys. David Hall, for instance, chairman of Wheeler Holdings Ltd — just recently moved into the area, met Miss Ridge in church, I understand. Became a visitor. But she didn't know him terribly well. And the others, Frimley, that buffoon Norman . . . it was a group brought together by Hertford. Almost like a Conservative Party Association deal. Something about it smacked . . . odd.'

'If she had asked Hertford for advice,' Arnold demurred, 'I imagine it would have been natural for him to seek out people of consequence and commitment who were known to him.'

'That's one way of looking at it,' Phil Martin commented in a sneering tone. Arnold glanced at him, wondering what stake really lay in all this for a hard-headed businessman like Martin — he did not seem the kind of man who would be interested in the preservation of ancient trust property of historical and archaeological significance.

'Don't get me wrong,' Harcourt-Fanshaw argued. 'I'm not saying there was anything amiss in the make-up of the group of trustees. No, they're committed enough, I suspect. But at the same time, apart from Hertford they were out-comers, you know what I mean? And then they appointed that chap Gaul.'

'I've met him.'

'Able enough, well qualified . . . but got some funny ideas,' Harcourt-Fanshaw muttered. 'And if he had his way, I think he'd take the whole project in quite the wrong direction. And then there's the terms of the Trust itself.'

'There's a problem there?'

Harcourt-Fanshaw pulled a face. 'Perhaps, perhaps not. Let's just say there are certain doubts . . .'

'But you said there was a Trust deed. Surely it would contain the necessary details.'

Harcourt-Fanshaw hesitated. 'Yes . . . and no. The Trust deed is clear enough. But it doesn't cover all of the property owned by Miss Ridge. You see, I was her legal adviser, and I know. The Trust deals with most of the land in the valley, including Ridgeway Manor and Ridge Hall up on the crag, but there are some odd omissions.'

'She left some property elsewhere? I don't see anything odd in that,' Arnold suggested.

'Nor I. But to whom did she leave the property? There's no will proved that covers the rest of her holdings. Ridgeway Home Farm, for instance — apparently it was sold, but it was to some kind of company registered in Jersey. And when I've asked questions there's been a degree of reticence on the part of the trustees, a reluctance to provide satisfactory answers. They say, in the end, it's none of my business.'

A stain of anger had reddened his cheeks; he sipped at his whisky and glanced uncertainly at Phil Martin. He was silent for a little while. Then he gathered himself and continued. 'Anyway, what with that, and the sort of unhappy feeling I had about the whole thing, I decided to take action.'

Arnold stared thoughtfully at the solicitor. Nothing the man had said so far led Arnold to believe he was motivated by anything other than a desire to salve wounded pride. He had been overlooked, ignored by the old lady when she had been facing the early prospect of death. 'So what action did you take?' he asked quietly.

'I set up the Friends of the Viking Research Trust, so I could keep an eye on the buggers,' Harcourt-Fanshaw said blandly, and took a long, satisfied swallow of whisky.

* * *

The drive to Ridgeway Manor was a pleasant one through winding lanes and high hedgerows that dipped through a valley thick with sycamore and alder and birch. Gradually, the valley widened, opening out as it joined the Ridge property, until Arnold caught a glimpse of the Ridge Hall folly on top of the crags and realized they were close to Ridgeway Manor itself, on the valley floor. As Harcourt-Fanshaw had said, it was only a short drive.

The solicitor and Phil Martin had driven ahead of Arnold, leading the way in Harcourt-Fanshaw's Jaguar. It gave Arnold time to reflect upon the meeting at Harcourt-Fanshaw's house. He was puzzled somewhat: it had been indecisive in the sense that he was not aware of any real reason for it being held. Apart from giving Arnold the background, and expressing his personal anxieties, Harcourt-Fanshaw had said little enough. Certainly, he had been punctilious in not attempting to influence Arnold in any way — other than by sowing seeds of suspicion about the motives of the trustees. Arnold suspected it had been little more than an attempt to give Harcourt-Fanshaw the chance to sum up Arnold Landon himself. Or maybe it had been for the benefit of Phil Martin.

Arnold was not clear as to how the businessman fitted into the scheme of things. He recalled there had been some considerable opposition to the suggestion at the Friends' meeting that Martin should take the chair. The cry of personal interest had gone up. Arnold had not yet determined where the problem might lie.

The meeting of the trustees was to be held in the dining room of Ridgeway Manor. When Arnold followed the others up the curved drive, parked near the colonnaded entrance and walked into the house, turning left into the dining room, he realized it was a room in the grand style. Some forty feet long, decorated with carved plasterwork, it was a handsome room built for entertaining in the grand manner. The house was seventeenth-century, but had been considerably restored — not always in the best tradition.

Sir Jock Hertford and David Hall were already there, and greeted each of them with a handshake and a smile.

David Hall was affability itself towards Arnold. His blue eyes were friendly and confident. 'I won't say I'm in any way disappointed that you're taking the chair of this meeting, Mr Landon,' he announced. 'It means it won't be left to me to keep old rogues like Jock Hertford and Joe Harcourt-Fanshaw in their place. They're old enemies, you know.'

Both Harcourt-Fanshaw and Hertford laughed loudly, but there was a forced edge to the laughter that did not escape Arnold. They stood side by side, the portly solicitor and the stocky, florid-faced man with the bad-tempered mouth, and they projected a false good humour. Tea was available to them all on a table in the corner of the room. Hall glanced at his watch and said he expected the others would soon arrive since the meeting was due to commence at six thirty.

Arnold took a cup of tea and moved a little apart from the others: he was not noted for his small talk. While he sipped his tea, Jock Hertford sidled across to him, where he stood admiring a full-length oil painting hung on the wall to the left of the door. 'That's the old man.' Hertford said.

'Who do you mean?'

'William Ridge — the nutcase who tried to build that house on the hill. Religious community, he wanted it for. Silly old duffer.'

'Different men, different dreams,' Arnold murmured. 'Suppose there's sense in that.' Arnold was aware of Hertford's eyes on him. 'You arrived the same time as Harcourt-Fanshaw, I noted.'

Arnold nodded. 'That's right. He showed me the way here.' He hesitated. 'We had a short meeting at his house before we arrived. Nothing significant. He just told me about Miss Ridge and his friendship with her. And the setting up of the Trust.'

'Hmmm. He wasn't around at the time, of course. That's why the old lady turned to me. Knew her for years. Harcourt-Fanshaw was a bit miffed about that. Hard luck, I say.' His piggy eyes dwelled on Arnold reflectively. 'You don't want to listen to everything old Harcourt-Fanshaw says. Got a bee in his bonnet. Everything in the trust is above board, but he's out to stir up trouble. David's a bit upset about it all.'

'Mr Hall?' Arnold glanced across to the chairman of the Viking Research Trust, talking animatedly to Harcourt-Fanshaw and smiling broadly. He did not seem upset at the moment. 'I would have thought he could handle the kind of problems that Harcourt-Fanshaw raised at the meeting.'

'Oh, he can, believe me.' Hertford replied with a certain grimness. 'He's tough, our David. Was in the paratroopers, you know. He can handle himself. Indeed, I'm not alone in admiring the way he's built up Wheeler Holdings Ltd. It was a run-down operation before he was drafted in. Turned it around in five years — real success story. Shares have quadrupled in value since then. Bit of a soft patch at the moment — recession, you know — but he'll come out of it, you mark my words. He's well thought of, is our David.' His voice dropped somewhat as he adopted a confidential air. 'Just between ourselves, there could be something coming his way.'

Arnold stared at the man's little red eyes. 'How do you mean.'

Hertford wagged his head sagely. 'There's a few of us in the Conservative Association believe his work for leisure in the north will not go unrewarded.' When he saw the puzzlement in Arnold's eyes he dropped his voice even lower. 'Next Honours list,' he half whispered. 'If an old duffer like me can get a gong there's every chance he'll be on the list.'

If the local association got its way, Arnold concluded. He turned, as he heard David Hall announce, 'Ah, they're here — the latecomers.'

Bill Norman came in first, clumping his way into the room, heavy-footed and powerful, then a few paces behind him the hawk-featured Sam Frimley. They appeared to have come in separate cars. The air of forced bonhomie as members of the group greeted each other did not escape Arnold: there were underlying tensions to be coped with.

Arnold called the meeting to order a little after six thirty.

They were seated along a broad mahogany table set with neat writing pads and pens: the pads bore the watermark of Wheeler Holdings Ltd, David Hall's company. Arnold noticed a curl of contempt to Harcourt-Fanshaw's lip as he fiddled with the pad in front of him.

'You will all be aware,' Arnold began, 'that I've been appointed as an independent chairman, and that necessarily means I'm not too familiar with the issues involved that have caused so much argument among the Friends of the Viking Research Trust. At the meeting, Mr Harcourt-Fanshaw proposed this working group to resolve contentious issues. As far as I'm aware, there is only one — the proposed sale of Ridgeway Manor.'

'Others might crawl out of the woodwork, if you don't manage to keep Harcourt-Fanshaw in check, Chairman,' Bill Norman growled.

'I think we can start with the proposed sale.' Harcourt-Fanshaw announced almost genially, disregarding Norman's intervention. 'Perhaps I could begin by making a statement?'

'Please do,' Arnold agreed.

'I think it would be worth my while recapping what my understanding of the situation was, immediately before the death of Miss Amelia Ridge.'

'Is that really necessary?' Sir Jock Hertford queried, his red-rimmed eyes narrowing angrily.

'In the interests of the chairman.' Harcourt-Fanshaw replied blandly. 'I think he needs to be aware of the . . . er . . . tensions that surround the *whole* matter.'

'I'd like to hear it' Arnold ruled.

'As Miss Ridge's legal adviser, up to the time of my wife's death, I had drawn up her will, by which she had made a number of bequests, the details of which we needn't go into. You can imagine my surprise, Chairman, when I returned from my trip to the Far East, after her death, to discover that she had drawn up an entirely new will—'

'With the assistance of an entirely reputable firm of solicitors in Morpeth,' Hertford snapped.

'I don't impugn them,' Harcourt-Fanshaw allowed. 'A well-respected firm. But I had conversations with the senior partner — we were at Cambridge together — and I understand that the final dispositions made by Miss Ridge were not entirely in accordance with the bequests he had drawn up for her.'

'We're all of us entitled to change our minds,' Sam Frimley commented, after a short silence. 'That's the law, isn't it?'

'Quite. But I've never understood just how it all happened.'

David Hall shifted in his seat, and sucked his teeth thoughtfully. 'Perhaps, Chairman, I might be able to help Mr Harcourt-Fanshaw. I don't see that it's at all relevant to *this* meeting, but let's not cavil about that. The facts are as follows. Miss Ridge did make a new will, after her heart attacks, with the assistance of the Morpeth firm, in Mr Harcourt-Fanshaw's absence. And about that time she also consulted me, and Sir Jock, about the discovery of the Viking grave in the valley. I had got to know her through the church,' he added almost apologetically, 'and she seemed to, well, value my advice.'

'That's right.' Hertford added firmly, glaring at Harcourt-Fanshaw.

'She told us — Jock and me — that she wanted to establish a trust to oversee, control and protect the site and develop it as a sort of heritage centre. We agreed to act as trustees ourselves, and find two others. But at the time we held those discussions we were left in no doubt as to how it would be established.'

'And just what were her intentions?' Harcourt-Fanshaw asked carefully.

'She made them quite clear. She repeatedly told us that the Viking grave area in the valley would be given to a trust which we would operate. The idea was that she would set up the Viking Research Trust as an entirely separate charity to own and manage that property. On that basis we went ahead. The Trust was established.'

'And her will?'

'She never discussed her will with us.' Hertford intervened.

David Hall nodded. 'As far as we were aware, whatever happened to the rest of her property, the Trust would be safe, independent, controlling the site and its environs. Basically, the valley floor, really.'

Arnold hesitated, glancing around the group. 'But that's not what finally happened?'

'Exactly.' Harcourt-Fanshaw muttered.

'If it had been just that, no problem would have arisen.' Hall suggested. 'But you can imagine our surprise when the truth emerged after Miss Ridge's death. Unknown to us as trustees, she had seen fit to leave to the Trust a large part of the valley holdings, including Ridgeway Manor itself, and the folly on the crags up there. This had never previously been communicated to us as her intentions, and it caused us some embarrassment.'

'That I can believe.' Harcourt-Fanshaw growled. 'What puzzles me — and a lot of other people — was that the bequest did not appear in the new will drawn up by the Morpeth firm.'

David Hall shook his head. 'I can't comment on that. All I can say is that Miss Ridge, shortly before she died, added a handwritten codicil without the benefit of advice from the Morpeth solicitors, it seems. It was in her own hand, and properly attested, so there was no legal problem with it.'

'But in that codicil she made new, additional bequests, including the gift of Ridgeway Manor to the trustees. Why did she do that?'

'We have no idea.' David Hall said flatly.

'And what were the other bequests?'

Hall shrugged. 'They are of no concern to us. Our interest lies only in the Trust bequests.'

'So you know nothing about the ownership of Ridgeway Home Farm or the company in Jersey?' Harcourt-Fanshaw challenged.

Sir Jock Hertford's cheeks were reddening. He turned to Arnold. 'Chairman, the question has already been answered by David Hall. Our interest here is in the Trust affairs. What the old lady did with her property is of interest to us only in so far as it affects the Trust — and the Friends.'

'I think that's right,' Arnold agreed, nodding to Harcourt-Fanshaw. The solicitor leaned back in his chair, hands placed flat on the table in front of him.

'All right,' he said, 'I'll leave that where it stands for the moment. But let me ask this question. Was the bequest to the Trust, in the codicil, made with any legal qualification or restriction?'

David Hall shook his head. 'There were none.'

'So why now do you wish to sell Ridgeway Manor?'

Hall looked steadily at Harcourt-Fanshaw. 'Decisions about the sale of the manor house are for the trustees. This is not — as you've already pointed out — a meeting of trustees. We are gathered together as a group of the Friends of the Trust, an entirely separate body and one not registered as a charity. You explained all that to us very well, Mr Harcourt-Fanshaw.'

'Glad you learned something the other day. But I still ask the question. The Friends were established to assist and help in the work of the Trust. I feel they're entitled to have a say in the sale of the manor.'

'Legally, they are not.' David Hall stated firmly.

'Maybe not legally, but morally they are!' Harcourt-Fanshaw insisted. 'What's there to hide in all this? Why can't you be open about it? Even though the Friends can't insist on knowing, or having a say in decisions properly to be made by the trustees, why all the secrecy? What the hell is going on, Hall?'

The emotional temperature was beginning to rise in the room. Arnold leaned forward, keeping his tone quiet and measured. 'Let's not get carried away by the kind of emotions we saw at the meeting of the Friends, gentlemen. I can see Mr Hall's point — legally, this is a matter for the trustees. On the other hand, Mr Harcourt-Fanshaw has the support of many of the Friends when he asks questions. Is there any reason why you cannot discuss with us in this group your reasons for the sale of Ridgeway Manor, Mr Hall?'

David Hall hesitated, then shrugged, capitulating. 'I knew Miss Ridge in the last few months of her life. She had become a frightened, confused woman. Jock and I, we were able to help her, give her some support that was lacking from her old friends.' Involuntarily he glanced at Harcourt-Fanshaw. 'I liked her — and she trusted me. That counts for something. I haven't wanted to expose what she was like in those last weeks — frail, confused, a little . . . I would appreciate if what I'm about to say could be kept in confidence. The situation is rather . . . delicate.'

'What situation?' Harcourt-Fanshaw demanded, anger staining his tone.

David Hall stared at him impassively. 'The bequest was made, as I said, without legal qualifications. On the other hand, it did not come unburdened.'

'What's that supposed to mean?'

'Miss Ridge had lost track of her affairs. She thought she was a richer woman than she really was.'

'She was wealthy!' Harcourt-Fanshaw insisted.

'It depends what comparisons you make.'

'She had landholdings, Ridgeway Manor itself—'

'It was burdened with a mortgage debt of three hundred thousand pounds — and no endowment.'

'I don't believe it!' Harcourt-Fanshaw gasped.

'Believe it or not.' Hall stated calmly, 'it's the truth.'

'But the property can't be worth half a million,' Phil Martin suggested in a cold voice.

'Therein lies our problem.' David Hall replied. 'If we managed to find a buyer, when all costs are cleared, the trustees would be lucky to come out with more than two hundred thousand pounds. And there is no endowment to the Trust — with little income arising from the land-holding gifted to us.'

'And the mortgage, if you don't sell?' Harcourt-Fanshaw asked.

'We can't afford to service it. Not when you take the other considerations into account.'

Arnold frowned. 'What considerations?'

David Hall sighed. 'There was also a memorandum of wishes drawn up by Miss Ridge. It made various suggestions about what she thought we should be doing with the site. We've since taken both legal and financial advice. The law firm in Morpeth tell us the memorandum does not form part of the codicil and therefore is not legally binding on the trustees. And financially — well, we are advised that the suggestions she made involve financial risks which are inappropriate to a charity.'

'So your answer is to sell!'

David Hall was nettled by Harcourt-Fanshaw's tone. 'What alternative do we have? We were given lands but no money; the manor house crippled with a mortgage — and suggestions for development and protection of the site. But we can't afford to service the mortgage and carry out development work on the site. We certainly daren't go along with Miss Ridge's wishes — which are not binding on us anyway. What alternative is there but to sell, and use the proceeds to further the work of the Trust?'

Phil Martin leaned forward, his cold eyes fixed on David Hall. 'As I understand it, you haven't explored the possibilities. I believe Ridgeway Manor could be put to other uses. I've already told Mr Hall, Chairman, that I can put together a consortium of businessmen who would be prepared to put money into the Trust in return for a long lease and use of the manor house—'

'We've already discussed that at length.' Sir Jock Hertford snapped testily. 'To start with, the uses you suggest would not be in keeping with the ambiance of the valley, there's some doubt whether a charitable trust could countenance such a deal, and in any case, what's this consortium you talk about? Eight businessmen, I've been told. Who are they? What are their plans? It's all so vague, undefined—'

'Like your proposed buyer?' Martin challenged.

Bill Norman hunched his powerful shoulders and glared at Martin. 'We have a buyer — but he wants to remain anonymous until all this furore has died down. That's his right.'

'You've only one buyer, and he's anonymous.' Harcourt-Fanshaw scoffed. 'Is that the way a charitable trust should behave?'

'We'd probably get more buyers if you and others in the Friends hadn't raised all this stink in the newspapers.' Sam Frimley argued.

'The newspapers wouldn't have been alerted if everything was all above board!' Harcourt-Fanshaw roared.

'What the hell's that supposed to mean?' Bill Norman shouted. 'Don't talk to me about things being above board! Your friend Martin's proposal for a long lease is fine, except we've never seen a firm proposal and I have the feeling that its terms won't be acceptable to those of us who want to see the Trust properly managed.'

'Are you suggesting that I don't act in the best interests of the Research Trust?' Harcourt-Fanshaw bellowed.

The meeting, Arnold concluded, was heading the same way as the meeting of the Friends of the Viking Research Trust.

4

The papers had piled up on Arnold's desk.

Karen Stannard had announced that his workload was to be changed so that what she regarded as 'executive' matters should be taken from him and left where they belonged with her or with the director. As far as Arnold could see, the decision had made little difference: he was unable to distinguish any particular change in the kind of work he was being called upon to do. He had spent three days preparing the paperwork for an excavation area around an abandoned quarry near Alston: there were an estimated six hut circles within what appeared to be a contemporary field system and a licence for further excavation was being sought. He stood in for the directorate — Brent-Ellis and Stannard — at a conference in Newcastle on funding of projects, and he had been called up to Galashiels to do an inspection of a proposed new road that would go through an ancient fort complex. He guessed there would be a public inquiry forthcoming as a result.

The consequence was his desk was covered in paper and there was a weary clerk telling him that Ms Stannard was breathing fire because he hadn't been in the office for three days and she wanted to see him.

'I've had Peter Gaul on my back,' she snarled at Arnold the moment he showed his face in her office. 'He wants to see me, and it's all because of you!'

'Me?' Arnold was nonplussed. 'What have *I* done?'

'It's what you haven't done,' she snapped. 'You haven't interviewed him to get his views on the meeting of the Friends.'

'But why should I?'

'Because you're an independent chairman of the working group and you should be listening to all sides in the matter.' She eyed him for a few moments, her lids languorous as though she were enjoying the silence. 'You didn't have much to say in your report to me.'

'There wasn't a great deal to say.'

'That's what I told Mr Gaul.'

'My report wasn't meant for him. It was a departmental report to you, as you'd requested, so that you were kept up to date about what was happening.'

'Well, it appears that Mr Gaul has other sources of information,' she replied. Her eyelids lowered for a moment almost as though she were wishing to hide something from him. 'However, the fact is he appears to think you might already be taking sides in the dispute. Just how accurate is his assessment, Landon?'

Arnold sighed. 'I've taken no position, as must be clear from my report to you.'

'Your very *brief* report.'

'As you say. The fact is, there are personal issues clouding the argument. Basically, the trustees under the chairmanship of David Hall have reached a decision — they wish to sell Ridgeway Manor because they can't afford to service the mortgage debt. There's no endowment with the Ridge bequest, and they're unable to give financial assistance to the work that needs to be undertaken on the grave site if it is to be properly carried forward. There is a government grant, of course, and we've given certain financial assistance, but if the excavation is to be completed and a report written up, a lot more money would be needed for the project — a project apparently dear to Miss Ridge's heart.'

'If it was so dear to her why didn't she leave more money to the Viking Research Trust?'

Arnold shrugged. 'It seems she was not as wealthy as some had suspected.'

Karen Stannard sighed. 'But you spoke of personal issues.'

'Harcourt-Fanshaw was a friend and legal adviser to Miss Ridge. But he had no part in the making of the bequests. He feels he was sidelined. It's clouded his judgement, I would guess, and he displays personal animosity towards the trustees. There also appear to be some undercurrents regarding Phil Martin — he's Harcourt-Fanshaw's nominee — but I've not worked out what they're about yet.'

'So the trustees want to sell, and Harcourt-Fanshaw . . . ?'

'Is against the sale. He wants further investigation of other possibilities. In particular, he wants time for Phil Martin to put in a considered paper on a lease and development proposal—'

'To do what?'

'It's a bit vague at the moment.' Arnold shook his head. 'The trustees are somewhat cynical about the proposal. They see it as an attempt by Harcourt-Fanshaw to slow things down. There were high words at the meeting. In the end I had to adjourn it so tempers could cool.'

'And consequently no decisions were taken.'

'That's right.'

'Peter Gaul sees that as a leaning by you towards the Harcourt-Fanshaw camp.'

'I don't know where he gets his information from. I'm in neither camp,' Arnold replied irritably.

'Peter Gaul wants you on his side.'

'I don't even know what he wants out of the whole thing.'

Karen Stannard rose from behind her desk and slowly walked across to the window. She stared out to the distant hills for a little while, silently, arms crossed. Then she looked back to Arnold across her left shoulder and smiled: there was no warmth in the smile.

'I'll be frank with you, Landon. You caught me somewhat on the hop with this Trust working group. I wasn't quick enough to find the right reasons to stop your involvement. And the director . . . well, we know he dislikes problems in his department. Now, I'm more certain than ever that you're not up to the job. But you've got it, and you're going to make a pig's ear of it. The fact is you're not strong enough, not tough enough to handle these people . . .'

Whereas you think you are, Arnold thought to himself.

'. . . but why should I interfere? There's a good reason — I think you could damage the department's reputation by your weakness. On the other hand, why should I haul you out of a mire of your own making? You see my dilemma?'

'I do indeed, Miss Stannard,' Arnold replied drily.

'So I've reached a decision,' she said, turning around and leaning against the windowsill, to face him directly. 'I'm not going to interfere. But I *am* going to watch you closely. And I'm going to start with Peter Gaul.'

'I don't understand.'

'You're going to see him.'

'For what purpose?'

'To be a properly independent chairman. To listen to his point of view.'

'But he's neither a trustee nor a member of the Friends, as I understand it. He has no status—'

'He's an employee. And he knows the protagonists. So you're going to see him. Today.'

'I'd have to contact him to fix an appointment—'

'I've already done it.' She smiled sweetly. Arnold was not fooled by the smile.

'I wonder why you would do that?' he said quietly.

'Because I'm coming with you. To get a first-hand account — rather than the biased, sketchy statement you're likely to give me, if your last report is anything to go by. And

I'll also be sitting in, on future occasions, at your meetings with the working group.'

'There might be an objection to that.'

'I've already spoken to David Hall. He sees no problem.' She smiled again. 'He says he'd welcome my presence. Thinks it might lighten the atmosphere.'

'He doesn't know you, Deputy Director.'

For a moment he thought he had gone too far. But then the spark in her eye faded, and she even seemed vaguely amused, in a cynical way. 'No, he doesn't. But then, perhaps *you* don't know me too well either . . . yet.'

Arnold nodded. 'You'll let me know the time and place, then. I have a deal of work waiting on my desk.'

'Yes. Because you've not been in your office.' She sat down behind her desk again, consulted her diary even though he knew she would already have the facts at her fingertips. 'Four thirty, this afternoon. You'll drive. You'll call for me here at three-fifteen. Meanwhile . . .'

He had turned to leave; now he hesitated, looking at her inquiringly.

'How are you getting on with Kirkby?' she asked, almost casually.

Arnold frowned. 'Fine. He came up to the Galashiels site with me, and I've passed over a few files to him, so he can get the feel of the department.'

'Enjoying having an acolyte, then?'

'He doesn't need me to mentor him,' Arnold replied shortly. 'He's perfectly capable of doing a decent job of work in the department and—'

'What do you think of him?'

Surprised, Arnold asked, 'How do you mean? As a colleague?'

She picked up a pencil and began to toy with it. 'Well, yes. I mean, you've spent time with him . . . what's he like?'

Arnold shrugged. 'Pleasant enough. Somewhat reserved. But capable — and he knows a lot about—'

'Does he have any social life? Any friends in the department?'

'Not that I'm aware of. But I haven't inquired.'

'He's not talked about his background, the other jobs he had before he came to Morpeth?'

'No.'

His shortness nettled her. Her mouth tightened. 'So he doesn't talk much about himself to you.'

'I don't talk much about myself to him,' Arnold replied edgily. 'Just what's this about, Miss Stannard?'

She kept her eyes on the pencil. 'Nothing really. I'm just . . . curious about him. I wondered whether he'd opened up to you at all, talked about himself, I mean, you being the humanist you are.' The sneer was clear in her tone. 'I gather he's a bit of a loner. He came to County Hall not very long ago, but kept himself to himself in the Education Department. And he's following the same track here, then.'

'Perhaps he likes his own company.'

'Or has something to hide.'

There was a short silence. 'We all have something to hide, I would guess,' Arnold said.

Her eyes came up to his: he had been wrong about their colour. They were steely-grey and cold. 'I've nothing to hide, Landon, even if you do. As for Kirkby, I make no bones about it. His history here in Morpeth is unremarkable, and yet, he's something of a man of mystery. Where he came from, why he came here . . . There's something about the man . . .' She stopped abruptly and threw down the pencil. It rolled along the desk and fell on the floor. She kept her eyes fixed on Arnold. 'But then, as you say, many of us have our little secrets.'

He turned to leave. As he reached the door she said, 'I'll be ready for you at 3.15.'

* * *

They drove most of the way in silence. The afternoon was warm and sunny and Arnold had no objection to the silence:

it enabled him almost to forget Karen Stannard was in the car. Once or twice he caught sight of her elegant profile, as she sat beside him, staring straight ahead at the road, and he wondered what inner devils drove her. She was doing well in her career, she had obtained early advancement and had built a reputation for herself with her book, and yet she seemed to feel that everything was a battle: her relationships with her staff and others was one conditioned by the belief that if she didn't move quickly, to stay one step ahead, she could go under. She trusted no one, it seemed.

It didn't explain her attitude towards Syl Kirkby, nor her interest in him. To Arnold, the man seemed unexceptional: a quiet worker, reserved, a little sad, and careful about his private life. Arnold saw nothing unusual or sinister in that. He was confident that Kirkby could do a good job in the department, given the opportunity, but he suspected that Karen Stannard would raise as many barriers to the man's progress as she could. Arnold could not understand why. From what she said, she had an intuitive dislike for Syl Kirkby. If so, that was her problem.

When they reached the study centre they were a little early, and it was locked. Arnold guessed Gaul would be up at the grave site so he suggested they walk up there to find him.

There was a small group of people there, working at the site. Peter Gaul caught sight of his visitors as they approached and detached himself, bringing with him a tall, square-shouldered woman with short-cropped dark hair and steel-rimmed glasses. She was dressed somewhat mannishly in a donkey jacket, jeans and heavy boots and her voice was deep and vibrant. Gaul introduced her as Dr Rena Williams, in charge of the dig.

Arnold was amused by Karen Stannard's reaction. Up to now she had been inclined to expose the dominant side of her nature; in the presence of Dr Williams, however, she became almost deferential. She smiled easily, she listened carefully as the team leader explained what they were doing, and Arnold was left to cool his heels for ten minutes while the two women walked around the grave site, talking animatedly. Gaul excused himself for a few minutes also, allowing Arnold opportunity to take a closer look at the activities of the dig team.

They were young — undoubtedly university students from Dr Williams's department. They were patiently scraping and sifting away, proceeding with care and circumspection: they were probably terrified of their leader whose reputation in the field was formidable, Arnold knew. He made his way across to the west side of the site and took another look at the old badger setts. He was still standing there, contemplatively, when Dr Williams and Karen Stannard came up.

'Badgers,' Rena Williams intoned in her deep, rich voice.

Arnold nodded. 'I was just wondering whether it would be worthwhile to make use of the setts as a sort of borehole.'

'Why? Waste of time.'

Arnold glanced over his shoulder. Karen Stannard was smiling slightly in genuine amusement.

'It might be a waste of time, but on the other hand,' Arnold said, 'it could lead to something interesting.'

'Such as?'

Arnold shrugged. 'I must take second place to the experts, of course, but when I saw the list of artefacts which have been discovered it did cross my mind we might have a boat burial here.'

'I would doubt that,' Dr Williams announced, sniffing.

'Well, I'm puzzled about the packing rocks. You see—'

'Our view is that the burial, if there is one, will be along the western side of the site. But we're not even certain what kind of burial it could be. And looking at the size of the site, a boat burial is highly unlikely.'

'Yet it's possible there was an outer compartment,' Arnold insisted stubbornly. 'The grave goods would have been left there, along with the gaming material, with an inner compartment leading to a burial chamber. If it is a boat burial it would have been achieved by a deep excavation on the east side of the site, near the badger setts, and the packing rocks would suggest—'

'And *I* would suggest we leave such matters to Dr Williams and her team,' Karen Stannard intervened smoothly. She flashed a brilliant smile at Rena Williams. 'It's not our job to offer gratuitous advice. We're here for other reasons.' She deferred to Rena Williams. 'I'm afraid my colleague gets carried away from time to time.'

'I've heard about Mr Landon,' Rena Williams replied. Her dark eyes were fixed thoughtfully on him. 'I understand he has demonstrated a certain . . . flair in archaeological matters.'

'Luck, others suggest,' Karen Stannard said, unable to keep an edge of malice out of her tone. Rena Williams looked at her curiously, and Karen Stannard's mouth tightened.

Peter Gaul broke the silence, as he came up to join them. 'Are we ready for our meeting?' he asked.

They took their leave of Dr Williams and turned to make their way back to the study centre. Arnold glanced back to the site as they walked away: Rena Williams was standing quite still, staring fixedly at the badger setts.

Peter Gaul unlocked the study centre door and took them through to a small lounge. He spent several minutes in the adjoining kitchen, making them some coffee and then he returned with a small tray and three mugs.

'I'm glad you were able to come out to join me here,' he said. 'It's a bit difficult getting away at the moment, with Dr Williams's party on site.'

'No problem for Mr Landon,' Karen Stannard replied smoothly. 'He's always out and about, aren't you, Landon? Never in the office, it seems to some of us. But it's your meeting, Mr Gaul. I'm along as an observer — it's Landon you need to be talking to.'

Gaul's dark brows bunched, and he nodded. He glared at Arnold fixedly. 'I'm not very happy with the way things seem to be going with the working group you're chairing.'

'In what sense?' Arnold asked.

'Delays in making decisions. It plays right into Harcourt-Fanshaw's hands.'

Arnold shrugged. 'I don't know what you mean by that.'

'You don't know what makes Harcourt-Fanshaw tick. The man's annoyed because he lost his power base with Miss Ridge before she died. And he wants to vent his spleen on the trustees. I don't hold any brief for them, because I think they're wrong the way they're going about things. But the longer this dispute bickers on, the less likely it is we'll reach sensible decisions about the future of development work at the Viking site.'

'And what decisions would you regard as sensible?' Arnold asked quietly.

Peter Gaul's powerful shoulders were hunched and he cradled the mug of coffee between two large, dark-haired hands. 'The important thing is to develop the site. But the trustees don't have the money to do that properly. On the other hand, the objectives laid out by Miss Ridge are quite clear. She wrote a memorandum, I understand, detailing her wishes—'

'Which are wishes only — and the trustees can't afford to carry them out,' Arnold intervened.

'That's so, but those wishes — which concern the development of the site, the writing of reports, the opening of the valley to a wider range of visitors, the creation of a heritage centre and museum — they're all valid objectives.'

'Desirable they may be — but the money isn't there. The trustees feel that by selling Ridgeway Manor they will at least be able to raise some money to carry out the completion of the grave excavation. But there's no way that would also cover the other things you mention.'

'But it can be done,' Gaul growled.

'How?'

'By giving me a free hand.'

There was a short silence. Arnold hesitated. 'I'm not at all sure where you fit into the picture. I'm even somewhat vague about the terms of your employment, Mr Gaul.'

'I'm employed by the Trust.'

'I appreciate that. But your salary . . .'

Gaul stared at his coffee angrily. 'I receive no salary as such.'

'I don't understand,' Karen Stannard said, leaning forward.

Gaul shrugged. 'I . . . I wanted the job. The trustees said they couldn't afford a salary. They pay me certain expenses.'

'But you can't live on expenses alone.'

'I also have a franchise,' he said uncomfortably. 'The contract I have allows me to make arrangements with schools, universities and the general public to make entry and car parking charges at the western entrance to the valley . . . and there's the artefacts shop at the far end of the valley, too. I receive the profits from that. But that's really the point. I make a living wage out of it, but it could all be so much better. If I was given a free hand, both to develop the study centre itself, and also to raise finance to expand the facilities at the shop, I'm certain I could make sufficient money to plough a good deal back into the site itself. I've put a proposal to the trustees. It would involve opening up Ridgeway Manor as an additional centre, selling off a part of the extensive library there and redeveloping that library to fulfil a specialist function, extending the grounds to take in leisure facilities—'

'Sounds very grand, Mr Gaul,' Karen Stannard remarked.

'It's very possible as a project.' Gaul replied sullenly. 'But the trustees threw it out. They said they were not confident it could succeed, and they were not prepared to give me a contract. Instead, they come up with this mysterious buyer whom they won't nominate — but I have my suspicions about that.'

'What do you mean?'

Gaul shook his head. 'Jock Hertford is a slippery customer. He's got his fingers in a lot of pies.'

The three were silent for a little while. Arnold observed Peter Gaul carefully. The man had a seething anger deep inside; its virulence puzzled Arnold. 'You have some . . . statement you want to make about Hertford, as a trustee?'

Gaul shook his head. 'Not at this stage. But I think you should look carefully at the motives of the trustees before you make any decisions on behalf of the Friends. They have no legal powers, I know, but they can raise a lot of noise in the right places. But don't be fooled by Harcourt-Fanshaw. He's not really interested in the Trust itself: he's just peeved that he's been sidelined, and he'll want to delay the whole thing or cause the kind of trouble that would end with him being called to save the Trust. I know what he's about!'

'I feel it only fair to say,' Arnold murmured, 'that your name came up in the discussions we held the other day.'

'I've no doubt.'

'You've had a . . . dispute with the trustees.'

Gaul's mouth twisted viciously. 'I don't like being called a crook.'

'It was hardly that, I gather—'

'You weren't there, Landon!' He glared around him and shook his head. 'It all started with that bastard Alan Crickley — the journalist. He's always looking for a dirty, muck-raking story, and he thought he found one with me. If I could have got my hands around his neck then . . .' Gaul glared fiercely at the table in front of him, his mouth working silently. 'Then, of course, the trustees took it up. The bastards said there were some queries about things being sold in the trading centre. They as good as accused me of lifting items from the site and selling them on. I challenged them to prove it and they backed off. All they had was the scurrilous article by Crickley, and a bit of gossip. But it left a sour taste in my mouth. There was no call for that kind of talk — that bastard Bill Norman was behind it: he's an old mate of Alan Crickley from his rugby days. He's got a loud mouth and a suspicious nature — thinks everyone is as badly principled as himself.' Gaul put down his mug shakily and balled his fists. 'I wouldn't mind taking him on face to face sometime — big man, he's supposed to be.'

Arnold gained the impression that Peter Gaul would not be averse to physical violence in response to any criticism he might face.

They carried on the discussion for some time, Karen Stannard taking little part, leaning back in her chair and watching, listening. The comments revolved around the same theme endlessly: Gaul was bitter about his employment contract, angry that the trustees had turned down his suggestion for the development of the site, and vaguely censorious of their motivation in the running of the Trust. He clearly felt Harcourt-Fanshaw was slowing things down for his own personal ends, and he was obviously concerned that Arnold was being made a dupe of by all parties.

When they finally took their leave and drove away from the centre, Karen Stannard was smiling cynically. 'It seems to me you're caged with a crowd of miserable tigers, blunt-clawed, niggly and spiteful.'

It wasn't a bad summation, Arnold considered. 'I don't know that I've learned anything in particular,' he said. 'But the argument Gaul had with the trustees was more serious than he made out.'

'You didn't mention it in your report,' Karen said coldly.

'I didn't think it was my place to do so. It was raised in the meeting by Bill Norman — he and Gaul are certainly not friends. It was clearly a matter of some seriousness at the time — and the comment was made to me that Gaul never sued Crickley over the article. No smoke without fire, was Norman's comment. But I wasn't given much detail and it has nothing to do with the sale issue.'

'But they believe Gaul's been lifting stuff from the site?'

Arnold shrugged. 'They can't prove it.' He frowned. They had swung around a bend in the road and ahead of them was a large tractor, trundling along slowly, scattering dried mud from its large wheels. The bends continued for a mile or more, and there would be no possibility of overtaking.

'This is going to be fun,' Karen growled in a surly tone.

'There's a way around,' Arnold replied. Some two hundred yards further on a narrow road ran off to the right, a side track to the one they had used on their approach to the field centre earlier. It was slightly longer than the main road but if he could pick up speed over the hill he would be able to rejoin the main road in about two miles and avoid the hold-up of the trundling tractor. He turned right at the intersection, and high hedges ran either side of the car.

As they breasted the hill the hedges became sparser. Below them to the left the tractor ground its placid way onwards. Arnold glanced across to the fields ahead of them, and to the left. There was a circling of excited crows in some number, high above a copse on the slope of the hill.

'You were saying there's no proof Gaul's been stealing,' Karen reminded him.

Arnold nodded. 'They received a complaint, I understand, which Norman investigated. A dealer up at Amble had been offered some Viking artefacts, and they were traced back to Gaul. When questioned, he claimed he'd purchased them years ago — he has a small private collection of his own and that they were nothing to do with the site here. But . . . he was challenged about it, and there was quite a bitter argument.'

'They didn't sack him.'

'Which would suggest they felt they were on unsure ground. He's got a three-year contract. They didn't think they could support Norman's suspicions, but I suspect they'll try to get rid of him when the contract runs out . . . What's happening there?'

Arnold slowed the car. There was a Land Rover parked close to the hedgerow, and in front of it a blue Ford saloon, slewed into the ditch. Beyond the hedgerow, in the field, a man was running down the slope towards them, waving his arms. Arnold stopped the car. 'Wait here a moment.'

Karen Stannard was not accustomed to receiving orders. As Arnold got out of the car, so did she. Across the hedge, the man was slowing, lurching, shouting incoherently, still waving his arms.

'What's the matter?' Arnold called.

The man was dressed in an old jacket, jeans and gumboots.

He stopped at a distance of some fifty yards from them, waving frantically, and pointing to the copse on the slope behind him, circled by the noisy, excited crows. Arnold climbed over into the field at the gate; Karen Stannard followed. The man turned, stumbled into a run back across the field towards the copse.

When they reached the copse the man was standing with his hands on his hips, chest heaving breathlessly. He was staring at the ground in front of him. Arnold and Karen Stannard moved to stand beside him.

In the thick undergrowth they saw what the farmer had found. He turned helplessly towards them, shaking his head. He tried to explain to them, in a ragged voice, that he had found the Ford, seen tracks across the field as though something had been dragged towards the copse. And he had seen the crows.

The body lay on its back, arms thrown wide. The eye sockets were sightless, blind to the early evening sky, and there was thick, matted blood in the man's hairline. The mouth was wide open, gaping in a savage rictus, but Karen Stannard was shuddering at the crow-pecked eye sockets. Then she gasped, a low note of horror.

'Landon . . . do you see who it is?'

Arnold nodded. In spite of the attack by the crows he had recognized the man who lay there. He turned to look at Karen Stannard. All the confidence had leached out of her face: she was pale, shocked, and trembling.

'You recognize him,' she said.

'That's right. It's Alan Crickley.'

CHAPTER THREE

1

The crows had gone.

Detective Chief Inspector Culpeper squinted up at the morning sun and cursed his luck. For years he had taken his wife Margaret to Seahouses for a break — they usually took a cottage there and spent their evenings in the Jolly Fisherman. This year, their son had arranged his leave to coincide with his father's and had arranged a visit for the family to Majorca. Margaret had not been very keen to go — she was a conservative soul, ample-bosomed, unimaginative and easily pleased — but Culpeper himself had been looking forward to it, and the opportunity to do some fishing off a strange, and warmer coast.

Now all his plans had been thrown into disarray. The killing of the journalist meant there would be no leave at this time, and the plane tickets would have to go begging. The thought did not please him. Nor was his temper improved as he saw Detective Inspector Farnsby trudging up the slope towards him: he had an uneasy working relationship with the man. They had respect for each other, but there was always an edge of competitive dislike between them.

He turned and looked again at the trampled scene in the copse. He had been called out late last night and had joined the team who had worked under arc lights on the hill. The body had been taken away in a shell some hours earlier, and the undergrowth had been searched thoroughly; a team had also walked the field, but there was little or nothing to be found. The marks that suggested the body had been dragged across the raw earth were still visible but there was now a general trampling from numerous feet that meant the likelihood of turning anything else up was negligible.

Coppers were always regarded as having big feet, Culpeper thought sourly, and the myth wasn't far from the reality. 'Just about finished now, sir?'

Culpeper flashed a jaundiced eye at Farnsby. The younger man was too bright and chipper in the morning sunshine: Culpeper was aware of his own unshaven state, and desire for a good hot shower. It would have to be back at Ponteland headquarters — there'd be no chance he'd get home today with all the paperwork that had to be completed.

'I suppose so. You got your end sorted out?'

Farnsby nodded. He was a product of the accelerated promotion programme for young graduates, and he prided himself on his quick responses and swift action. He was seen as a high-flyer by the chief constable, and chances were he would not be too long in the Northumberland area — things were different for Culpeper, thick-waisted, late forties and going nowhere.

'I've been in touch with the *Journal.*' Farnsby said. 'They are more than prepared to cooperate, of course — the editor is torn between regret at having lost a good journalist, and excitement at having an inside track on knowing the victim. He'll be enjoying the thought of the banner headlines for the next few weeks.'

'You're getting cynical, Farnsby,' Culpeper said, almost daring the younger man to say he'd learned in a good school.

Farnsby ignored the comment. 'We've got two men down there already, packing up Crickley's files, and interviewing the editor on the assignments Crickley's been working on recently.'

'Any preliminary thoughts?'

'Early to say.' Farnsby crinkled his brow. 'Crickley's been with the *Journal* for some years and was accustomed to working on his own. Comes out as a bit of a loner, from what the editor told me over the phone. Didn't seem to have much by way of a social life — kept himself to himself. No girlfriend, no buddies on the paper. Lived for his work, it seems.'

'And maybe died for it,' Culpeper growled. 'So what do you reckon happened up here?'

Farnsby shrugged. 'You've seen as much as I have, sir. But the way it looks to me, Crickley met someone in the roadway down below. His car is pulled into the side—'

'I don't agree with your initial hypothesis,' Culpeper interrupted.

'How do you mean, sir?'

Farnsby was a little nettled. Culpeper liked that. 'You suggest he met someone in the road. I doubt that. The Ford — it looks to me that it was slewed into the hedge, maybe by someone not used to driving it. We agree Crickley was not killed up here at the copse?'

'Almost certainly. He was killed elsewhere — I assumed down in the roadway. Then the body was dragged across the field, dumped out of the way in the copse.'

'When?'

Farnsby shrugged. 'The pathologist will give us a probable timescale in a few days — you know how cautious they are — but early suggestions are that the body's been there for maybe forty hours before discovery. It had rained, you'll recall, but the ground under the body was dry. Also, the crows had had time to have a go at it and—'

'And you'll need to have a good look at the car,' Culpeper interrupted. 'Do we know whose it is?'

'Crickley's. We ran a check on the computer — it's his car all right.'

'Well, my guess is he didn't drive it here. He met the killer somewhere else. I think he was killed at some distance from here, then driven to this spot in the late evening, dragged across the field and disposed of in the copse. The road down there, it's not particularly busy, and anyone coming past who saw the car in the hedge wouldn't necessarily assume there was a problem. The farmer, I suppose, thought otherwise.'

'He reckons he saw the car the previous evening when he drove past. When he came to the field later the next day and saw it still there he decided to take a look around.'

Culpeper nodded. 'Right. Well, there could be signs, forensic evidence in the car—'

'They've started working on it,' Farnsby said. 'But why do you assume the dead body was driven here?'

'Hunch.' And the fact there was no sign of another car on the verge, except the Land Rover parked by the farmer. But it was early days, and Culpeper was tired and irritable and maybe he was too concerned to get a rise out of the detective inspector.

It was only a theory, anyway, and it was foolish to construct elaborate theories before the forensic evidence was in. Too many cases went sour from coppers trying to make facts fit theories instead of the other way around. There had been that bad series of cases some years ago, with that crazy pathologist O'Connor in the Midlands, who'd seemed to think he had a God-given mission to put people behind bars. He'd been backed by coppers who were only too keen to take his statements at face value. Bad business. Culpeper shook his head. 'What about the people who found the body?'

'I've got them sorted out. The farmer who first stumbled across the body . . . he's at Morpeth now, making a statement. The other two — the ones the farmer called to help they'll be at Ponteland later this morning. They made a brief statement here last night, before you arrived, but they were then allowed to go home because they came on the scene after the farmer found the body, so don't have much of a story to tell. Just confirming the farmer, really. They'll be available for questioning later. I thought you might want to be in on that.'

'Why?'

'One's the deputy director of the Museum and Antiquities department at Morpeth. The other . . . you've met before.'

'I have?'

'Arnold Landon.'

Culpeper's autumn-brown eyes were lidded. He nodded. 'Landon. Yes, I've certainly met him before.'

* * *

Culpeper blinked when he saw Karen Stannard.

She was dressed in a grey suit of a somewhat severe cut but it only served to emphasize her femininity. The white blouse was open at her throat and her skin was tanned. He thought he had rarely seen such classical beauty and she reminded him of some of the cool-featured models he'd seen on television catwalks — controlled, elegant and slightly superior. She had come into his office, shaken hands with him, and taken a seat as though unaware of the effect she had upon him. But he guessed the truth would be different: Karen Stannard was the kind of woman who would always know exactly the impact she made upon men. It gave her some of her strength and confidence.

'So you're the new deputy director of the Department of Museums and Antiquities.'

'I took up my appointment a few weeks ago.'

'You're enjoying the work?'

'It's interesting,' she replied noncommittally.

Culpeper lowered his eyes to read again notes of the brief statement Karen Stannard had made at the field. After a short silence, he looked up at her and said, 'So you were in the area on departmental business, Miss Stannard?'

'That's right. We'd gone up to the study centre owned by the Viking Research Trust. It's a private dig, of course, and we have no control over it, but we'd been to see the man who runs the centre — Peter Gaul.'

'We?'

'My colleague Mr Landon was with me. He had an arranged meeting with Gaul and I'd decided to go along. For departmental reasons.'

'Ah yes.' There was something in her tone that interested Culpeper: he could not get a fix on it, but there was a certain edge there. Culpeper's eyes flickered again to the notes. 'Now, according to your statement at the scene, you were driving. On your way back to Morpeth when the farmer—'

'Mr Coleman.'

'—waved you down. He called you into the field . . .'

'He was clearly disturbed. He wanted to show us something. I think he was scared, wanted support.'

'You didn't stay in the car?' Culpeper asked.

Her eyes were a strange, shifting hue. He couldn't place the colour. Her voice was cool. 'He wanted support. When Landon got out, I got out too.'

He ignored the challenge in her tone. 'According to your statement, you . . . recognized him?'

'The dead man? We both recognized him.'

'So you knew Alan Crickley well.'

'I knew him. Not well. We'd met a couple of times.'

Culpeper detected a note of hesitation in her voice. 'In what capacity did you meet him?'

She shrugged. 'He interviewed me. About my job. He came to my office. And there was another time, later. We met by chance, casually, in Newcastle.'

'So you weren't friends.'

'Hardly.'

Culpeper leaned back in his chair and stared fixedly at her. 'You saw the car slewed into the hedge. And you saw the body. Do you have any thoughts about what happened?'

She met his gaze directly. 'Not really. When I saw the car I thought maybe it had gone out of control . . . but it could equally have been just bad parking. Then, in the field . . .'

'I don't want to distress you, Miss Stannard.'

'I'm not distressed.'

He was certain she was not. But there was something about her that puzzled him. She was nervous, underneath the cool exterior, and she held his eyes too long. It was as though she saw the interview as a challenge, a hurdle to climb over. She was a competitive woman, but it was not the explanation for the unease she felt. 'I assumed Crickley had been dragged across the field and dumped in the copse. We all three of us assumed that. We talked about it, while we waited for the police.'

'It was you who made the call.'

'I had a mobile phone.'

And a cool temperament. 'Is there anything you want to add to your statement at this time, Miss Stannard?'

Again, a brief hesitation. Then she shook her head firmly. He thanked her for coming in, explained he might wish to see her again in due course, and saw her to the door. She was the kind of woman a man always saw to the door.

* * *

After she had gone Culpeper turned to the files that Farnsby had placed on his desk. They included a breakdown of Alan Crickley's movements and diary appointments for the last few weeks, and a briefer summary of his appointments over preceding months. Farnsby had worked quickly: he'd left a note in the file stating that the details needed further checking for accuracy but he'd felt it would be useful if Culpeper had some early intimation of the range of matters that had attracted Crickley's attention of late.

Culpeper grunted. High-flying efficiency.

There was also a breakdown, supplied by the editor, of the pieces that Crickley had recently published, and a note of some of the items the editor believed he had been currently working on. Once again, Farnsby had added a note.

'These are the matters Crickley informed his editor about. I am making further inquiries — it may be there were other stories Crickley had been chasing up, which he had not told the editor about.'

Culpeper looked through the list. The items seemed pedestrian enough: some personal profiles, including one of Karen Stannard; a report on mining in Northumberland; a series on Victorian murder cases in the northeast; the discovery of the Viking grave; meetings of the Viking Research Trust and the controversy surrounding the proceedings of the trustees.

Culpeper spent a little while musing over the list of articles and then he turned to the next file, which contained the summary of diary and appointment entries. Slowly he went through the names, then checked them against the actual diary entries in the hard-backed, page-a-day diary that had been supplied by the editor with the files. He made a note of some of the unfamiliar names. There were a few names he recognized — these he placed in a separate list, in the careful, looped hand that was the result of his childhood schooling.

The phone rang. It was reception. 'Mr Landon has arrived, sir.'

'Send him along.'

Culpeper rose heavily and opened the door. There was an automatic coffee machine standing against the far wall. He poured two coffees into plastic cups, added milk from an open glass bottle and took the cups back to his desk. A few minutes later Arnold Landon entered, somewhat warily. Culpeper smiled, amused by Landon's concern.

'Well, Mr Landon, it seems we keep stumbling over each other in the course of our separate duties.'

'It's not a situation I actively seek, believe me, Mr Culpeper.'

Culpeper believed him. He smiled complacently and waved Landon to a chair. He placed a cup in front of his guest and carefully moved the second cup behind his files. He stared dreamily at the cup for a few moments. 'So, you have another manager to contend with.'

'I beg your pardon?'

'Miss Stannard. A formidable lady, and a beautiful one.'

Arnold Landon smiled, but made no reply. Culpeper caught a gleam in his eyes that could have spelled cynicism but he could not be sure. 'You showing her the ropes, then?' he asked.

'Hardly. She would resent even the suggestion.'

'Oh, I got the impression you were maybe holding her by the hand in taking her up to Ridgeway Field Centre.'

'Hand-holding is the last intention I would have with Miss Stannard,' Landon replied briskly. 'No, you're far from the truth, Mr Culpeper. She was really along as a sort of check.'

'How do you mean?'

Somewhat guardedly, Landon said, 'I think she feels I need watching.'

Culpeper chuckled. 'I can go along with that. Anyway, I've got notes of the statement you made . . . Would you mind going over what happened again?'

He listened while Arnold repeated his version of the events at the field. They tallied both with his earlier statement, and with that made by Karen Stannard. When Arnold at last fell silent, Culpeper sighed. 'So, really you just sort of stumbled over the thing — I mean, you got called in by Coleman, the man who actually found the body.'

'That's right.'

'On the other hand, you knew something the farmer didn't.'

'Did I?'

Culpeper spread his hands wide. 'Of course. You knew the dead man's identity. As did Miss Stannard.'

Landon shrugged. 'I'd met him a few times. He interviewed me over the *sudarium* business. And I came across him again at the Friends' meeting. But I didn't know him well.'

'Not many people did, it seems . . .' Culpeper glanced at the list of names he had copied from Farnsby's list. 'You were up at the field centre to meet a Mr Peter Gaul.'

'That's right.'

'It seems he also was an acquaintance of Alan Crickley.'

Arnold Landon hesitated, then he nodded. 'I'm not surprised. Crickley knew all the people involved with the Viking Research Trust. He'd been covering the meetings of the Friends and the controversy that had arisen over the proposed sale of Ridgeway Manor. I believe he had written about it recently.'

'So he had.' Culpeper nodded thoughtfully. 'But it seems he might also have had other dealings with Mr Gaul. Do you know about those?'

Landon frowned. He held Culpeper's glance. 'I'm not sure what you mean.'

'Neither am I,' Culpeper admitted. 'But Gaul's name appears in the diary, and the notes suggest they didn't see eye to eye. Would you know what that was all about?' Landon's hesitation was palpable. 'Maybe you should ask Mr Gaul about that.'

'I certainly shall. But since you're involved with the Trust, I thought maybe you could throw light on it.'

Arnold Landon shrugged. 'I know little more than the gossip—'

'I love gossip.'

There was a short silence. Then Landon said, 'I believe there was some sort of . . . quarrel. Crickley wrote a piece suggesting there had been pilfering from the Viking grave site. The trustees investigated it. They questioned Gaul. The results were, I gather, somewhat inconclusive. Certainly, nothing was proved against Gaul. He kept his job. On the other hand . . .'

'Yes?'

'A degree of resentment survived. But that's a long way from saying that Gaul had anything to do with the death of Alan Crickley.'

'I'm suggesting nothing of the kind,' Culpeper replied amiably. 'But the body was found on a minor road that leads to the field centre, indirectly. You didn't use that road on your way to the centre?'

'We used the main road.'

'Hmm.' Culpeper eyed Arnold carefully. 'Gaul disliked Crickley. Did you dislike him, Mr Landon?'

'I didn't know him well enough to form an opinion.'

'He was not a popular man.'

'Journalists often fall into that category.'

'Like policemen,' Culpeper smiled. 'Anyway, you knew Crickley . . . as a matter of interest, I wonder if you know any of these other names that he had listed?'

Arnold Landon shrugged. 'I don't know. Who are they?'

'What about David Hall? Bill Norman? A Mr Frimley?'

'They're trustees of the Viking Research Trust. He'd known them well from his covering of the controversy. Along with Harcourt-Fanshaw, and Sir Jock Hertford.'

'Ah yes, there's a record of several meetings with him. What about Fred Brierley?'

Landon shook his head. 'I don't know him.'

'Syl Kirkby?'

Landon's head came up; there was surprise in his eyes. 'His name appears on the list?'

'You know him?'

'He's a colleague of mine. But to my knowledge, Crickley only met him once, at the Friends' meeting. I can't imagine why he would have made a note of his name.'

Culpeper smiled thinly. 'Nor I. But I suppose it's not important.' He observed Landon carefully for a few seconds. 'Do you have any thoughts about why Crickley was killed?'

Arnold shook his head. 'None.'

'So there's nothing you can think of, in your acquaintance with Crickley, that might be significant . . . something you'd want to mention to me about him, or his activities?'

'Nothing I can think of.'

Culpeper sipped his coffee. 'Well, let's leave it there for the moment. They'll take a formal statement from you shortly. Meanwhile, why don't you tell me about the grave site and the people who are working there. Just as a matter of interest, of course.'

Because you never know, Culpeper thought as Arnold began, just what pieces might fit when they were all on the table.

After Arnold Landon had finished his coffee and gone, Culpeper looked again at the list of names he had compiled. He went down them slowly, ticking off in his mind the possible relationship they might have had with Crickley. The man would inevitably have made some enemies — but who among this list might have disliked him sufficiently to smash in the back of his head with a heavy, blunt instrument?

Or more likely, feared him?

2

The staff in the department at Morpeth were somewhat subdued during the next few days. It had been a matter of gossip that the deputy director had been interviewed by the police regarding the killing of Alan Crickley and at first Arnold had been pressed for details, but he had refused to discuss the matter. Some of the gossip must have got back to Karen Stannard for she finally took some of the girls in the typing pool to task in no uncertain manner, and thereafter an uneasy atmosphere prevailed. It was one Arnold was pleased to eventually get out of when he and Syl Kirkby were called upon to visit a prehistoric site in the West Alien valley that the department had been mapping. It gave Arnold the chance to visit one of his favourite pubs for lunch, near the Blue Back bridge.

The dale itself was one of sharp contrasts — a sweeping fell, wild and peaceful, but in the valley there was the precipitous Allen Gorge, a descent from the broad heather moor and a change from the high, wild Pennine views into an ordered landscape of estate lawns, shaved plantations and well-stocked pastures.

Kirkby was silent and preoccupied as they drove, so Arnold was able to concentrate on the views, recalling the old days with his father, when they had walked the fells and heard the swish of sedge grasses in the autumn wind, and the cry of the curlew as night drew in over the darkening hills. They drove down at last through Thornley Gate and along the Burn Tongues road and parked at the Blue Back inn, for a bar snack. Arnold pointed out to Kirkby the view up the valley from the bridge, in his estimation one of the finest in the north country: past birches and hazels to the thin spire of Whitfield Church rising gracefully above the top of the trees and the curve of the river.

They leaned on the old bridge and admired the view in the late afternoon sunshine. Kirkby had said little all day, at the site or during the drive, and Arnold respected his silence. Now, as the warmth of the sun touched their faces and the shadows grew longer on the river banks, Kirkby suddenly said, 'There's a lot of talk in the office.'

'About what?'

'The killing.'

'It's inevitable. The gossip will die down.'

'You knew Crickley, of course.'

'Not very well.'

'What did you make of him?' Kirkby asked in a guarded tone.

Arnold glanced at his companion. He shrugged. 'Not a very pleasant man . . . but I suspect one who'd been scarred in some way, in his past. Maybe it affected him. Or maybe it was his job. He was always trying to ferret out stories. That can affect a man's relationships with his fellows — and maybe sour him too.'

There was a short silence.

'You remember that day at the Friends' meeting — when you introduced him to me? He seemed to think he knew me.'

'I remember. You said you'd never met.'

'That was true. We'd never met,' Kirkby said nothing for a while. He seemed to be struggling with some kind of decision. Arnold remained silent. At last, Kirkby said quietly,

'He wasn't convinced, you know, about our never having met. He contacted me again, later.'

'What on earth for?' Arnold asked in surprise.

Kirkby shrugged evasively. 'He had some bee in his bonnet. Said he was sure we'd met. Wanted to have a talk with me — said he thought I could help him. I refused to meet him. Then, one day, he buttonholed me in the street in Morpeth.' He smiled wearily. 'He could be a very persistent man.'

'What was it he wanted from you?' Arnold asked.

'We never got around to discussing it. I didn't like the man — he was typical of his kind.' He hesitated. 'But I took the trouble to go back through newspaper files — read some of the stuff he'd written over the years for the *Journal*. It confirmed me in my view of him. Muck-raking: that was his interest. They're all vultures, people like him. Nothing they like doing more than picking over old bones.'

There was a resigned bitterness in his tones that made Arnold feel uncomfortable.

After a little while they returned to the car and Arnold drove them back to Morpeth. Kirkby was silent, hunched in his seat, and since he seemed to be in a dark mood Arnold made no attempt at conversation. When they reached Morpeth, feeling a little sorry for the man, Arnold suggested they might meet for a drink that evening. Kirkby seemed a little embarrassed by the offer, though grateful, and declined.

Arnold suggested they meet at ten the following morning in his office so they could go over the papers prior to the next meeting of the Friends' working group. It would be useful if Kirkby could come along to take notes: Arnold felt that a fuller, contemporaneous note-taking might be more acceptable for report purposes as far as Karen Stannard was concerned — even though she was going to be at the meeting herself.

Arnold spent a troubled night thereafter.

He rang Jane Wilson at her home in Framwellgate Moor — he had not seen her for some weeks because of his workload

— and he would have appreciated a long chat, but she had to cut him short. She was going out to dinner — a function at the University of Durham to which Professor Dennis had invited her. Arnold was unreasonably put out by the news: Dennis had never made any secret of his admiration for Jane and for some reason the attention he paid her annoyed Arnold. Yet Jane was nothing more than a good friend.

Nevertheless, Arnold found it difficult to sleep, and consequently he was somewhat edgy the following morning when he arrived at work.

His temper was not improved by the manner in which Karen Stannard swept into his office at nine thirty. 'Where's Kirkby?' she snapped imperiously.

'At his desk, I imagine. I'm not due to see him until ten.' Arnold massaged his temples with his left hand: he had the vague beginnings of a headache. 'I've suggested Kirkby comes with us to the trustees' working group meeting. He can take a full note of the proceedings. That way, Deputy Director, you'll get a comprehensive report in due course.'

'You've invited him to the meeting? With what authority?' she demanded, her voice rising sharply.

Arnold's own temper began to flare. 'I didn't think I needed authority — he's my acolyte, remember? Your words. It was your idea that he tied himself to me so—'

'Well, I'm untying him as of now,' she cut in, her eyes flashing. 'Don't overreach yourself, Landon. Now, go tell him I want to see him in my office.'

'You pass his room on your way back to your office,' Arnold remonstrated.

She paused, stared hard at him, and her mouth was a thin line. 'You'll instruct him, nevertheless — as I'm instructing you.'

Arnold almost began to wish that the halcyon days of Simon Brent-Ellis were back again.

He walked along to the office used by Kirkby and two clerks. The door was open. He leaned against the doorjamb. Wearily, he announced, 'You're wanted.'

'What?'

'Her Highness. In her office. *Now.* I should tread carefully: it's not one of her best mornings.'

Kirkby rose slowly to his feet. He was pale, but there was a firmness about his mouth that made Arnold suspect he was holding something in check, but only with difficulty. He brushed past Arnold and walked down the corridor. Arnold made his way back to his own room.

Twenty minutes later Kirkby stood in front of Arnold's desk. 'It seems I have fledged — or been fledged. I no longer report to you.'

'The umbilical cord has been cut? Congratulations.'

'I don't think it was done in that frame of mind,' Kirkby replied bitterly.

Arnold stared at him. The man's eyes were flecked and he was trembling slightly. His fists were clenched and it suggested to Arnold that he was enraged, but was keeping control of his emotions.

'What's happened?' Arnold asked quietly.

Kirkby managed a ghost of a smile. It lacked humour. 'You might say Miss Stannard tried to carpet me, and I resisted.'

'Good for you.'

Kirkby's eyelids flared briefly. 'She certainly put her point across forcibly — but she also went too far. We ended up, shall I say, in an atmosphere lacking in mutual respect. Anyway, the long and the short of it is I will receive tasks directly from her — and you need no longer be burdened with me.'

He paused, and some of the bitterness faded from his mouth. He stared at Arnold for a few moments, as though struggling to find the right words. 'I'm sorry about that, Landon. I . . . I quite enjoyed our trips together.'

Arnold nodded. 'Maybe there'll be others.'

Kirkby sneered and turned towards the door. 'Not if Miss Stannard has her way.'

* * *

Sir Jock Hertford owned a late-thirteenth-century hall-house near Aydon. It was half hidden in deep woods above a small but steep ravine, in what Arnold considered to be a secretive but very beautiful location. Oddly enough, he had visited the grounds some years previously on a walking tour: now he found that he was to be a guest there, for the meeting of the Friends' working group.

It was a fortified house, an answer to the increasing lawlessness and the attacks of the Scots in the border wars: in the fourteenth century a pele tower had been added to the existing house and new surrounding walls erected to give it an appropriate measure of protection.

The interior of the house was rather bare and cheerless since many of the old farmhouse fittings had been torn out, possibly under the direction of Lady Hertford, who turned out to be a rather faded, desiccated woman of indeterminate age, who greeted them on entry but once the group was gathered, disappeared to the back of the house. They stood around in the drawing room sipping an elderly sherry and admiring a small collection of mediaeval armour that Sir Jock had collected over the years.

'I'm pleased you've joined me in my little home,' Sir Jock announced expansively, 'since we have a great deal of affection for it. It's been in my wife's family for a couple of centuries—' He glanced at Harcourt-Fanshaw with a hint of malice. 'Not unlike your situation really, old chap.'

He waved his glass to take in the whole group. 'Anyway, I thought it might be sensible to hold the meeting here, to get away from Ridgeway itself. Give us a rest from the sort of pressures that bear on us all, I guess, connected with the property — and then there's been this murder business, as well. Since it occurred not too far from Ridgeway Manor, I thought it a good idea to meet here. Put it to Mr Landon, and he agreed.'

Behind him, Arnold felt the displeasure of Karen Stannard like a physical hand on his shoulder. She had not been aware he had been consulted on the matter — presumably she felt she would have wanted him to discuss the suggestion with her. She could be touchy about such things — even though Arnold was entitled to make such decisions for himself.

Hertford, enjoying himself as the affable host, smiled around the group of trustees in the room — Frimley, Norman, David Hall — and bowed slightly in the direction of Karen Stannard. 'We're delighted to see Miss Stannard here, of course, as an observer — she lightens and graces the room. But I also took the opportunity, Mr Landon, of inviting the solicitor who advised the trustees on the matters in issue. Mr Enwright, from Morpeth. I hope there will be no objection to his sitting in on our meeting — he might be able to clear up a few matters.'

Arnold glanced briefly at Harcourt-Fanshaw. For a moment he thought the solicitor was about to object, then Harcourt-Fanshaw managed a wintry smile. 'Mr Enwright and I are old friends — and antagonists in the courtroom. How are you, George?'

'Well enough, Joseph,' Enwright replied easily. He was a tall, thin man, quite bald, but with thick black eyebrows and heavily bagged eyes. There was no smile in those eyes, however, and Arnold suspected that the two lawyers held little liking for each other.

'I'm sure there'll be no objection from the working group,' Arnold intervened, 'since it may well mean we can move a little faster towards decisions.'

'I'm not a great believer in speed, myself,' Harcourt-Fanshaw informed them, in warning, 'if it leads to mistaken or inappropriate solutions.'

'I'm sure we'll all bear that in mind,' David Hall said smoothly.

'Good,' Sir Jock Hertford boomed. 'Well, Chairman, if we've all finished our sherry, the meeting room awaits. It's the old billiard room, actually — I've arranged for us to sit around the table — got a cover on to protect the baize. But if we get bored, we can always take up a cue or two, hey?'

There was the clink of glassware as they replaced the sherry glasses on the silver tray, and Hertford led the way to the billiard room. When they were all settled around the table, Arnold opened proceedings.

'I'm afraid we left matters in a somewhat indeterminate state at the last meeting,' he began. 'The discussion was somewhat heated, and I thought it best to terminate and adjourn the meeting so we could all have time for reflection. But I'm reluctant that matters should drag on too long. The Friends have every moral right to have a say in the decisions of the trustees, but it is clear, of course, there is no legal restraint upon them—'

David Hall leaned forward and smiled faintly. 'While we're concerned to get matters sorted out as soon as possible, Chairman, we're also aware that our actions are open to public scrutiny. However, as Sir Jock and I have already discussed, we believe that the presence of Mr Enwright might help to expedite matters considerably.'

'In which case,' Arnold suggested, 'we might begin by asking Mr Enwright to make a statement about the outstanding issues.'

Enwright cleared his throat importantly, his Adam's apple bobbing in his scrawny throat. 'There's not a great deal for me to say, Chairman. I understand from Mr Hall that certain points have already been made, and that my task would be to confirm the accuracy of the understanding that the trustees have of the legal position. The points are as follows.' He flicked up a bony finger. 'One, Miss Ridge made provision for the Viking Research Trust but did not see fit to establish an endowment to support it. It was the designated landholdings only—'

'Which did not include certain properties.' Harcourt-Fanshaw interjected.

'Quite so. Ridgeway Home Farm, for instance, and the adjoining lands. But the overall result is that the Trust itself is, in my view, remarkably short of funding capacity. Second—' he flicked up another finger — 'certain desires and objectives were expressed in Miss Ridge's additional memorandum. They have no legal standing, and do not form part of the Trust bequests. Consequently, though the trustees might feel there is a certain moral obligation to conform with her wishes, there is no *legal* obligation — and the financial situation should inevitably override any such moral obligations.'

'Are you speaking as a lawyer now, Enwright?' Phil Martin asked with a sneer. 'Or as a financial expert?'

'I simply state the facts as I see them.' Enwright replied in what he clearly considered to be a dignified manner.

'So that brings us to the encumbrances on the property bequeathed to the Trust,' Arnold suggested.

'Quite so, Chairman. I am able to confirm that Ridgeway Manor was heavily mortgaged, and was the major bequest made. While there were no legal constraints placed upon the use made of the premises, there was the wish stated in Miss Ridge's memorandum that the house be used as a museum and library.'

'Ahah!' Harcourt-Fanshaw ejaculated.

Enwright stared at him coldly. 'But those wishes are not legally binding, and it is clear from discussions I've had with Sir Jock and David Hall that the future of the Trust must lie clearly in the liquidation of assets held by the Trust — namely, the sale of Ridgeway Manor and repayment of the indebtedness.'

'Which is where we'd got to at the last meeting,' Phil Martin argued. 'What you're saying is that the manor needs to be sold.'

'It is an encumbrance the Trust cannot afford.' Enwright intoned.

'And the trustees have found a buyer?' Arnold asked.

'There's one in the pipeline.' David Hall agreed, nodding.

'Are you able to say who it is?' Arnold asked.

'We're in a delicate situation, Chairman.' Hall replied, almost pleadingly.

Harcourt-Fanshaw moved his chair, the arms thudding against the table. 'I wonder whether the delicacy has anything to do with the rest of the Ridge estate?'

Stiffly, David Hall turned to face him. 'I'm not sure what you mean.'

'The bequest to the Viking Research Trust was not sufficient to carry out the objectives of the Trust. But I knew Amelia Ridge well — and as her former legal adviser, I knew she was pretty well-heeled, as the saying goes. So what happened to the rest of her property?'

'That's not the concern of the trustees, or this meeting.' Sir Jock Hertford snapped.

'But perhaps our eminent legal friend Mr Enwright might be able to enlighten us.' Harcourt-Fanshaw sneered.

Enwright grimaced and consulted his bony knuckles. 'I find myself in an embarrassing situation, Chairman. Strictly speaking, I must agree with Sir Jock — these matters are not within the purview of the meeting.'

'The information is of concern to some members of the working group,' Arnold suggested gently. 'Is there no way you can help us on the matter?'

Enwright shrugged. 'I suppose there's no real harm . . . The fact is, Chairman, I drew up Miss Ridge's last will and testament, but she saw fit to make a codicil later, without my advice. It's perfectly legal, of course, even though she was an old lady—'

'And susceptible to all sort of influences.' Harcourt-Fanshaw sneered.

'I wouldn't know about that.' Enwright replied coldly. 'All I can say is that there were certain bequests made, quite legally, to a properly incorporated company. I can understand the reasons—'

'Chicanery?' Phil Martin queried cynically.

'There were clear tax advantages to the estate.' Enwright replied, colouring slightly. 'The company is situated in Jersey, outside the tax jurisdiction and—'

'The name of the company?' Harcourt-Fanshaw asked.

'I don't see it's of consequence, Chairman, but as I recall it is the Islands and Mainland Property Company Limited. I—'

‘And its directors?’ Harcourt-Fanshaw pounced swiftly.

‘Are not known to me, nor need they be disclosed to me.’ Enwright announced. ‘Chairman, I feel we’re moving from the point. We’re concerned here, as I understand it, with the possibility of the sale of Ridgeway Manor.’

‘And that.’ intervened Sam Frimley snappishly, ‘is all.’ His hawkish features were pinched with suppressed anger and his narrow eyes flickered sharp glances around the table. ‘I don’t know what Harcourt-Fanshaw is driving at, or what he hopes to dig out of the woodwork, but the issues are clear as far as I’m concerned, and I’m tired of beating around the bush.’

‘My sentiments entirely.’ Bill Norman added roughly. ‘Let’s stop pussyfooting around. As trustees we know what has to be done. We’re going along with the wishes of the Friends, and we’re being good guys in explaining everything, but we’re not legally bound by the wishes of the Friends. Chairman, I think we need to thrash out a statement from this working group that you can take to the Friends, and that’s the end of the matter. And part of that statement will be that the trustees are selling Ridgeway Manor.’

‘Not putting it out to tender?’ Phil Martin asked swiftly.

‘You’ll never get your bid together in a month of Sundays.’ Norman snapped, hunching his heavy shoulders as he leaned across the table. ‘We’ve got an offer on the table and it’s a fair one. We don’t have to discuss it with you, or disclose the details — and I move we don’t do that in any case. But your so-called consortium bid — I don’t believe it really exists. It’s just a blind that you and Harcourt-Fanshaw have cooked up between you. You want to delay everything, not for the good of the Trust, but for your own purposes. I don’t know what you’re up to, Martin, though I guess it’s something personally advantageous to you, but for Harcourt-Fanshaw, all he’s interested in is slowing things down, throwing mud at the existing trustees, in the hope that he can come in and head the whole thing himself. You never could accept that you lost your way with the old lady, could you,

Harcourt-Fanshaw? Well, I can tell you, your prevarication, it ain't going to work. No way, not never!'

Inevitably, everyone wanted to speak at once.

* * *

'Well, you made a cock-up of that,' Karen Stannard observed with a degree of satisfaction in her voice. 'We've ended up with a decision of the trustees to get on with the sale, Harcourt-Fanshaw has stormed out threatening a lawsuit, there's the inevitable production of a minority report to the Friends, criticizing your chairmanship and the decisions reached by the trustees, and almost certainly a comeback against the department since you're an employee. Yes, a real balls-up, if you don't mind me saying so.'

'Miss Stannard.' Sir Jock Hertford boomed as he lurched towards them with a bottle and two glasses, his normally bad-tempered mouth now widely grinning, 'I think the occasion calls for a glass of champagne. Will you indulge?' He waved the bottle in her direction and nodded to Arnold.

'Splendid job you did there, Landon. Cool chairmanship. And we reached absolutely the right decision.'

'Miss Stannard was making a similar point a moment ago.'

Arnold confided, arching an eyebrow in the deputy director's direction.

'Splendid!' Hertford intoned. 'You ought to promote this fellow, Miss Stannard. Got a cool head — when all about him are losing theirs, hey?' He poured each of them a glass of champagne. 'To be honest with you, glad it's all over. The buyer we have — point of withdrawing, I suspect. Time going on. Had to resolve the issue. That chap Martin, he's a fly-by-night; would never have come up with a bid.'

'So the trustees won't go to tender?' Arnold asked.

'No need. Good price. Better than market value.' Hertford winked. 'It means we'll be able to get rid of the manor itself, and walk away with money in hand. Money we can use to satisfy some of Miss Ridge's objectives in the Trust. The dig can be completed, the report written up . . . all good stuff.'

'Why are the projected buyers prepared to pay above market price?' Karen Stannard asked coldly, clearly put out by Hertford's eulogy of Arnold's chairmanship.

'Philanthropy.' Hertford said and waved the bottle in the general direction of David Hall and Bill Norman. 'Those are the guys you have to thank. They've done the negotiations with the buyers — persuaded them that they have a duty towards the Trust — to support it, all that sort of thing.'

'Duty?' Arnold asked, puzzled. 'Why should they have a duty to the Trust? Who are the buyers?'

Hertford stared at him, his eyes glazing slightly. He took a deep breath. 'Well, you know—'

David Hall was at his elbow, smiling benignly at Arnold and Karen Stannard. 'Jock's looking after you pair, but not the rest of his guests. Anything left in the bottle, Jock?'

'We were just talking about the buyers of Ridgeway Manor,' Arnold said. 'How you'd persuaded them to pay above market price.'

'Bill Norman's doing, not mine.' Hall replied, smiling. 'He pulled in old rugby contacts, talked of ancient games, charmed them out of the trees.'

'Sir Jock suggests they saw it as their duty.'

There was a brief silence. Hertford reddened slightly. 'I was just saying—'

'Duty is perhaps an overstatement.' Hall said smoothly. 'I talked to them when we discussed price . . . I pointed out that we were involved in a charitable trust, and maybe there was some way they could build up the price by way of a charitable donation. I think that's how they'll work it — in the end, it's all about tax advantage, isn't it? Anyway, you'll excuse me . . . I want a word with Bill Norman before he goes.'

'So Bill's away, is he?' Hertford said, recovering his composure. 'That's cutting down the group. Pity Harcourt-Fanshaw and Phil Martin wouldn't stay on for a drink. No need to take things so personally. Bad losers . . . Now David Hall, there's a winner, take it from me.'

'A winner?' Karen Stannard asked. 'In what way?'

Hertford grinned at her. 'Haven't you seen the way his shares have picked up recently — in Wheeler Holdings, I mean? The way he's turned that company around . . . I was telling Landon, last time we met, how the shares quadrupled from the time he started with them. Made a packet out of it myself. Then last year there was a bad time, they plunged to an all-time low — recession, all that sort of stuff — but the man's bounced back. There's been some strong institutional investment recently, as you'll have seen from the financial press . . .' He winked. 'And though I shouldn't say it, there's going to be an announcement soon. Keep your eyes open, chaps, keep your eyes open!'

He wandered away, grinning broadly. Karen Stannard stared at his waddling back with distaste. 'Announcement? What's that supposed to mean?'

Arnold sipped his champagne. 'It seems Mr Hall has been put up for an honour by his friends locally. Services to industry in the northeast . . . or to the Party.'

'I thought those things — preferment to honours, I mean — were supposed to be kept secret.'

'I get the impression,' Arnold replied, 'that Sir Jock Hertford would have difficulty keeping anything secret. When he's been drinking, at least.'

* * *

Arnold reached home about eight o'clock. He made a light meal for himself and was just finishing it when the phone rang. He was surprised to discover it was Syl Kirkby.

'Landon? You suggested the other evening we might have a drink together.'

He sounded wary, diffident, and his words were a little slurred. There was the sound of music in the background. 'That's right,' Arnold said.

'I wonder whether you might like to have one tonight?'

Arnold glanced at his watch. He was not keen about going out again tonight, but something in Kirkby's tone made him feel sorry for the man. 'Not a bad idea. I could make it in about half an hour.'

'The King's Head?'

'In thirty minutes.'

Kirkby was in the lounge bar, seated at a table in the corner behind the door, when Arnold arrived. There were two glasses in front of him. 'Got you a whisky,' Kirkby announced. 'Thought you wouldn't be averse, though I don't really know your tipple.'

'That'll be fine,' Arnold replied, sliding into the seat across the table from him. He glanced around the room: he could hear faint sounds from the juke box in the bar. Kirkby must have phoned from the passageway just outside the bar. He looked at Kirkby: he suspected the man had been here for some little while.

'So how are you?' Arnold asked.

There was a certain defiance in Kirkby's eyes as he returned Arnold's glance. 'Bloodied but unbowed. Undeterred by the slings and arrows. What other cliches can I think of?' He blinked owlishly at Arnold. 'I'm tougher than I look, you know.'

'I don't doubt it,' Arnold replied soothingly.

'I just wish that people would leave things alone. That bloody woman . . .'

'Karen Stannard?'

'She was insufferable. While I'm in that bloody office, all right, she has the right to deal with my work schedules. But she's no right to pry into my private life!'

'Is that what she's doing? I shouldn't take too much notice—'

'What I do with my time is my affair! And what I've *done* with my time is even less of her business. She's had my files out, you know.'

'Files?'

'There's damn all in them, of course,' Kirkby smiled wolfishly. 'Here, hold on, I need another drink.'

'Let me.'

Kirkby shook his head and lurched to his feet. He went up to the bar and ordered another round of drinks. Arnold realized the man must have been drinking steadily for some time before he had phoned for company. Kirkby was badly bothered about something — it was in his eyes and in his manner. He watched him carefully as Kirkby slumped heavily down in the seat again. He'd brought back a couple of double whiskies.

'She was mad as hell, of course,' Kirkby confided, grinning maliciously. 'It's really gone to her head, hasn't it, being made deputy director! She thinks she's God Almighty — and believes she has the right to know what goes on in every nook and cranny. That's why she's so bloody frustrated!'

'I don't understand.'

'Ahah! No reason why you should. But you're all right, Landon. You don't pry. You respect a man for what he is . . . not what people say about him. But her . . . she's mad as hell because there's nothing in my personal files and she thought she could browbeat me; insist I tell her what I did before I came to Morpeth. But I faced her down, I'll tell you! It's my business, and anyway it was part of the deal . . .'

His voice died away and he took a swallow of whisky.

When he looked up at Arnold his mood had changed again. There was pain at the back of his eyes and his shoulders were hunched. 'Drink can make you maudlin. But the last few weeks have been OK, you know? You've been good company, Landon. No questions. Just . . . friendship. Colleagues.'

Arnold nodded, but said nothing: he was getting worried about Kirkby. The man's voice was getting shaky and thick, the words blurring.

'But like it or not, I think it's time to move on. That bitch will never let up. And in the end, something will blow. I've always known it. I wouldn't mind really if it was true. But it never was, you know? I'm dogged with it . . . and you'll never know what it was like, Landon. The bestiality of it all . . . you'll never know.' He sipped at his glass again, and there was a sudden surge of drunken courage. 'But she can go to hell. I told her straight enough in her office that she should keep her nose out of my life, and I'll tell her again if she pokes around anymore. I've got contacts . . . I've got muscle on my side, you know? The bastards owe me, and I can bring pressure to bear . . . You want another drink?'

Arnold shook his head. 'No. And I think maybe you've had enough. Let me take you home.'

'Home?' Kirkby snorted. 'I got a rented flat just up the street. And I live alone. No friends. Nothing. Home? No chance of that now. Where the hell can I go when there are people like Stannard and that bastard Crickley around?'

Arnold felt something move in his chest. 'Crickley? What's Crickley got to do with this?'

'Ah, with what, my friend? What did Crickley have to do with anything? Another long nose, poking into dusty corners. And look where it got him! He got just what he deserved, believe me, and if I had the chance again . . .'

His eyes grew wary suddenly, and he leaned back in his seat. He stared at Arnold as though he were a stranger, a defensive barrier rising between them. 'Home. Yes, maybe I should get back. It's only just after ten o'clock, but it's been a long day.' He sat silent for a little while. 'It's a pity, you know. I could have liked this job, better than pen-pushing in the Education Department. But that was the best offer they could come up with at the time. Now . . . to hell with it all. I don't need this hassle, from Stannard. And I didn't need it from Crickley either. Even though that's resolved, isn't it?'

He leered suddenly at Arnold and a cold knot grew in Arnold's stomach. He rose and put out his hand. 'Come on, I think you'd better go home.'

Outside, the street was quiet, and the moon was high. As they walked along the roadway and under the arch that led towards the terraces where Kirkby had a flat, Arnold heard the man giggle.

'Education Department! What a bunch of idiots they were there! Refugees from the classroom, most of them — couldn't teach, so went into administration! I could teach, not like them. But look at me now. Not real; a wisp of imagination; a ghost.' He stopped, stared up at Landon and laughed harshly. 'I did classics, you know . . . nobody teaches classics in the schools now, do they? But it was my subject. I loved it. I remember my classics teacher at school — he was good. Even introduced us to the texts they used in schools in Roman times, think of that! And there was one phrase from a Roman school text that's always stuck with me. Question and answer. *"What is Man?"* was the question. You know what the answer was?'

'No.'

'The answer given was *"A short-lived ghost"*. Philosophy, see? You can teach language and philosophy at the same time. But I never understood when I was a kid. Now, it's different. I understand. Could have been meant for me. A ghost. A short-lived ghost.'

'Is this where you live?' Arnold asked, pausing at the door of the three-storeyed Victorian house.

'This is the place. You're all right, Landon. Thanks for the company — brief though it was. I needed someone to talk to.'

He fumbled with his keys. 'Even a ghost needs someone to talk to, from time to time . . .'

3

'So, what have we got?' John Culpeper sighed, leaned back in his chair and stretched his arms behind his head.

Farnsby laid the files on the desk between them and opened the top one. It was a summary file, carefully written, in the neat, precise hand that Culpeper hated. Somehow, it epitomized Farnsby in Culpeper's mind: small, controlled, never swayed by emotion. A man who knew where he was going: a man who had somewhere to go.

'I've had two men working on the materials given to us by the *Journal,*' Farnsby began. 'Much of it is routine, but by looking at Crickley's diary and comparing it with rough notes Crickley kept, I think there's a few areas we could concentrate on, where we might get some leads.'

'You're working on the assumption that Crickley was chasing up some story that made someone edgy.'

'Maybe edgy enough to kill. Yes, sir. We've nothing else to go on, really, since Crickley lived alone, had a few acquaintances but no real friends . . . but could have made enemies. I'll come back to that in a moment, but first of all there's this Fred Brierley entry in his diary.'

'You traced him?'

Farnsby nodded. 'I don't think it has much relevance other than general background, but I've spoken to Brierley on the phone. Apparently he came up north to interview Crickley—'

'Not the other way around?'

'No, sir. The reason for the interview was that Brierley's writing a book on James Thornton.'

'Our crusading QC?'

'The very same.'

'So what information was Brierley expecting to get from Crickley — about James Thornton, I mean?'

'Ah. Well, that's the thing, sir. Did you know that there was a personal link between Crickley and Thornton?'

'I did not.'

Farnsby smiled. 'A very interesting one, in fact. It would seem that our journalist Alan Crickley was the adopted son of James Thornton. And, according to Brierley, the relationship was not a good one. From what our friend Crickley told him, Thornton was a bit of a cold fish. Keen to right wrongs perpetrated by the police—'

'Yes, we all heard about that,' Culpeper remarked grimly.

'But not a home-loving man. Brierley reckons that Crickley carried a big chip on his shoulder; hated Thornton; got away as soon as he could, and had nothing more to do with our do-gooding MP, QC.'

'Hmmm. So while Thornton was chasing up and down the country, beating the drum about miscarriages of justice, bent coppers and incompetent pathologists, his own home life was a bit bare.'

'That's about it.'

Culpeper frowned. 'Fascinating bit of gossip, but it doesn't get us very far. You don't see this Brierley chap fitting into the frame at all?'

'No, sir. He says he was up in the north-east a few weeks back, to see Crickley, but since then he's been back home, working on his book. But as I said, it's just background.

Maybe it explains Crickley's character — a loner, not given to making friendships, bit of a chip on his shoulder.'

'Right. So what else have we got?'

Farnsby gestured to the papers in front of him. 'I've made a list of the current files Crickley was working on. Methodical chap — he had a disk on the computer in the office. The editor's copied it for me. It seems he was concentrating on maybe three or four stories. The first one concerns a guy called Peter Gaul.'

'I've seen something about that in a file you've already given me,' Culpeper growled.

'That's right. Gaul works for the Viking Research Trust. You'll have seen something about the article Crickley wrote in the *Journal* — Gaul was hauled over the coals by the trustees after the article appeared. While Crickley named no names in the article, there was plenty to read between the lines. It all came down to Gaul really — a suspicion that someone had been lifting artefacts from the site — and he is the site director, after all. It all blew over, in the end. But it remains as an active file on Crickley's disk. He was still worrying over it like a dog with a bone. So I think it's something we need to follow up. As far as I gather, Crickley had no time for Peter Gaul — and Gaul certainly had no reason to like Crickley.'

'Gaul works at Ridgeway, you say . . .'

'At the field centre.'

'Not too far from where the body was found.' Culpeper sniffed. 'We'd better get someone checking up on Mr Gaul. Find out what his movements were at the period in question. I suppose there's nothing in the diary?'

Farnsby shook his head. 'Not specifically naming Gaul. The night he died, Crickley did have an evening appointment. There's a time fixed — seven o'clock — but no name. Instead, there's an odd kind of doodle. Here it is, sir.'

Farnsby turned the file around so Culpeper could see it more clearly. He stared at it, puzzled. It comprised a square, on which was printed a letter F; adjoining it and linked to it below was an oblong, with the designatory letter M. Across the linked boxes was a shaded area, lightly scribbled in pencil.

'What the hell's that supposed to be?'

Farnsby frowned. 'I don't know, sir. It might mean nothing . . . just a doodle. But it's on the page with the appointment time, so we can't ignore it.'

'Hmmm.' Culpeper stared at the sketch for a little while, but could make nothing of it. At last he looked up to the expectant Farnsby. 'So what else was he working on?'

Farnsby took a deep breath. 'There's another name. Sir Jock Hertford.'

Culpeper's eyes narrowed. 'Tell me.'

'Nothing specific. Just a series of queries in short notes. But the lines of inquiry that Crickley was working on were, in the first instance, undue influence, and secondly, suspect share dealings.'

'Hell's bells,' Culpeper groaned. 'I have a feeling I'm not going to enjoy this. What are the details?'

'There aren't any. Just the notes. Along with another name — Bill Norman.'

'The ex-Northern player?'

'That's right. His name seems to be linked with Hertford. But the notes don't lead anywhere specific. If we start digging in these areas for links between Hertford, Norman and Crickley, I'm afraid we're going to be guessing. The only way forward is to haul Hertford in and confront him — and do the same with Bill Norman.'

'He used to be a bit of a thug on the field,' Culpeper mused. 'Temper on a short fuse. Not above getting his retaliation in first, as they say.'

'Maybe he heard about Crickley's interest in him and decided to do something about it.'

'That's galloping on a bit, Farnsby,' Culpeper warned. 'We've got to go canny on this one. All right, what else was our busy little journalist friend working on?'

Farnsby shook his head. 'Something I'd have thought was a little out of his line. Technical stuff, which I wouldn't have thought was suitable for the *Journal.* Rather more for a specialist magazine.'

'An article?'

'Outlines for one, I'd guess. He's got notes about cassiterite, arsenopyrite, rock gradings . . .'

'What the hell is all that about?'

'I'm not clear, sir. But I think he was preparing an article on tungsten and wolframite mining. Oddly enough, he's also got references to geological surveys of 1890 for some of his information, but I haven't had time to look up the survey. If it's of any significance at all to our investigation, it escapes me.'

'Let's not waste time on it,' Culpeper said. 'Better stick to what's more obvious. Maybe that was a hobby of his. I think we'd better concentrate more on Gaul . . . and Hertford. And Norman, I suppose.' He paused, eyeing the file in front of him with a sour expression. 'Gaul Norman and Hertford. They all have a connection with this Viking Research Trust.'

'That's right, sir.'

'Better dig up a list of all the trustees,' Culpeper suggested thoughtfully, 'and see if any of the others turn up in Crickley's purview.'

'You think there may be a connection?'

'There's a physical connection, in distance terms, and there's Hertford . . .' He eyed Farnsby coldly. 'You're aware we could get trouble over this investigation, aren't you?'

Farnsby hesitated. 'Hertford, you mean?'

'Sir Jock Hertford.' Culpeper sighed; he disliked complications. 'I think, in the circumstances, we'd better have a meeting with the chief constable. Just to make sure.'

'I think you're probably right.' Farnsby agreed heavily. 'I'll set it up for Friday — I believe he's in Kent at the moment.'

'Right. And now, I gather, a certain Mr Harcourt-Fanshaw wants to see me.'

A few minutes later Mr Harcourt-Fanshaw walked into Culpeper's office. He wore a tweed suit, with a red spotted handkerchief displayed in his breast pocket. His jacket was open, and his bulging waistcoat was bright hued.

'I've come to see you, Detective Chief Inspector, as a public-minded citizen. I feel it is only right that I should impart to you matters that I had previously discussed with the unfortunately deceased Mr Alan Crickley . . .'

* * *

'DCI Culpeper . . . Take a seat.'

The chief constable remained standing, leaning against the radiator on the wall beside the window, arms folded across his burly chest. His thin mouth was set grimly and his baggy-pouched eyes were stern. Culpeper knew the interview was going to be difficult. He took the seat offered, and waited.

'Farnsby suggested that you and I should talk, so I called for the files you've kept so far on the Crickley killing.' the chief constable announced. 'Have you got any further with matters?'

Culpeper nodded. 'Farnsby's interviewed Peter Gaul concerning his whereabouts on the evening Crickley was killed. We've had the pathologist's report and his calculation is that Crickley died from a blow on the back of the head with a blunt instrument, between eight and nine in the evening. He's also confirmed the view that we had already reached — Crickley was not killed at the place where he was found. There were stains in the car, on the seat and the carpet, that suggest he was killed elsewhere, and driven to the field.'

'Just to be dumped, and hidden?'

'Some attempt was made to hide the body, but our guess is the killer began to panic, wanted to get away from there.'

'But he left Crickley's car where it was.'

'Half stuck in the hedge. Maybe another sign of panic the driver lost control in the road. Anyway, it means that the killer must have walked away from there—'

'Unless he had an accomplice.'

'Of course.'

'So tell me about Gaul.'

'As I said, Farnsby's interviewed him. There was certainly no love lost between Gaul and Crickley: Gaul was incensed about the treatment given to him in the *Journal* — if only indirectly. But there was no question of suing, it seems.'

'He was accused of theft, indirectly, according to your file.'

Culpeper nodded. 'That's right. But Gaul didn't sue — he says he couldn't have afforded to. And he didn't lose his job. The trustees decided nothing was proved, so he stayed on.'

'And his movements that evening?'

Culpeper shrugged. 'His story is a bit shaky. He claims he worked late at the site — denies that Crickley came there to see him. Late in the evening he went down to the local pub in Hart village — but it's not something he does regularly, and we've found no one who can vouch for the fact he really was there.'

'How far is his office — it's at the field centre I take it — from the spot where Crickley was found?'

'Three or four miles. Not a long walk.'

Culpeper was silent for a while as the chief constable stared at him, broodingly. 'So you've still got Gaul firmly in your sights.'

'That's right, sir. He's about the best we've got at the moment: Farnsby has some people still checking on the pub story. But I have to admit, forensic haven't come up with anything yet which would tie Gaul to the car, though they're still checking fibres and so on . . .'

His voice trailed away in the face of the chief constable's cold eyes. 'Which brings us.' the chief constable said quietly, 'to your file comments about Sir Jock Hertford and one of the other trustees of the Viking Research Trust.'

'Bill Norman,' Culpeper said unhappily.

'And you've a little more information since you passed in the file, I take it?'

Culpeper nodded. 'Yes, sir. I had a visit from a solicitor called Harcourt-Fanshaw. It would seem he had some kind of relationship with Alan Crickley. He'd been using him — or they'd been using each other. Harcourt-Fanshaw is a member of the Friends of the Viking Research Trust, and he's clearly unhappy about the way the trustees are behaving. To that extent he's driven by . . . personal motives, I suspect. But what he told me more or less ties in with notes kept by Alan Crickley.'

'Tell me.' the chief constable said softly.

'Harcourt-Fanshaw had been feeding stories to Crickley for use in the *Journal.* The guy might be a solicitor, but he's not exactly brimming over with principles. He denied it when I asked him, but I suspect he's been feeding juicy items to Crickley for some time. It's my guess he put Crickley on to the Gaul story in the first instance. However . . .'

The chief constable moved away from the radiator and walked slowly to his desk. He sat down, drew a pad towards him and began to doodle on it with a pencil.

'. . . the important thing he wanted to talk to me about,' Culpeper went on, 'was what Hertford and Norman have been up to. Or what he claims they've been up to.'

'And what exactly was that?'

'Crickley had notes about share dealings linked to Hertford's name. Harcourt-Fanshaw reckons that Hertford and Norman have been working together in certain share purchases which wouldn't stand the light of day.'

'He's been specific?'

Culpeper shook his head. 'No. But he reckons that it's come to his attention on the grapevine that both men have been using inside information to make some dealings. He reckons Norman doesn't have two quid to rub together — but has plenty of contacts. Hertford has no money of his own — it's his wife holds the purse strings. But both men have been investing heavily — and making a killing. So he thought it public-spirited to advise me: Sir Jock Hertford and Bill Norman have been acting outside the law. And Alan Crickley knew about it.'

The chief constable was silent for a while. He tapped the pencil against the table edge. 'So you have notes written by Crickley — which contain no details — and a statement offered gratuitously by Harcourt-Fanshaw — whose motives are open to suspicion.' His grey eyes were suddenly fixed on Culpeper. 'It's not a great deal to go on, is it?'

Culpeper nodded in agreement. 'No, sir. But I don't think we can ignore it. We'll have to take some soundings at the Exchange in Newcastle, and maybe . . .'

His voice died away as the chief constable's mouth tightened. He waited, a cold feeling in the pit of his stomach.

'This is a very delicate situation we find ourselves in, Culpeper. Sir Jock Hertford is a prominent man . . . one might say, very prominent. He's chairman of the Party in the north, he's well known in charitable circles, a man of independent means — even if they are his wife's — deputy master of the Hunt . . . we are talking *political* matters, here, Culpeper.'

'I know that, sir.'

'And then there's Norman.' the chief constable added grimly. 'Not so heavyweight as Sir Jock Hertford but still with a good reputation socially — and he has extensive, important connections as a result of his playing days. He has lots of well-placed friends who could make a lot of noise. Do I need to spell it out?'

'No, sir.'

'Spell it out I will, nevertheless, Culpeper. You've got to go very, very carefully on this one. No wild allegations. No incautious steps. No pressurizing unless you're very sure. It's not just that we have two prominent northern people here in your gunsights — from what I see of the evidence against them, if you can call it that, is little more than unsubstantiated gossip from a source that is quite possibly tainted.'

'Harcourt-Fanshaw is a solicitor with a reasonably sound practice and—'

'And has come to the forefront recently for the noise he's been making about the management of the Viking Research

Trust. The newspapers have been full of it — and that, I suppose, was the result of his link with Alan Crickley.'

'I guess so, sir.'

'Consequently, I'm not sure we can place a deal of reliance on what Harcourt-Fanshaw says.'

'There's also the matter of undue influence,' Culpeper replied stubbornly.

The chief constable's eyes gleamed. 'Ah, yes. The will of the late Miss Ridge. Another of Mr Harcourt-Fanshaw's fantasies, I believe. He claims . . . exactly what?'

Culpeper's tone was gritty. He did not care for the veiled contempt in the chief constable's voice. He knew what was behind all this. 'Harcourt-Fanshaw reckons that he was ousted from Miss Ridge's confidence by Sir Jock Hertford. He claims that Hertford persuaded the old lady to change her legal adviser—'

'Who was previously Harcourt-Fanshaw.' the chief constable intervened.

'—and then later persuaded her to add a codicil leaving a large part of her property to a Jersey-based company. He's certain that Hertford is a director of that company, and had used undue influence to sway her, to his own financial advantage—'

'If this really happened, it's a civil matter, Culpeper, and nothing to do with us.'

'It could also be a motive,' Culpeper insisted doggedly. 'If Harcourt-Fanshaw is right, and Alan Crickley was digging, with the threat of exposing Hertford's shenanigans—'

'Alleged shenanigans.' the chief constable objected.

'—it could have provoked Hertford to violence. Or even Norman. And it's well known that Bill Norman could be goaded to violence.'

'On the rugby field, a decade ago. That's thin, Culpeper, very thin.' The chief constable was silent for a little while. 'But I take it, then, you'll be wanting to do some checking on Hertford and Norman.'

'That's my intention, sir.'

'I don't like it, Culpeper. Your premisses are thin . . . and the investigation could be dangerous. It could blow up in your face.'

'I don't think we have any choice, sir.'

The chief constable grimaced. 'All right, but let's be clear. You keep this very low profile. I think it's all very shaky depending as it does on this Harcourt-Fanshaw character and the information is suspect in itself. Harcourt-Fanshaw's bile recently has been obvious. He could be using us for his own purposes, as it seems he used Crickley.' He paused. 'I suppose you'll be checking out Harcourt-Fanshaw's movements, too?'

'We've not got him in the frame, sir.'

'Well, I suggest you put him in.' the chief constable replied crisply. 'If you're going after Norman and Hertford on such slim pickings, you'd better look at your solicitor friend also. He was involved with Crickley, after all.'

'They were working together, sir,' Culpeper protested.

'And friends do fall out, Culpeper.'

'Yes, sir.'

There was a short silence. At last the chief constable made his decision. 'My advice, in the circumstances, is that you should concentrate on Peter Gaul. He sounds a more promising lead. He's not got an alibi that is supported, so see if you can break it. The rest . . . is on your own head . . .'

That figured, Culpeper thought sourly.

The chief constable put his hands flat on the desk and stared at Culpeper. 'So, I hope I've made myself clear. If you are going to take a close look at the trustees of the Viking Research Trust you'd better do it discreetly. I want no screams back in this office. There are well-connected people out there who won't take kindly to the suggestion that some of their own are being suspected of murder. And that means they'll head for one phone number in particular. Mine.'

* * *

And that was where the rub was, Culpeper thought cynically as he left the chief constable's office. It was all about bridge, and golf, and the Hunt, social affairs, limousines, organized guns on the moors and politics. The chief constable was well-connected, and if it got out that one of the set was being investigated, he'd be forced to defend the situation, personally.

But that was *his* problem, Culpeper decided grimly. He had a job to do.

On the other hand, he didn't trust Harcourt-Fanshaw. The old man could be right on that one. The flamboyant solicitor had an axe to grind. He obviously had a down on the trustees, and a little muck-raking for his own ends was just what he clearly enjoyed. He'd lost Alan Crickley as a conduit for gossip — maybe he was not above using the police for the same purposes.

So maybe the chief constable was right in that, at least. It would do no harm to put Harcourt-Fanshaw into the frame.

He turned into the corridor and made his way towards his room. He had just reached the door when Farnsby came walking quickly towards him. There was an odd light in his eye.

'So, what's up, Farnsby?'

'Just had a phone call, sir — a woman whom you've already interviewed.'

'Yes?'

'Karen Stannard.'

'So?'

'She says she thinks she knows who killed Alan Crickley!'

CHAPTER FOUR

1

Arnold Landon parked his car at the back of County Hall and checked his watch. He was not due in the office until nine thirty, and there was some shopping he needed to do, so he walked briskly into the high street and spent ten minutes waiting behind a chatty, middle-aged woman who clearly saw visits to the butcher's as occasions for social gossip. He had time in hand, however, and was not unduly disturbed. As he was leaving the shop he heard his name called.

He turned. It was Dr Rena Williams.

'Good morning,' Arnold greeted her. 'I didn't know you lived in Morpeth.'

'I don't.' Her voice was deep and husky, and she had her hands thrust down into the pockets of a voluminous trench coat. She seemed dressed more for the high fells than for the town. 'I've got an appointment to see Miss Stannard.'

'Then we can walk to the office together.'

'That will be pleasant.' They fell into step down the high street, back towards the car park. Rena Williams glanced at Arnold quizzically. 'How are you getting on with Miss Stannard?'

'Well enough,' Arnold replied guardedly.

'I get the impression she's a woman of firm views.'

'I can endorse that,' Arnold smiled. 'And I suppose she feels she has to make an impression in the department new brooms and all that.'

Rena Williams laughed. 'And she's a woman.' She glanced again at Arnold covertly. 'Have you and she clashed much?'

Arnold hesitated. He did not know the archaeologist very well and was reluctant to indulge in office gossip. He shrugged. 'We've had our little differences. It's inevitable, really. But why do you ask?'

'She seems to disagree with you on various points.'

'Such as?'

'Oh, I don't know . . . the dig up at Ridgeway, for instance. She advised me to disregard you. She emphasized that decisions about digs should be left to the experts — not to amateurs like you.' She paused. 'I hope you're not offended.'

Arnold was not offended. He smiled at her. 'It's a viewpoint I've heard before. It seems sensible, really.'

'Superficially, yes. But I'm not so sure it always applies. I'm well aware of your reputation. And you seem to have an eye. Your comments, for instance, about the possibility of a boat burial . . . I've been thinking a lot about it.'

'Yes?'

'It could be you're right,' she said slowly, as they crossed the road and entered the car park, heading for the rear entrance to the offices. 'And in other circumstances, I'd be inclined to take up your suggestion and follow it through. But, I don't know . . .'

'In other circumstances?'

'If we had the money. And the time. Though it's the same thing, I suppose. That's the reason why I'm coming in to see Karen Stannard, really. We're conducting this dig on a shoestring. I've already spoken to David Hall and the trustees and it's clear there simply isn't enough money to continue, not unless Ridgeway Manor is sold off. I take no sides in that dispute, it's none of my business, but I suspect from what Mr

Hall says, that even if the sale goes through, money will still be tight. So I want to see Miss Stannard to find out if there's any way we can obtain further grants, from the government, the local authority, one of the funding agencies . . .'

'I see. But it wouldn't take much work to open up the badger setts and undertake a sectional survey.'

'I agree. But it would be at the expense of digging elsewhere — and your suggestion, while being attractive, was not in our original brief.' Rena Williams sighed. 'We're using cheap labour as it is — the university students . . . I don't know how we can possibly complete the dig in the circumstances.'

'I understand it was a project dear to Miss Ridge's heart,' Arnold said, opening the door for her to walk into the building.

'That's so — and I got a very sympathetic hearing from David Hall. But we're all stuck in the same bind. We need a rich benefactor — and there's not too many of them around these days.'

They took the lift up to the third floor. At the door of his room, Arnold pointed down the corridor. 'If you just follow the corridor along, and turn left at the end, you'll find Miss Stannard's secretary. Don't be put off by her formidable appearance! She'll take you in to the deputy director's office. Nice to see you, Dr Williams.'

'And you, Mr Landon.' Rena Williams smiled. 'Will we be seeing you up at the site again soon?'

Arnold shrugged. 'Not in an official capacity. I will have to come up to Ridgeway Manor for the meeting of Friends, when I'll be reporting on the working group—'

'Do call in at the site then,' she said crisply. 'We could talk further about the possibilities at the dig.'

'I look forward to that.'

Dr Williams began to walk down the corridor and Arnold turned to go into his room when a woman's voice shouted down the corridor.

'Mr Landon!'

It was the dark-visaged Miss Sansom. She was waving at him urgently. Rena Williams looked back over her shoulder. 'I think you're wanted,' she said, smiling.

'Miss Sansom?'

'You're to come to the deputy director's office. Immediately.'

There was no mistaking the peremptory note in her voice. Arnold walked quickly down the corridor and as Rena Williams stepped aside, Arnold asked the secretary, 'What's the problem?'

'There are always problems around here!' she snapped irritably. 'And Mr Brent-Ellis is out of the office, as usual, not available.'

It was the first time Arnold had ever heard a word of criticism of the director from the lips of the loyal, loving servant. He glanced at Dr Williams. 'Sorry about this. I know you have an appointment . . . '

'Needs of the service,' she said cheerfully.

Arnold tapped on Karen Stannard's door and opened it. The first person he saw was Detective Chief Inspector Culpeper.

Karen Stannard was standing behind her desk. Red spots of anger marked her cheeks; when Arnold glanced at Culpeper he saw that the chief inspector also looked somewhat put out. He gained the impression that the two were not getting along terribly well.

'You wanted to see me, Deputy Director?' Arnold asked.

'Where's Kirkby?' she rasped.

Arnold stared at her. 'I've only just got in—'

'He's not in his office,' she interrupted, her eyes cold and hard. 'You seem to be the only person in the office he has any kind of relationship with, so you must know where he is.'

'I know where he lives, if that's what you mean,' Arnold replied stiffly. 'And I know him only because you made him my "acolyte" as you put it. But what's the matter? What's all this about?'

There was a short silence. Culpeper cleared his throat.

Karen Stannard glanced at him and then abruptly sat down. She was angry, and clearly upset about something.

'Why don't you sit down, Mr Landon?' Culpeper suggested reasonably.

Arnold took a seat.

'How well do you know Mr Kirkby?' Culpeper asked.

Arnold glanced at Miss Stannard before replying. 'Not very well. We've worked together these last few weeks, but he keeps very much to himself.'

'He's a bit reticent, then?'

That's right.'

'Hasn't talked much about himself?'

Arnold nodded. 'I don't think he's given to confidences. We've talked a little . . . I gather he doesn't look back on his childhood with much pleasure, but that's about all I've learned of him. Except . . .' He hesitated.

'Yes?'

'I don't think he's terribly happy in this department.'

'Why?'

'I don't think it's for me to comment.' He was aware of tension in Karen Stannard's body. 'I just get the impression he feels . . . unwelcome in this department. And under pressure.'

There was a short silence. At last, easily, Culpeper asked, 'Have you spent any time with him socially?'

'I've been for a drink with him at the King's Head. Once. The other evening.'

'He didn't unwind then?'

'He got drunk. It was because he felt unhappy. I believe he'd had . . . words with Miss Stannard.'

She hissed slightly. Culpeper ignored her. He scratched his cheek thoughtfully. 'He's told you nothing about his background, then.'

'What's this all about, Mr Culpeper?' Arnold asked.

Culpeper regarded him owlishly for a few moments and then turned to Karen Stannard. 'I think the deputy director might answer that.'

Karen Stannard sat upright and glared at the policeman. 'I don't think this is at all appropriate.'

Culpeper inclined his head in disagreement. 'I think it's quite appropriate, Deputy Director. You mentioned Mr Landon's name in your . . . allegations. It seems to me quite in order that you should repeat your story in front of Mr Landon. That way we can check out just how seriously I should take what you say.'

Karen Stannard was not pleased. For a brief moment there was a hunted look in her eyes, but then her natural iron took over and her lips tightened. 'All right, Chief Inspector. If that's the way you want it.' She raised her chin defiantly and glared at Arnold. 'I rang Ponteland yesterday and spoke to the police. I told them I thought I knew who killed Alan Crickley.'

'You did?' Arnold said in surprise.

There was a short silence. Culpeper said quietly, 'She thinks it was Syl Kirkby.'

Arnold laughed.

'You're amused,' Culpeper said.

'It's a preposterous suggestion!'

'Why do you say that?' Culpeper asked keenly as Karen Stannard looked furious.

Arnold shrugged. 'He's a quiet, reserved man who minds his own business. It's true, I've seen him show anger—'

'When?'

'After a session with the deputy director.'

Karen Stannard snorted indignantly. 'The little worm—'

'Please.' Culpeper held up an admonitory hand. 'Go on, Landon. You've seen him angry—'

'But it was controlled. The other evening it was different, of course, he'd been drinking . . .'

'He was angry then?'

Arnold shrugged. 'Not so much angry as . . . maybe frustrated, because people wouldn't leave him alone.'

Karen Stannard shot a quick, triumphant glance at Culpeper.

The policeman ignored it. 'People . . . How do you mean, Landon?'

Arnold hesitated, recalling the conversation he had had with Kirkby. He hadn't understood much of what the man was talking about. He shook his head. 'I don't know, really. You should ask Kirkby about it—'

'He's not in the office,' Karen Stannard snapped. 'That's why we're asking you. Did he say anything about Crickley?'

Reluctantly, Arnold nodded. 'He said he'd had a sort of run in with him. He objected to the man. Apparently Crickley insisted they'd met before — Kirkby denied it. But that's all it was, I think. Kirkby was irritated — he is an intensely private man, and doesn't care for people probing into his life.'

'Does that seem normal to you?' Karen Stannard asked, sneeringly.

'We all like our privacy,' Arnold replied.

'When you saw him in the pub . . . he was drunk, you say? Did he make any comment about Crickley's death?'

Arnold hesitated. 'I think he made some comment . . . that Crickley deserved what he got. Something like that. He didn't like the man — thought him a muck-raker.'

There was a short silence. Culpeper sighed, and settled himself more comfortably in his chair. 'All right, Miss Stannard, we don't seem to be getting very far so I think you'd better repeat what you've told me — in Mr Landon's hearing. It might be he can shed some further light on the whole thing.'

The deputy director did not like it. She had clearly expected her statements to the policeman to have been kept private: she was not keen to expose the remarks in front of one of her minions. She gritted her teeth and glared at Culpeper.

'I can't say I cared for Mr Kirkby the first time I met him. He's a rabbit and he was dumped upon us from another department — but there's also something about him that bothers me. Call it feminine intuition, if you like,' she challenged them. 'But I put it down to instinct and an intelligent summing-up of people. There's something . . . odd about Kirkby. The way he looks at you . . .'

'Tell us about his relationship with Alan Crickley, as far as it went,' Culpeper suggested.

'I think Alan Crickley felt the same kind of shiver that I did,' she continued. 'I met Crickley first when he came to see me here at the office. He was interviewing me — my reactions to getting this job, that sort of thing. But at the end he asked me about Kirkby.'

'What was his interest in Kirkby?' Arnold asked.

She shrugged disdainfully. 'I didn't inquire. But he'd met him at the AGM of the Friends of the Viking Research Trust—'

'That's right. I introduced them,' Arnold added.

'And it seems that Crickley thought they'd met before . . . that he'd recognized him from somewhere. Kirkby denied it. Quite vehement about it, it seems. So, when Crickley met me here he asked me about Kirkby. I knew nothing about the man, but I was curious . . .'

'You told me earlier that Crickley asked you to take a closer look at Kirkby, and his background,' Culpeper corrected her.

Karen Stannard shot a furious glance in his direction. 'All right, he asked me to check on him. So I did. And that's when I began to get suspicious. I met Crickley a few days later, in the Greenmarket in Newcastle. I told him that there was something odd.'

'So you were sort of spying on one of your colleagues for a newspaperman,' Culpeper suggested almost cheerfully.

'I did what I thought was right,' she replied coldly. 'As deputy director I'm responsible for the staff in the department — to the director. I need to know the staff — their strengths, weaknesses, and backgrounds. And if I think there's something odd about one of them, it's only right I should check. Which is what I did. I got out the personnel files. That's when my curiosity became really aroused. The one on Kirkby was extremely slim. No history. No background. No record of previous employment.'

Arnold frowned. He did not approve of the way Karen Stannard had behaved, but he was nevertheless surprised at what she had found.

'He came from the Education Department, on transfer. They'd have held the full record there,' he suggested.

There was a triumphant note in her voice when she replied. 'I checked there too. Same thing. No details, going back from the time he joined the authority. So then I made a few more inquiries — I know people in the county — but it was all very peculiar. I simply drew a blank.'

'You mean you'd come across a man of mystery,' Culpeper drawled.

Her tone was cold. 'I was intrigued. When someone is appointed to the authority forms have to be filled out. Details of previous experience. Kirkby's was very sketchy. So I made some inquiries in the chief executive's office. They had nothing, and the chief executive was not available. So . . . I met Crickley—'

'When exactly was that?' Culpeper asked.

'The week before he was killed. I told him I was puzzled. He seemed very interested. Then I called Kirkby in and asked him directly.'

'That was discreet of you,' Culpeper said.

The sarcasm did not escape her. Stubbornly, she went on, 'I felt I had a right to know what was going on. He was in my department . . . my responsibility. So I asked him direct. Told him about the personal file. Asked him whether there was anything he had to tell me. He got angry. We had words. He insisted his private life was just that — private. I replied I didn't see this as private life, but professional. He stormed out . . .'

'He was somewhat depressed when he was out with me at Galashiels,' Arnold said. 'He was upset.'

Karen Stannard was silent for a few moments, then she seemed to gather herself determinedly. 'I was puzzled, and, I admit, angry. I didn't like the way he stood up to me — as though he had a right to keep his past professional life secret. Because that's the way I saw it — secrecy. I worried about it for a day or so — then I got a phone call from Crickley.'

'And when was that?' Culpeper asked.

'It would have been two days before he died. He sounded pleased. He told me not to bother about Kirkby any more. He said he'd tied it all in, remembered where he'd seen Kirkby . . . he suggested he'd found out something that would cause quite a stir in northern circles.'

'Did he say he was going to confront Kirkby?' Culpeper asked.

Karen Stannard shook her head. 'He didn't actually say he was . . . but he sort of implied Kirkby had a shock coming. It was then that I hauled Kirkby in again — and confronted him with the fact that Alan Crickley was investigating him. I wanted to know exactly what it was Syl Kirkby was hiding.' She paused. 'He became quite . . . vicious.'

'It was after that, I guess, that he rang me to join him at the King's Head,' Arnold said quietly. 'He was very upset.'

'And so was I,' Karen Stannard flashed. 'And then I realized what probably happened. Kirkby has something to hide in his past. Crickley knew about it, once he had pieced it together. He was going to expose him in the newspaper. I thought and thought about it — and I decided I'd better call you. Because I think Crickley had a meeting with Kirkby. I think Crickley threatened to expose him, they quarrelled and Kirkby killed him!'

The room grew silent. Culpeper stared at his shoes. Arnold waited, anger seething in his veins at the way Karen Stannard had behaved. She was flushed, determined in her glance, waiting. Culpeper sighed.

'So you rang the police,' he said, 'and dragged me out here.' He looked at her sourly. 'But what is it you've got, Miss Stannard? Second- and third-hand stuff — a mystery man because there's not much in his personal files; a murder motive because Alan Crickley thought he'd recognized Kirkby from somewhere? What's it all about?'

'He's not in the office today.'

'So maybe he's ill. Or maybe he's upset about the way you've treated him and taken off. It's hardly a criminal offence.'

'But you'll follow it through,' she insisted, her glance pinning him to the chair.

Culpeper shrugged. 'I've better things to do, but I'll get someone on to it. Unless you've got something to add, Landon, that'll clear things up.'

'I think it's ridiculous to even consider that Kirkby would have killed Crickley. He doesn't seem to me to have that kind of explosive anger. As for his absence today, I don't know, but you could check at his flat—'

'We'll do that, of course. But unless you can come up with something rather more concrete, Miss Stannard, I'm afraid you've just been wasting time for all of us — yourself included. And your time, I'm sure, is valuable . . .'

2

The level of interest in the affairs of the Friends of the Viking Research Trust had clearly declined. The room at Ridgeway Manor that had been set aside for the meeting was half empty. The main protagonists were there in full force, of course: Harcourt — Fanshaw and Phil Martin, the group of trustees comprising David Hall, Sam Frimley, Bill Norman and Sir Jock Hertford. Peter Gaul was present and, Arnold noted, so was the tall, square-shouldered Dr Rena Williams. Their glances met across the room when he entered and she gave him a slight smile.

The thin turnout was probably due to the fact that time had passed and tempers cooled. Arnold was not certain it would make his task any easier, however — the people present would be those more committed to the cause, whatever the cause might be.

He took the chair at the small dais alone, and in silence. He began by reiterating his function as an independent chairman of the working group and by stating that he would be presenting a report which was in his view fair and unbiased. He then read out the formal statement that he had prepared.

'Considerable discussions took place within the working group where all possible arguments would seem to have been aired. Legal and financial advice was taken. The facts of the matter would seem to be resolved into certain precise issues. Firstly, there is only a limited amount of money held by the Viking Research Trust and it is insufficient to support the work currently being undertaken at the grave site on Ridgeway.'

He paused to let the statement sink in. It was important that they all understood the situation. Rena Williams looked grave behind her steel-rimmed glasses. Near her, Peter Gaul sat bolt upright, concentrating.

'Second, it is a fact that Ridgeway Manor, which was an important part of the bequest to the Trust from Miss Ridge, is burdened by a heavy mortgage, the servicing of which takes up most of the resources of the Trust. With current interest rates, in fact, it is virtually impossible to service that burden and continue work at the grave site.'

Arnold hesitated and glanced around the room. Everyone seemed to be listening to him intently; Harcourt-Fanshaw had a furrowed brow, and Phil Martin had a cynical twist to his mouth.

'These points are basic,' Arnold continued, 'but the third point is equally important. It is clear that although Miss Ridge may well have wished otherwise — as far as can be discovered from the memorandum she left — there is no encumbrance or legal constraint placed upon the trustees as to how they can deal with Ridgeway Manor. They have placed a case before the working group and although it did not result in a unanimous agreement, I am forced to say that as chairman I agree with the undoubted logic of the trustees' intentions.' He paused, staring intently at the faces in front of him. 'In other words, the trustees have persuaded me that unless the manor house is sold it will be impossible to continue the work at the site — and that in itself would destroy the main objective of Miss Ridge's bequest.'

There was the scraping of a chair. Peter Gaul stood up. His dark face was suffused with anger. He waved a hand violently. 'You say the sale is the only way. But you wouldn't take evidence from me. I insist there is another way — a lease, financial support, making the whole thing a commercially viable venture. In my hands . . .'

He had no support. He felt it, the indifference at his back. Harcourt-Fanshaw had his adherents, but Peter Gaul was alone. It might have been due to the rumours about his activity on the site, Arnold guessed, but it was clear no one trusted Peter Gaul to save the development work at Ridgeway.

The room was silent. Peter Gaul sat down.

'One further issue remains,' Arnold continued. 'It relates to the procedures involved in the sale of Ridgeway Manor. If that sale is to go forward, and I see no logical reason why it should not, there is a question of how it should be done. Certainly, the practice in the public sector is to go to tender, or seek sealed bids. But the Trust is bound by no such rules. It is the duty of the trustees only to seek the best value, or a fair market price. I would agree that there is much to be said for open tenders being sought, but I do not believe that the Friends as an organization can have any legal say in the matter. The sale is a matter for the trustees themselves, and no one else, provided they comply with their duties as trustees.'

He paused again, waiting for any comment. There was none, though he could see Harcourt-Fanshaw had his head down, conferring with Phil Martin.

'Consequently, since the trustees have stated to the group that they have found a purchaser, this is all they need to communicate to the Friends. The identity of the purchaser is not known to me — but the purchaser's desire to remain unnamed at this stage is a matter over which the Friends can have no control, or say.'

His mouth was dry. He closed the folder in which he had placed his notes, and in silence faced the audience.

There was a vague rustling, and he sensed some disappointment in the room. He was not surprised when Harcourt-Fanshaw rose to his feet, one thumb hooked into the pocket of his flamboyant waistcoat. 'You have made your statement, Mr Landon, and I agree that it is a report with which the majority of the working group concur. But that's hardly surprising, is it, since they are the trustees! You will not be surprised, however, if I indicate the dissent of myself and my colleague, Mr Martin.'

'You had already warned me that you would be dissenting,' Arnold agreed. He did not add anything about the heated way in which the decision had been communicated to him.

'And I'm sure you will not object if I speak to the matter today.' Harcourt-Fanshaw added.

Arnold made no reply. He had, in effect, done his duty. 'Mr Landon, I believe, has acted with fairness,' Harcourt-Fanshaw intoned, half-turning ponderously to look around the room, 'but has failed to carry through one of the points he has made. I listened to his report with care. There is one comment he made which I would like to draw your attention to, relating to the sale.' He paused, for effect. 'You will all be aware that I oppose the sale — at least, the manner in which it is being conducted. But setting that aside, I wish to draw attention to Mr Landon's own words — he said: the matter of the sale is a matter for the trustees themselves, and no one else, *provided they comply with their duties as trustees.* This is the issue to which I desire to refer. It is my contention that the trustees have in fact been guilty of a breach of trust — and in carrying out the sale they will be compounding that breach.'

A babble of voices broke out. Harcourt-Fanshaw waited for it to die down. Arnold glanced at the group of trustees. They appeared strangely unmoved by the charge.

'Let me be specific,' Harcourt-Fanshaw continued. 'We have all heard of the memorandum written by Miss Ridge, which is specific about the objectives she wished completed. The trustees will tell you it is not legally binding. But I say it is *morally* binding, and in equity the trustees should bind themselves to it. Why? Because the whole position of a trustee is a moral one. He must comply with the law, of course, but he must also comply with the wishes of the benefactor. In equity he must do so.'

Bill Norman twisted in his seat, looking around the room behind him. He muttered something to David Hall, but the chairman of trustees ignored him.

'And then I would wish to go back beyond the memorandum itself,' Harcourt-Fanshaw announced. He paused, dragged a handkerchief out of his top pocket and wiped his mouth. It was the first sign of tension Arnold had noted in the solicitor: he guessed that Harcourt-Fanshaw was gambling a last throw, because Arnold's report had effectively cut the ground from under him.

'I wish to charge the trustees with more than defalcation of duty. There are guilty men among the group. I charge those guilty men — whoever they may turn out to be—' he fixed his gaze on Sir Jock Hertford — 'with having taken advantage of a confused old lady. I charge them with having twisted the objectives of the Trust for their own benefit. I charge them with having deliberately misled her in the setting up of the Trust itself, and in the disposition of her holdings—'

Someone at the back of the room shouted out, catcalling at Harcourt-Fanshaw. It seemed to break down a barrier: a lady in the front row waved her fist at the trustees, a number of voices broke out into an altercation in the middle rows and for a moment Arnold feared they would be back to their earlier situation, where pandemonium had broken out in the last meeting of the Friends.

Then David Hall stood up.

He was calm in his grey, sober business suit, his thick shock of dark hair carefully smoothed down, handsome features serene. He stood there stiffly, unmoving, saying nothing. The noise burst and rumbled around him but he simply waited, holding Arnold's gaze, and gradually the noise began to subside. Harcourt-Fanshaw was still on his feet, waving his handkerchief, but as the room grew silent he seemed to become edgy, and nervous. He glared defiantly at David Hall.

'I still have the floor, Mr Landon!'

'Sit down, Harcourt-Fanshaw — you're blocking the light!'

‘In more ways than one! Let’s listen to what the chairman of trustees has to say!’

There were more calls making a similar point, and at last, unwillingly, Harcourt-Fanshaw resumed his seat. His face was flushed and he seemed angry. Phil Martin, sitting beside him, was stony-faced.

‘I’d like to begin,’ David Hall said, ‘by thanking Mr Landon for the balanced and fair report he’s made to the meeting. It summarizes the discussion admirably. He has also allowed Mr Harcourt-Fanshaw to make his own comments. I don’t wish to allude too closely to them, except to say they amount to a farrago of nonsense—’

He paused while some of the solicitor’s supporters called, ‘Answer! Answer!’

‘—but answer them I will — or rather, would — if Harcourt-Fanshaw had the temerity and foolishness to raise them in a court of law. The trustees have done nothing wrong, and I will stand by that. So I treat Harcourt-Fanshaw’s rabblerousing tactics with the contempt they deserve. However, it may well be that I can resolve all these issues at once, and overcome the objections raised by many of you, as Friends of the Trust, by bringing you up to date with recent events.’

Arnold looked around the room. David Hall’s calm bearing was having its effect: they were all listening to him now, even the hecklers.

‘Mr Landon was absolutely correct in saying the sale of Ridgeway Manor is a matter for the trustees, and perfectly within their powers. The procedures for sale are also a matter for the trustees. I am able to tell you that we have had a buyer in the wings for some time — a buyer who wishes to remain anonymous. I make no comment on that. At this stage, such anonymity is of no relevance, bearing in mind that the sum being offered for the property is considerably in excess of its true value.’ Someone at the back stood up and tried to interrupt but sat down again when Arnold raised his hand.

‘Why should the sum be in excess of true value? For the same reasons that Miss Ridge made her original bequest. The buyer is interested in seeing the further development of the Viking Research Trust. It's as simple as that.' He paused and glanced down at Bill Norman. 'Mr Norman and I have been involved in the negotiations, but it is to Mr Norman that most of the credit must go. For he has been able to persuade an even greater response from the purchasers than we could possibly have hoped for. Mr Norman, perhaps you'd like to tell us all about it?'

With a show of reluctance, Bill Norman rose to his feet. He stood there, broad-shouldered, injecting sincerity into his somewhat battered features, and waved a deprecatory hand. 'It was a team effort, believe me. David is too modest. We pulled together on this one. He's the kind of guy I could have done with years back, packing down with me when we played the Aussies. No, we did this together. The fact is, not only did we extract a high purchase price from the buyers, but we gave them a solid spiel about the Trust itself, and the importance of the grave site. We were able to point out to them that there are considerable tax advantages to be gained by making a gift to a charitable trust — which is the status enjoyed by the Viking Research Trust — and, to cut a long story short, they were swayed by our arguments.'

He took a deep breath, and smiled. 'I'm pleased to inform you that the purchasers are prepared to make a contribution of half a million pounds to the continuation of the Trust, and the development of the grave site itself. The donation will be made directly to the Viking Research Trust and will thus ensure that all of the objectives desired by Miss Ridge will eventually be secured!'

'Half a million!'

There was a gasp, and a ripple of excitement in the room. Arnold stared at Norman, standing there so pleased with himself, and something churned over in his mind.

Harcourt-Fanshaw was on his feet again. He began to say something, then stopped. He spluttered incoherently, and it was clear he was angered rather than pleased by the statement. He was aware of the sense of excitement generated in the room by Norman's announcement and he could find no immediate way to dampen it down. At last he struggled out with a question. 'Is this . . . generous donation without any strings?'

Norman smiled. 'Absolutely none.'

'But why should they do it?' Harcourt-Fanshaw floundered.

'I've told you. Tax advantage. And public philanthropy.'

'There are no preconditions?'

Norman was about to speak when David Hall placed one hand on his arm, and rose. Norman sank down in his seat. David Hall smiled at Harcourt-Fanshaw. 'It depends on what you mean by preconditions. There is one obvious one, naturally. The charitable gift will be conditional upon the sale of Ridgeway Manor going through. But that must be obvious, of course. It's why the purchasers are even talking to us in the first place.'

'It's a bribe!' Harcourt-Fanshaw snarled.

'Bribe . . . commission . . . there is usually a price to be paid for everything.' Hall replied smoothly. 'It depends on how you look at things. The way I look at this offer is simple. We can't go on as we are. We can't fulfil the objectives of Miss Ridge's Trust. By selling Ridgeway Manor we can take not only the one small step we had anticipated — now we can actually complete the task she had set us initially — albeit without giving us the financial support to do it. That, as far as I'm concerned, is a good deal — call it what you will, Harcourt-Fanshaw.'

And that, it seemed, was the general consensus of the meeting.

* * *

Tea was available in the room after the meeting, and some thirty people stayed on. Peter Gaul was notable by his absence but Rena Williams came up to join Arnold. She was smiling. 'That was quite a brilliant stroke, it seems to me,' she said.

Arnold nodded thoughtfully. 'Quite brilliant.'

'Removed all our problems in one fell swoop. And I won't have to go cap in hand to the department again.'

'Did you get no help from Miss Stannard?'

'She was not in a receptive mood. Something had upset her.' Her eyes glinted at him behind her steel-rimmed glasses. 'I suspect it was you.'

Arnold smiled. 'Not me, for once.'

'Anyway, if this marvellous donation is for real, it means we can now enlist a better qualified workforce — and we'll also be able to open up those badger setts, Mr Landon, and investigate your theory. Wouldn't it be exciting if we did find a boat burial there!'

'Very.'

She looked at him carefully and raised an eyebrow. 'You don't seem as infected as I with the excitement of this news.'

Arnold laughed. 'Oh, I am, don't get me wrong: I'm hugely pleased for you and for the Trust. It solves all the problems, as you say. On the other hand . . .'

'Yes?'

Arnold shrugged. 'I just hope there'll be no slip-up.'

'How can there be?'

'I don't know. This has been so sudden. The announcement . . . it's almost too good to be true. I mean, David Hall knew what I was going to say today, and he also knew there'd still be a row, orchestrated by Harcourt-Fanshaw. I'm just a little surprised he didn't mention these charitable donation arrangements to me before the meeting started.'

Rena Williams managed a husky giggle, incongruous in a woman of her build and appearance. 'Well, Mr Landon, you have to admit it was a very effective piece of theatre.'

Theatre.

Yes, it was that, Arnold mused. But why was he left with a small niggling feeling of unease?

He was aware of Sir Jock Hertford moving in his direction. The man's face was flushed and beaming. 'Landon — and Dr Williams! All most satisfactory, hey? A brilliant stroke! Look, we've set aside a small room where we can get together for a celebratory drink. Would you both care to join us? It's just the trustees, you know.'

Arnold was inclined to refuse, but Rena Williams linked her arm into his and giggled again. 'We'd love to, Sir Jock!'

Arnold allowed himself to be dragged from the main hall into a side room. A silver tray with several decanters had been placed on the table in the centre, and the trustees stood there against the background of eighteenth-century oil paintings, beautifully carved wall panelling and ornate plasterwork in the ceiling, hugely pleased with themselves, glasses in hand. Arnold looked around him: this room was in good condition but Ridgeway Manor as a whole needed a great deal spent on it before it could be rendered habitable. He wondered what the new owners would do with it.

Arnold accepted a glass of whisky and suffered the excited, inane chatter of Sir Jock Hertford for some minutes, feeling vaguely out of place, until Bill Norman came over and congratulated him.

'What for?' Arnold asked.

'For supporting us as well.'

The heavy face was smiling, confident, as Arnold stared at him. 'I wasn't actually supporting anyone,' he said. 'I tried to be objective.'

'You still ended up supporting the trustees though, didn't you?' Norman said cheerfully.

'Because the case was logical.' Arnold was slightly nettled at the implication in Norman's tone that he had in some way stepped aside from his independent, objective position. He felt a light touch at his elbow and turned: it was David Hall.

The man's tanned features were relaxed and confident. He held a large whisky in his hand and he waved it negligently. 'Dr Williams, nice to see you here. Jock, Bill — do you mind if I whisk Mr Landon away for a moment? I'd like a private chat with him.'

They both grinned and nodded, bobbing their heads conspiratorially, Jock Hertford winking at Arnold. David

Hall gestured towards a seat in the window embrasure at the far end of the room. 'Let's take a seat over there.'

Arnold wondered what the reason for the conversation was going to be. He suspected it might have something to do with his chairmanship of the working group — Norman had already misunderstood his position — perhaps Hall felt the same.

'I'd like you to understand,' Arnold said as they sat down, 'that I had no bias towards the trustees in my statement. I exercised an independent judgement. I said what I did because I felt it was the only way forward.'

Hall smiled, his piercing blue eyes reflecting the smile. 'Of course, my dear chap, we all appreciate that.' He paused, glancing around the room. 'It doesn't mean, nevertheless, that we're not grateful for what you've done.'

'Thanks are neither necessary, nor in order,' Arnold replied shortly.

David Hall's eyes dwelled on him for a long moment. He nodded. 'As you wish, Landon. Anyway . . . you'll be aware I'm a busy man.'

'So I understand.'

'I'll make no secret of the fact that Wheeler Holdings have been through a pretty traumatic period over the last two years. We took a battering in the recession and our share price fell through the floor. It was touch and go . . . believe me.' He smiled, disarmingly. 'However, we all pulled together and by rustling up some financial support I managed to reverse the situation. We're almost back up to where we were.'

'I'm pleased for you.'

'Hmmm.' Hall's eyes strayed, his glance wandering around the room. 'But the story doesn't end there. Really, it can't end there. A business moves on, or it dies. We need restructuring at Wheeler Holdings, an aggressive push into the European market . . . in short, Landon, I feel the company is going to need my full attention over the next few years.' He paused, fixing his glance on Arnold. 'Which leaves me with a problem.'

'In the company?'

'No. In the Viking Research Trust.'

There was a short silence. Someone laughed across the room and Hertford was heading for the whisky again, his red face gleaming. Arnold was not sure what was coming, but he had a vague idea.

'Once the sale of Ridgeway Manor is completed — and all the paperwork is already in place — the work at the site can sail forward. But I'm not sure I'm the right man to see it through. Quite apart from the fact that I'm not sure I can afford the time, in view of the situation at Wheeler Holdings, I also feel that someone more in tune with the needs of the site would be a more sensible choice. I'm a wheeler-dealer, I admit that: but the Trust now demands someone more sympathetic to the world of archaeology as such. Do you know what I mean, Landon?'

'I can see your point, but—'

'I'll be frank with you. I can't afford the time to continue as chairman. And Bill Norman will be joining Wheeler Holdings as PR man in the next few months. I can't see him being able to afford much time for the Trust. Jock is fine, but can be . . . erratic; Sam Frimley is not sufficiently forceful . . . What I'm saying is we need two new trustees. And one of them should become chairman in my place. Hertford and Frimley aren't suitable to lead the Trust; we could manage with just one new trustee for the time being — but that person should take the chair.'

He paused, eyeing Arnold seriously. 'We've all been impressed by the manner in which you took the working group and presented your unbiased report. You thought only of the best way forward for the Trust. That's the kind of drive and projection the new chairman of the Viking Research Trust should demonstrate. In other words, Landon, I'm saying to you that once I complete the paperwork for the sale of Ridgeway Manor, it's my intention to resign as chairman of the Trust.'

He watched Arnold with careful eyes. 'I'd like you to take over in my place.'

Arnold wondered what Karen Stannard would make of that.

3

She was not pleased.

Surprisingly, however, she put up only token resistance to his statement that he intended taking up the offer.

'Can David Hall just make you an offer like that and carry it through?' she asked frostily.

'The existing trustees have the power to appoint new trustees — and choose a chairman. Hall tells me they are all in agreement that I should take over.'

'It's a conflict with your duties here.'

'I don't see that. It's unpaid, it's part-time, I can do it outside my working hours and it shouldn't affect my activity here at all. Moreover, in one sense it's a useful appointment — it gives the department, indirectly, more control over the future of the grave site.'

'Maybe there'd be objections from Dr Williams.'

'She has no say in the appointment of trustees. As it happens, I've already mentioned it to her, and she seemed pleased by the news.'

Karen Stannard sniffed. She still didn't like it, but Arnold was left with the impression she would no longer oppose the situation. It was another peg on which she could hang her dislike, but it was not a battle she felt she needed to win.

'I'll make a report to Brent-Ellis,' she said coldly. 'I'll place on the file my disagreement with your decision. The rest is up to you.'

Arnold had the feeling there would be a number of items on his personal file before he and Karen Stannard were through.

When he was back in his room he got down to clearing his desk of some of the litter of files that had accumulated there. He had been working for an hour or longer, absorbed in the minutiae of minutes of meetings, reports of site investigations and a first draft of his notes on the Galashiels visit, when a light cough disturbed him. He looked up. Jerry Picton was standing in the open doorway.

'Hard at it, Landon? Won't do you any good with Her Highness. I reckon she's got it in for you, good and proper.'

Arnold stared with distaste at the little man with the pitted skin and narrow, mean eyes. 'Anything I can do for you?'

Picton snickered and advanced into the room, perching himself on the edge of the table. 'Don't be so touchy. I'm just taking a break from the weary grind. I hear there was an interesting meeting between you, Stannard and the coppers.'

'You shouldn't believe all you hear,' Arnold replied, returning to his report.

'So why has your friend and mucker Syl Kirkby disappeared?'

'He's a colleague, not a personal friend.'

'Whatever you say. But he *has* done a bunk.'

'I wouldn't know.'

Picton was peering at him uncertainly. 'Don't be so bloody close, Landon. I'm only repeating what I hear. The story is that She-Who-Must-Be-Obeyed has blown some sort of whistle on our colleague Kirkby and he's shot off into the sunset to avoid being clobbered by the coppers. And a little bird tells me it's tied in with the topping of this Crickley character. Is that true?'

Arnold leaned back in his chair and stared coldly at Picton. 'I get the feeling it's not so much what you *hear* in the department, Picton, as what you *say*.'

'You suggesting I'm spreading rumours?'

'Malicious rumours,' Arnold corrected him. 'But for the sake of the record, I've no idea what's happened to Kirkby. Beyond that, I've nothing to say.'

Picton shrugged, grinned unpleasantly, and removed his haunch from the table. He sauntered to the door. 'Well, I suppose you'll know if anyone does, Landon. Keep me posted, anyway. I like to know what's going on.'

* * *

The man seated in the chief constable's room was small, dark-suited and neat in his striped shirt, sharply creased trousers and highly polished shoes. He had a thin, closed face and heavily lidded eyes that made Culpeper think of a snake. He was a man who would be used to knowing secrets and keeping them. He was called Cunliffe.

The chief constable waved Culpeper to a chair. 'Mr Cunliffe is from the Home Office,' he announced.

Culpeper waited. There was a short silence and then the chief constable cleared his throat. 'We have a problem, Culpeper. Mr Cunliffe will explain it.'

Cunliffe pursed his thin lips. 'The matter I wish to discuss is a delicate one. It has caused us certain . . . problems in the past, and we had hoped that the matter had been settled. But a few days ago we received a rather disturbing phone call. And now . . .' He hesitated, glancing at the chief constable. 'I imagine you will have heard of Dr Steven O'Connor?'

The chief constable grunted. Culpeper nodded. 'He was a pathologist based in the Midlands. He was . . . removed from his job.'

Cunliffe's nostrils were pinched with distaste. 'O'Connor was a wild card. It's clear that he was suffering some form of dementia. He later claimed to have been hearing voices. The long and short of it is that he caused us severe embarrassment.'

'He manufactured evidence,' Culpeper said.

'With some collusion from the local police,' Cunliffe replied frostily. 'They were happy to accept conclusions from O'Connor which were not based on evidence supplied. O'Connor himself believed he had a mission — and that the people he helped put away deserved their fate. The whole thing came to light after pressure was brought by the late James Thornton.'

Culpeper glanced at the chief constable. His face was impassive, but Culpeper guessed the chief constable was not pleased by Cunliffe's visit.

'Thornton's investigations brought a great deal of embarrassment to the Home Office; there is no disputing that.'

Cunliffe continued. 'There were several appeals from people who had been convicted on O'Connor's perjured evidence. In three cases arrangements had to be made. Convictions having been quashed, as unsafe, the individuals were released and compensation awarded. Ex gratia.'

The mandarins in Whitehall wouldn't have wanted to admit their mistakes, Culpeper thought sourly.

'It was also put to the Home Office,' Cunliffe went on, 'that financial compensation alone would not be enough. The publicity of the original trial, the noise generated by O'Connor's disgrace and the overturning of the convictions, would mean that the individuals would continue to be affected — unless they could fade away, and obtain complete privacy. So . . . in a couple of cases it was agreed that we would furnish them with a new identity. And in one case, we also agreed to help him get a job.'

He was silent for a moment, inspecting his sharp striped cuffs with care. 'In such a situation, of course, it is absolutely necessary that as few people as possible know what has been done. Even the local police force are not informed. It could lead to leaks.'

Culpeper saw the chief constable move in his chair, a reflex movement, indicative of his annoyance. Cunliffe appeared not to notice it, or, if he did, he decided to ignore it.

'You will no doubt recall that one of the cases in which O'Connor was involved related to a man called Simon Ford. It caused a certain sensation at the time because the man was a teacher who had been accused of the rape and murder of one of his own pupils. A girl called Annette Wentbridge. When the case came to trial Dr O'Connor stated categorically in his forensic evidence that there were several quite clear links that could be established between the girl and Ford. In particular, he cited pubic hair specimens, blood and semen samples, fibres . . . it was quite an accumulation.'

He paused and looked up at Culpeper. His eyes were blank and grey, expressing no emotion. 'Unfortunately, when O'Connor fell from grace, the conviction against Ford was deemed unsafe. He was released. He was paid compensation. He took, I believe, a long holiday, to the Far East. He was also assisted in other ways.'

He flicked a non-existent speck from his sleeve with a disdainful finger. 'It was not possible, of course, to return Ford to a teaching situation. That would have been . . . unwise. So the Home Office made arrangements to place him in a field similar to his previous employment. Negotiations took place between the Home Office and the chief executive of a local authority, all in the strictest confidence. The man was found a job, in an Education Department. All seemed to be well.' His eyes flickered to the chief constable. 'Then we received a phone call from this man. He was complaining that his . . . ah . . . cover was about to be blown, as he put it.'

There was a short silence. The chief constable turned to Culpeper. 'It would seem from what Mr Cunliffe's already told me,' he said heavily, 'that Simon Ford has been working in Morpeth. He's been using the name of Kirkby.'

Culpeper felt cold. His mouth was dry. He said nothing for a little while. Then he asked quietly, 'I think it was a mistake not to have information here about this man.'

'I disagree,' Cunliffe replied distantly. 'Security was essential. The outcry . . .'

The chief constable was watching Culpeper suspiciously. 'Did you know anything about this?'

'About Ford being up here? No, sir,' Culpeper said hastily. 'But—' he turned to Cunliffe — 'you said this man complains his cover's been blown. How did he think that happened?'

Cunliffe pinched his nostrils between finger and thumb, reflectively. 'From what we gather, Ford — or Kirkby as he now calls himself — met a journalist who recognized him. It's doubtful that they ever met previously, but the journalist must have recognized him from some publicity in the past, done some checking, and reached the correct conclusion. He went back to Kirkby and questioned him. Kirkby realized the man knew who he was. There was some veiled threat to expose the story. That was when Kirkby phoned us.'

'For what purpose?'

'He was angry. He felt we were in some way to blame goodness knows why. Anyway, he wanted us to provide him with another identity — get him away from Northumberland. And then . . .'

'You heard the name of the journalist in question again,' Culpeper growled. 'You heard he'd been murdered.'

'Precisely.'

The silence grew heavy in the room. A fly began to buzz noisily against the windowpane. Culpeper sighed heavily.

'In the course of our investigations into the death of Alan Crickley we took a statement from a man called Fred Brierley. He's been researching a book on the late James Thornton. That meant, naturally, he would have been looking closely at Thornton's crusade against the convictions of people like Ford. He met Crickley — who happens to be the adopted son of Thornton — and my guess now is that Brierley showed Crickley a photograph of Ford. That's how the connection was probably made in Crickley's mind. Moreover . . . '

'Yes?' the chief constable growled.

'We've had a suggestion that maybe Kirkby — or Ford, or whatever he's called — could have murdered Crickley.'

'You haven't told me about this,' the chief constable complained.

'We didn't really take the claim very seriously,' Culpeper protested. 'You'll recall, sir, we decided in this office that a clear line to follow on the Crickley killing would be to check closely on the movements of Peter Gaul. When Karen Stannard contacted us—'

'Who is she?' Cunliffe interrupted sharply.

'She works at County Hall — deputy director of the Museums and Antiquities Department. Kirkby had been transferred there from Education.' He glanced at the chief constable. 'She told us Crickley had been asking her about this man Kirkby. Implied he had something on him — a story he was going to write. So, when Crickley was killed, Stannard put two and two together, and contacted us.'

The chief constable frowned. 'You didn't follow it up?'

Culpeper shrugged uneasily. 'It seemed a bit thin. And Kirkby wasn't available.'

'What's that supposed to mean?' the chief constable snapped.

Reddening, Culpeper replied, 'He wasn't in the office — or his flat. But we had no reason to put out a call. Stannard's story was a bit vague. And we had other leads to follow. I thought Miss Stannard was overreacting. She doesn't like Kirkby, finds something creepy about him . . .'

His voice died away.

'Quite,' Cunliffe said.

'It looks as though what Mr Cunliffe tells us is some kind of confirmation of the suspicions Miss Stannard has.' the chief constable suggested menacingly, glaring at Culpeper.

'If only we had known earlier, sir—'

Cunliffe raised a delicate hand. 'I've explained the reasons. We shouldn't dwell on the past. The thing is, now, while Kirkby has contacted us and said he wants help, there has been only the one communication. It was prior to Crickley's death. Since then, silence. So, it seems to us that there is nothing more we can do at present. Except warn you — which is what I'm doing — of the facts. Crickley was clearly putting pressure on Kirkby. And now Crickley's dead and Kirkby is . . . out of touch.'

Culpeper grimaced, catching the chief constable's scowl. 'I'll get on to it immediately, sir.'

'There's just one other thing,' Cunliffe said, staying him. 'You'll be aware, of course, that this has been a source of considerable awkwardness to the Home Office. O'Connor's breakdown, the trials, the adjudication of the convictions as unsafe — and now there is the possibility of further embarrassment. If at all possible, it is to be avoided, gentlemen.'

'What's that supposed to mean?' the chief constable asked, displeased.

Cunliffe shrugged. 'While you conduct your search for Mr Kirkby, I think it would be to the advantage of all concerned if his true identity were not revealed. We should keep a veil over the past. The search should be for Kirkby — not Simon Ford.'

'I think you can trust us to keep our mouths shut.' the chief constable rasped unpleasantly.

'Yes. I'm quite confident of that,' Cunliffe replied with a thoughtful smile. 'But if I may make one further point.' He hesitated, inspected his cuffs again before he spoke. 'We all know about Dr O'Connor's . . . mistakes. There is no doubt he was unbalanced, and was instrumental in sending innocent men to prison. It was embarrassing that his . . . unwise actions caused suffering, and absolutely right, of course, that the innocent people involved were later released through the persistence and doggedness of James Thornton.' He permitted himself a wintry smile. 'James Thornton was not, of course, terribly popular with us in the Home Office. However, the convictions were overturned, the men compensated. But . . .'

There was a short silence, as Cunliffe chose his words carefully.

'There is a considered view in the Home Office that in at least one case, justice perhaps was not done, by the prisoner being released. One prisoner was given his liberty and compensated when, in all probability, he really *was* guilty.'

There was no need for him to pronounce the name. His eyes glittered as he looked at Culpeper and the chief constable.

'And one is left with the thought, I suppose, that if a man kills once, he may well be prepared to kill again.'

* * *

Arnold was surprised to see Detective Chief Inspector John Culpeper again at the office. When the policeman tapped on his door and entered the room Arnold rose awkwardly. 'Are you wanting to see Miss Stannard? I gather she's out this afternoon, and—'

'No, no,' Culpeper said, shaking his head. 'It's you I wanted a word with.'

Arnold was not sure he liked the sound of that. His palms were damp, and he felt nervous. 'What's it about?'

Culpeper walked across to the window and stared out across the car park. 'Just a follow-up, really, from my visit the other day.'

'How can I help you?'

Culpeper continued to stare out of the window. 'Miss Stannard pointed a finger at this man Kirkby. She thinks he's involved in the death of Alan Crickley.'

Arnold was silent. After a moment, Culpeper turned and looked at him. 'Kirkby's not turned up for work.'

'It appears not.'

'We checked his flat: there's no sign of him.'

Arnold shrugged, conscious of a dampness around his shirt collar.

'You've no idea where he might be?'

Arnold frowned. 'Why do you think I'd know?'

'He had no friends in the department; it seems he made none during his time in Education. But Miss Stannard assigned him to work with you . . . and I've had hints that if he saw anyone as a friend in this department it was probably you.'

'I told you. We're colleagues — and he kept himself pretty much to himself.'

'So you don't know where he is,' Culpeper repeated deliberately.

Arnold looked up and held his glance. 'I've no idea where he might be.'

Culpeper sighed. 'It's quite important that we get to see him, and talk to him soon. I think I can rely upon you, Landon — if he does get in touch with you over the next few days, let me know immediately. Will you do that?'

Arnold nodded dumbly.

After Culpeper had left, Arnold stared at the phone, miserably. He wished that Syl Kirkby had not phoned him, just twenty minutes before the policeman had entered the room.

CHAPTER FIVE

1

It was a relief to have dinner with Jane Wilson.

She had recently finished her latest historical novel and was inclined to relax; also, they had not met for several weeks so it was an opportunity to catch up with news of each other's activities. They met in Durham and ate at the County Hall Hotel — Jane was paying, by way of celebration.

But although it was a relief for Arnold, some of his anxiety must have shown through because Jane finally asked him, shrewdly, what was bothering him.

Arnold sighed. 'It's a bit complicated. A colleague of mine at the office has . . . sort of gone missing. The police want to interview him.'

'About what?'

'The death of Alan Crickley.'

Jane looked serious. 'They've been to see you at the office?'

'A couple of times. Our old friend Culpeper.' Arnold grimaced. 'The colleague — he's called Kirkby — is a bit of an oddball. Very reserved, keeps himself to himself, but it was Karen Stannard — you know, our new deputy director who started this hare running. She seems to think Kirkby's involved with Crickley, she called in the police . . . and now Culpeper wants to know if I know where Kirkby is.'

'Why you?'

Arnold shrugged. 'Kirkby has no friends in the department, but we've spent time together. On projects assigned by Miss Stannard.'

'But if you can't help the police, you can't help.'

'Ah, well, there's the problem.'

Jane watched him carefully for several seconds, and sipped her wine. 'You know more than you've told the police.'

'Sort of,' Arnold replied miserably. 'I don't know where Kirkby is, so when Culpeper asked me directly I wasn't lying when I told him I didn't know. But, shortly before Culpeper came to me, I had a phone call from Kirkby. He wants to see me. So, though I don't know where he *is,* I do actually know where he's *going* to be.'

Jane sniffed. 'I think you're splitting hairs, Arnold.'

He sighed. 'I guess so. But Kirkby . . . he made me promise not to tell anyone. He wants to meet me, talk to me, but just me.'

'I don't understand.'

'Neither do I, exactly. But I think he feels . . . beleaguered. The police want to talk to him, and he must have shot off like a startled rabbit. He's turning to me . . . I guess, because I'm the only person he feels safe with.'

Jane smiled. 'I can understand that.' The smile faded and she frowned. 'But what if he is mixed up in the killing of Crickley? You've agreed to meet him?'

'I couldn't really do otherwise. He sounded depressed . . . distraught. I did try to tell him he'd be best advised to go to the police, but he wouldn't hear of it. So . . . I arranged to meet him.'

'Where?'

Arnold grimaced. 'It's a bit out of the way. But that's the way he wanted it. There's a ruined, half-built folly on the hill on the Ridgeway estate. He wants to see me there.'

'Why there?'

Arnold toyed with his wine glass, frowning. 'I don't know really. But when I showed him the place in the first instance he was sort of taken with it. He became dreamy . . . introverted, and yet he began to talk. About himself, I mean. Not a lot, but there were hints of an unhappy background. I think he has some kind of affinity with the place.'

'So, are you going?'

Arnold nodded. 'I promised. I have my first meeting as chairman of the Viking Research Trust at Ridgeway Manor — I've promised to go up to the folly afterwards.'

'And alone? Is that wise? Meeting someone who might be involved in a killing, in a lonely place . . . Are you sure you should go?'

Arnold shrugged. 'Somehow, I don't see him as a killer.' Jane was silent for a little while. Arnold topped up her glass with Cabernet Sauvignon. At last, she said, 'Arnold, I think you're making a mistake. This is too much of a chance. And by withholding information from the police, there could be trouble. Particularly if there's some foundation to the suggestion Kirkby was involved in Crickley's death.'

'I see that . . . but I promised.'

'You know Culpeper. You can trust him.'

'I don't know. Kirkby sounded distraught, at the end of his tether. He might do something stupid . . . I think I need to go to see him.'

'Then take Culpeper.'

'I'm not so sure about that.'

She shrugged. 'That's my advice. If you're too stubborn to take it, that's up to you.' She glanced covertly at him. 'Anyway, enough of that. Let's not have the evening spoiled. There's gossip to catch up with. You first. So . . . tell me all about this Miss Karen Stannard.'

* * *

The following morning Arnold parked his car behind County Hall and collected a number of files from the boot. He had taken them home earlier to catch up with some work. As he was lifting them from the boot he heard his name called.

Charlie Graves was a short, tubby man about sixty years of age. He had worked at County Hall all his life, and for the last thirty years he had been based in the Planning Department, which Arnold had recently left. Oddly enough, though they still worked in the same building, they rarely saw each other.

'So how are things going, Arnold? Enjoying life more in the DMA?'

Arnold smiled. 'It's different, anyway.'

'I hear you've already crossed the new deputy director.' Charlie Graves grinned. 'Still, you were always crossing people in Planning, too, bonnie lad.'

'Not deliberately, believe me.'

Graves fell into step beside Arnold as they made their way towards the doors. 'I hear one of the things Miss Stannard is upset about is this job you've taken on outside hours. This trustee thing.'

'It's hardly a job,' Arnold protested. 'It's unpaid, it's only a few meetings a year . . . and it's none of her business, really.'

'It's the Viking Research Trust, isn't it?'

'That's right.'

'It was set up by Miss Ridge.' Graves said, musing, as he opened the doors to allow Arnold to slide in with the files. 'She lived up at Ridgeway Manor, didn't she? Now, there was something on my desk . . . I was looking at it the other day . . . Yeah, I remember now. There was some sort of application came in relating to the Ridgeway estate. I turned it up, because it's been around for three years or more. Out of time. Never proceeded with. I was moving the dust around, you know, throwing out old stuff. Didn't really know what to do with this. Maybe, since you're on the Trust now, you ought to be able to tell me whether we keep it, dump it, action it, or what.'

Arnold looked at him, puzzled. 'You mean the application hasn't been actioned?'

'No . . . Came in. Put on hold at the request of the applicants. Then, I guess, forgotten. And as I recall it was tied in with some kind of old survey. But to be honest, I can't remember too much about it. I didn't do anything with it, didn't pay much attention, in fact. But — you want to see it?'

Arnold shrugged. 'I suppose so, if it's likely to be reactivated at some time. Though I can't imagine why . . . Anyway, shove it down to me sometime and I'll have a look at it. Now, I've got to move, Charlie. I have an appointment with the solicitor to the Trust this afternoon and I've got a pile of stuff to get through first. Good to see you, Charlie. We ought to have a drink some time.'

'If it's on you, bonnie lad, I'll be there.'

* * *

Arnold was busy with the files all day and he had still not completed his work at five thirty. Normally he would simply have stayed on to complete the details but his appointment with the solicitor Enwright was at six so he was pushed for time. He locked up his office, spoke to some of the cleaning ladies who were coming on duty and made his way out to the town.

Enwright's office was tucked away down a narrow side alley behind the main street. The entrance was unimposing and the stairs somewhat rickety, but the receptionist was a pleasant, middle-aged woman who smiled readily, and talked to him, while Enwright kept him waiting the statutory five minutes, even though she was ready to leave for the day. She had her coat on and was leaving when Enwright finally called him into the narrow office with its old-fashioned furniture and dark mahogany table.

Enwright waved Arnold to a seat. 'I'm glad you've been able to come in so promptly, Mr Landon. You have a meeting of the trustees to attend soon, I believe?'

Arnold nodded. 'My first meeting.'

'And I understand that it is at that meeting that Mr Hall and Mr Norman will tender their resignations. Does that mean you will be taking over the chair?'

'That is the intention, I understand.'

Enwright nodded sombrely and opened his desk drawer. He was not much given to small talk. He took out several sheets of paper and placed them in front of Arnold. 'Mr Hall asked me to undertake the necessary formalities relating to your appointment to the Viking Research Trust and he has already been in a couple of days ago to complete from his side. I will just need your signature here . . . and here, and then we can get the papers off to the Charity Commissioners. You may read them first, of course — so you make sure you're not signing your life away.'

Arnold guessed it was the nearest Enwright would ever come to making a joke. He read the documents quickly. They related to his appointment to the Trust, and the resignation of David Hall and Bill Norman. They were to be placed before the next meeting of trustees. Arnold signed them and handed them back to the solicitor.

Enwright solemnly locked them away in his desk. He looked up at Arnold. 'Good. Now, it may be that this would be a convenient time for me to let you have any information you require regarding the Trust.'

Arnold shrugged. 'I don't really know that I have any particular questions. I've been aware of the work of the Trust, and I know the site fairly well where most of the work is being done.'

Enwright hesitated. 'I was referring not so much to the archaeological activity as . . . the Trust itself.'

'Is there anything I need to ask about?'

Enwright looked grave. He placed lean, bony fingertips together and inspected Arnold. 'That is not really for me to say, Mr Landon. However, may I say that I approve of your appointment? It is entirely appropriate that Mr Hall should . . . leave the Trust at this time, in my view.'

'I don't understand.'

'You are not, of course, familiar with the bequests made under the will of Miss Amelia Ridge.'

'That's right, I'm not.'

Enwright nodded. 'You will no doubt have heard that we were called in relatively late in Miss Ridge's life to act as her advisers. Formerly, she was represented by Mr Harcourt-Fanshaw. We became involved, really, through the good offices of Mr Hall — we've acted for him on several other matters. He recommended us to Miss Ridge in the absence, overseas, of Harcourt-Fanshaw. It was all . . . quite legitimate, in spite of what Harcourt-Fanshaw might imply.'

He sniffed, deprecatingly. 'So, we gave Miss Ridge advice on the drawing up of her will. Unfortunately, she later changed her mind — and some of the bequests — by way of a codicil. It wasn't very . . . neat. And in my view it raised certain ethical issues.' He hesitated, peering at Arnold. 'I say this to you in confidence, of course, and because I think that as a new trustee you should be aware of the position.'

'I understand,' Arnold replied, not understanding at all.

Enwright leaned forward, lowering his voice as though fearful of being overheard by eavesdroppers. 'Do you understand the concept of the secret trust?' he asked.

Arnold shook his head. 'Not really.'

'Hmmm. Well, in its origin it was based upon the attitude of the courts of equity — where the idea of the trust originated. The courts of equity would not allow statutory provisions to be used as an engine of fraud. In many cases, however, the concept related to cases where no fraud existed . . . and so in modern law it is generally the case that the secret trust operates outside a will, not being testamentary in nature.' He paused, watching Arnold closely as if to make sure he was following. 'Secret trusts do arise, however, out of testamentary dispositions in most cases.'

Arnold frowned. 'I don't understand.'

'It's quite simple, really. What happens is that the testator or testatrix — makes a will, but wishes to provide for someone without the world knowing about it. In other words, he or she makes a bequest to one person, Mr A, but secretly informs another, Mr B, that the property is really to be held for the benefit of someone else, Mr C. That is known as a fully secret trust. There is also the half-secret trust.'

Slightly dazed, Arnold nodded. 'So how does that work?'

'A half-secret trust arises where the will expressly states that the gift is made on trust — but does not state the details of the trust. In other words, the outside world will know a trust exists, but is not aware of its details, objectives, etc.'

Arnold was silent for a little while. He stared at the careful closed face of the solicitor. Finally, he asked, 'What does this have to do with the Viking Research Trust? The objectives there are clear cut.'

Enwright held up a finger. 'Please, I made no reference to the Viking Research Trust. But, in a way, it is affected, which is why I'm mentioning this business to you, You see. I've been slightly worried for some time. I don't believe there is anything wrong, legally, but . . . I am worried about the position of . . . certain people. And it is as well if you were to be aware of this before you take up your chairmanship of the Viking Research Trust.'

'So what's the problem?' Arnold asked.

'I need to go back to the death of Miss Ridge. She left a will, amended by codicil without benefit of our advice. She set up the Viking Research Trust in the will and made quite significant bequests in support of it.'

Arnold frowned. 'That's not the way it ended up.'

'Because the codicil changed it. It's been one of my worries.' Enwright explained. 'When I heard that the Viking Research Trust is not really a viable financial proposition, I remembered thinking what a pity it was that the original bequests had not been maintained. You see, they were changed by the codicil — in which we had no hand.'

'She had no legal advice?'

Enwright spread his hands in doubt. 'She was given *financial* advice.'

'Which led her to do what?'

'Effectively, to split the estate. She left Ridgeway Manor and the surrounding lands, to the Trust. But the major part of her holdings — and she was a fairly wealthy woman — she willed to a property company, established in Jersey. It is that property company which holds the major part of Miss Ridge's estate — Ridgeway Home Farm and the lands to the north of the valley. She took the step on financial advice, it seems.'

'And it's legal?'

'Quite. The idea may or may not be a good one. It was a tax avoidance device, I'm told.'

'So where does the secret trust come in?'

Enwright hesitated. 'Well, let me explain that the codicil does appear to state that the property is to be held for the benefit of the Jersey company. On the other hand there is a phrase in the codicil which suggests that the gift is on trust — but nowhere in the codicil are the objectives of the Trust explained. In other words, it would seem a half-secret trust has been established, and that the Jersey company holds the property for the benefit finally of someone else.'

Arnold was silent for a little while. 'I presume there were witnesses to the codicil?'

Enwright licked his lips, and nodded slowly. 'There were two witnesses. One was Sir Jock Hertford. The other was David Hall.'

'I see.' Arnold frowned. 'You were not given any details of the half-secret trust?'

'No. But if it does truly exist, one imagines the witnesses to the codicil would have received some communication from Miss Ridge before she died.'

'Have you asked them?'

'It is not my place to do so.'

Arnold shook his head. 'I'm afraid you're getting me into a bit of a legal tangle. I still don't see why you feel it necessary to confide in me, just because I'm to be a trustee of the Viking Research Trust.'

Enwright began to drum his fingers nervously on the table in front of him. He was clearly on edge, not knowing how far he could legitimately and ethically go. 'I . . . I merely think it would be better that you know these things, so that you are as fully informed as other trustees before you go to your first meeting. As I understand it, a document will be tabled at that meeting, requiring your signature.'

'What document?'

'The conveyance of Ridgeway Manor. David Hall has been to see me and all details are completed — a very generous price, in fact, it seems to me. But he has suggested to me it might be better were you to sign as chairman, rather than he.'

'Why?'

Enwright hesitated. 'The purchaser is the Islands and Mainland Property Company Ltd.'

Arnold frowned grimly. 'That name rings a bell.'

'It should, Mr Landon. It was mentioned at the meeting you chaired the other day — the working group I attended. The Islands and Mainland Property Company was the main beneficiary under the will of Amelia Ridge.'

Arnold stared at him, puzzled. 'And now the company wants to buy Ridgeway Manor?'

Enwright inclined his head. 'And is paying a handsome price for it. Moreover, it is the same company, of course, that is making a large donation to the Viking Research Trust.'

Arnold leaned back in his chair, slightly puzzled. 'Well, I suppose, in a sense, it's rather as if the original wishes of Miss Ridge were coming true. Her heart was in the Viking Research Trust, I am told, so perhaps it's only right that her money and the gift should come back to the Trust.'

'It's one way of looking at it.' Enwright agreed drily.

'But why didn't David Hall deal with this himself? Why does he suggest I should sign the deed of conveyance? He could do it equally well.'

'Perhaps because Mr Hall feels he must be scrupulous in his business dealings.'

'How do you mean?'

'It would not do for Mr Hall to sign in two places.'

'I don't understand.'

'Mr Hall is also a director of Islands and Mainland Property Company Ltd.'

There was a long silence between the two men. Arnold stared at the table, trying to fix in his own mind a sequence of events that would have led them to this present position.

At last, he looked up at the solicitor. 'I'm grateful for this information. Tell me — is there any reason you can think of why I should not sign the deed of conveyance, in my capacity as chairman of the Viking Research Trust?'

Enwright considered his fingertips and slowly shook his head. 'Mr Hall has neatly removed himself from any suggestion of conflict of interest by resigning from the Trust. Moreover, the price payable by the Jersey company is more than generous. It is also backed by a further significant amount by way of gift to the Trust from the company. In these circumstances.' Enwright intoned, 'I can see no logical reason why you should not with confidence sign the deed of conveyance.'

'But you thought I ought to be fully informed of the background to the sale and purchase.'

'That is it exactly, Mr Landon.'

* * *

But it wasn't the situation exactly, Arnold thought as he made his way back to his car outside County Hall. He remembered his conversations with Harcourt-Fanshaw, and the claim of undue influence he suggested had been used by Sir Jock Hertford over the ailing Miss Ridge. Perhaps to some extent, Harcourt-Fanshaw was now proved right. It was quite likely that Miss Ridge had been advised by Hertford when the codicil was drawn up; and maybe the financial advice had come from David Hall. They had witnessed the codicil, which had overturned certain provisions in the will in favour of the Jersey-based company.

But did it really matter in the end?

She had left the bulk of her estate to the Jersey company, and left the Viking Research Trust financially inviable. But now it was all coming right again. David Hall had persuaded the company to pump a great deal of money back into the Research Trust — money that had originally been Miss Amelia Ridge's.

And yet . . . there was something niggling at the back of Arnold's mind. Somehow, somewhere, he felt there was a link missing. The situation seemed . . . odd. And Enwright's talk of a half-secret trust,' he had left the thing in the air, really.

Something moved again in the back of Arnold's mind.

What was it Charlie Graves had said? It had been something to do with Ridgeway Manor. As he got in his car, Arnold decided he'd better go see Charlie Graves, first thing in the morning.

2

The trustees were already gathered when Arnold arrived.

David Hall greeted him with a warm smile as he entered the room and shook hands with him effusively. The others were already drinking coffee or tea: Arnold was offered either but refused. There was a general air of pleased excitement in the room, as though they had gathered to celebrate the completion of a desired task, but Arnold was somewhat subdued. They seemed to notice nothing untoward, however, and chatted away. Sir Jock Hertford beaming, Bill Norman telling old rugby jokes, and David Hall presiding with charm. Sam Frimley seemed somewhat bemused by the occasion, as though he was not quite clear what all the goodwill was about.

David Hall took the chair at the end of the gleaming table. 'You'll all be aware that this is to be a brief chairmanship on my part this evening. Indeed, all I want to do is fulfil two tasks. The first is to thank each of you for the support you've given me as your chairman over these last three years; second, to welcome Mr Landon to the board of trustees, and indeed, to the chairmanship of the Trust itself. I'm sure that for me it's the right time to stand down. A new hand is needed at the helm. I perhaps flatter myself when I say I've played my part in putting the Trust on an even keel, but what is now required is a man who has a deep knowledge of the kind of work the Trust should be undertaking — and I believe the Trust has that man in Arnold Landon.'

He smiled at Arnold. 'So, with those few words, perhaps I may now formally resign from the chair, declare that this will be my last meeting of trustees, and hand over to you.'

There was a brief flutter of applause. Ceremoniously, David Hall rose, vacated the chair he held and invited Arnold to change places with him. As he did so, Hall said, 'Since I have now formally resigned, I have no further right to remain in the meeting, Chairman, but—'

'I think, Mr Hall' Arnold interrupted him, 'it might be useful if you were to stay, in view of what is on the agenda.'

Hall beamed. 'You mean the sale of Ridgeway Manor. Of course, I appreciate that you might wish me to speak to the matter. And since Bill Norman was involved in the negotiations, it might be sensible if he also were to stay.'

'Mr Norman hasn't yet formally resigned,' Arnold said. Bill Norman hunched his powerful shoulders and leaned forward. 'I would like to do that now, Chairman, and formally tender my resignation.'

Arnold nodded coolly. 'And I'm sure the trustees would wish you well for the future, and your new job with Mr Hall's company, Wheeler Holdings.' He glanced around the table. 'That now clears the matter up, I believe. As a matter of form, now neither Mr Hall nor Mr Norman are trustees of the Viking Research Trust, I have taken over as chairman, and the number of trustees are now three — Sir Jock Hertford, Mr Sam Frimley and myself.'

'Rather formally, but quite accurately put.' David Hall replied, laughing.

'Now that we are all clear on that,' Arnold announced, 'and aware that Mr Hall and Mr Norman have no standing in this meeting other than that accorded them by the chairman, I suggest we can proceed to business. Mr Hall, I imagine you have a statement to make?'

Slightly puzzled, Hall nodded, and glanced at Bill Norman. 'Only very briefly, Chairman. I understand you've already been to see Mr Enwright. I had suggested he might wish to attend this evening, but he was unable to do so, and in any case assured me that the necessary formalities are simple enough and do not require his presence. The deed of appointment of yourself, and the resignations of Mr Norman and myself have been duly signed and registered with the Charities Commission. In the folder before you I have supplied the deed of conveyance of Ridgeway Manor to the purchasers: it merely requires your signature as chairman of the Trust. I'm not sure if you want me, for the sake of the record, to make a statement regarding the sale, Chairman?'

'I think that would be advisable,' Arnold replied, making a brief note, while Frimley scribbled at more length in his normal role as minute-taker.

David Hall nodded, and paused thoughtfully. 'As I announced at the recent meeting of the Friends of the Viking Research Trust, I and Bill Norman have been involved in lengthy negotiations with a purchaser who wishes to acquire Ridgeway Manor. Those negotiations have been successfully completed only a short time ago and, if I may say so, the result exceeded our expectations.'

He glanced around the table and smiled. 'As you are all aware, the Trust itself is in financial difficulties and cannot afford to service its debt and carry out the work needed at the grave site. In the event, we managed to persuade the purchasers not only to agree a very good price for the manor, indeed, one significantly higher than the market price, but also to make a considerable donation by way of a charitable gift to the Trust itself.'

'And a damn fine job, too.' Hertford interrupted.

'The donation is, as you might expect, contingent upon the sale going through.' Hall added, smiling at Hertford. 'Once the deed is signed, the donation will follow.'

'Do we have any assurances regarding that?' Arnold asked.

'In the file, along with the conveyance, you will find a bank draft for the sum involved.' Hall replied. 'All that is required, Chairman, is that you now sign the deed.'

Arnold opened the file and looked at the conveyance. On top of it was a small envelope; he opened it and saw the bank draft. He nodded. 'It seems to be in order.' He glanced around at the expectant trustees. 'I have taken legal advice from Mr Enwright and he's advised me there's no good reason why I should refuse to sign this document. Before I do so, is there anything any of the current trustees would want to say?'

There was silence, and a general shaking of heads. Arnold waited for a few seconds, and then glanced at David Hall. 'I wonder, nevertheless, since I'm a new trustee and don't know the background to the sale, whether you'd mind explaining, Mr Hall, why you found it necessary to resign from the Trust, and bring me in as chairman.'

Hall shrugged. 'As I explained to you, Mr Landon — my business interests, the need for new blood—'

'But it was your business interests that amounted to the paramount reason,' Arnold interrupted.

'If you wish to say so, I suppose that's right. Wheeler Holdings—'

'I wasn't referring to Wheeler Holdings, Mr Hall.'

There was a short silence. Hall's body was very still, his hands flat on the table in front of him. He stared at Arnold but his eyes were expressionless. 'I'm not sure what you mean.'

Arnold peered in an exaggerated fashion at the deed of conveyance in front of him. 'The purchasers of Ridgeway Manor are named as Islands and Mainland Property Company Limited. Do you have any comment to make, Mr Hall?'

The silence grew around them, Hertford frowning, Frimley looking puzzled at Arnold's tone.

Hall stared at Arnold contemplatively. 'I'm not sure what comment you desire to be made, Chairman.'

Arnold shrugged. 'That's for you to decide. But, for the sake of the record, you might wish to state whether you have any interest to declare.'

A thin smile touched Hall's lips. 'I'm no longer a trustee of this Trust so declarations of interest are not relevant.'

'That's true,' Arnold said blandly. 'But even so, for the sake of the record, is there anything you want to say?'

Hall hesitated, weighing up Arnold's question. Then he shrugged. 'I see no reason why it should not be said. As I imagine you know, from the thrust of your query, I am a director of the company named as purchasers. But there is no conflict of interest, since I have resigned.'

'Quite so,' Arnold replied coolly. 'And once I sign the deed, there'll be no problem, since none of the other trustees present have an interest to declare. I presume that is the case . . .'

There was silence. At last, Bill Norman leaned forward.

His face was dark with displeasure. 'I don't quite know what's going on here,' he said harshly, 'but to keep the books straight I'd better mention that I too am a director of Islands and Mainland Property Company Limited.'

'But you too have resigned,' Arnold replied pleasantly, 'so we're all clear and above board, aren't we?'

Sir Jock Hertford's mouth was ugly. 'Do we have a problem here that I haven't recognized, Chairman? Are you suggesting that the deed of conveyance should not be completed?'

'Not at all,' Arnold replied cheerfully. 'I merely wish to ensure that since this is a meeting of trustees, who have a duty to exercise good faith in their Trust dealings, we have everything out on the table — for the sake of the record. As I explained earlier, Mr Enwright tells me there's no reason why I shouldn't sign.'

Hertford puffed out his cheeks and sighed. 'So what more do you want to know?'

'Whatever any of you might wish to tell me.'

Bill Norman let out an exasperated grunt. 'This is sounding like a game played by the Inland Revenue: they won't tell you what they know — they want you to expose your hand. Just what is it you're after, Landon?'

Arnold leaned back in his chair. 'I'm not sure . . . anything you want to tell me, as I say. But particularly relating to the setting up of the Trust, and the offer of purchase from the Jersey-based company. And, perhaps, what happened in between.'

'I don't understand.' Hertford blustered.

'Perhaps I do.' David Hall said quietly. He was looking carefully at Arnold, as though he felt he had underestimated him. 'I think our chairman is aware that the Jersey company was established by Miss Ridge herself — or at least, at her behest.'

Arnold said nothing but simply stared expressionlessly at the former chairman of the Trust.

'I don't think we should go into—' Hertford began.

David Hall held up a confident hand. 'Please, Jock, I don't think we have anything to hide, or worry about here. There's no reason why we shouldn't satisfy Mr Landon's perhaps natural curiosity . . . and perhaps his desire to be assured that all is above board.' He paused. 'It's all quite simple, Chairman. Miss Ridge received financial advice shortly before she died. She was a wealthy woman, and she had set up the Viking Research Trust but a large part of her estate would have been swallowed up in tax. So, she decided to move part of that estate into a company established off-shore. There were certain tax advantages in doing that.'

'Unfortunately, that left the Viking Research Trust rather short of money,' Arnold suggested. 'Miss Ridge made a miscalculation.'

'In spite of advice.'

'The codicil was in her own hand.'

'Witnessed by you and Sir Jock Hertford.'

'We were witnesses only to her signature.' Hertford expostulated. 'We weren't consulted on the detail of the codicil. Indeed, I wouldn't have understood the bloody thing!'

'As Sir Jock says.' Hall added blandly. 'But once the decision was made, Miss Ridge asked me to set up the company in Jersey. She also asked me to act as a director of the company. Later, I asked Bill Norman if he would join me on the board. That way, there were two trustees of the Viking Research Trust acting — it was a way of keeping an eye on things. It meant the trustees had eyes and ears on the Jersey board.'

'Sounds a good idea,' Arnold murmured.

'I'm pleased you think so.' Hall said ironically.

'So what happened then?' Arnold asked.

Hall shrugged. 'It wasn't long before we realized that the Trust was financially inviable. There was plenty of money in the Jersey company, and we all knew that Miss Ridge had dearly wanted to see the research work go on successfully. We had her memorandum of objectives to evidence that. So Bill and I, we started to put pressure on the Jersey company. And in the end we persuaded them that it would be a good idea to buy Ridgeway Manor, pump some much needed finance into the Trust, and also top that up with a charitable donation. Once again,' he added drily, 'that would be a tax efficient way to behave.'

'I see. So really,' Arnold said, 'the whole thrust behind this purchase is designed to benefit the Trust?'

'Certainly. And, perhaps in a roundabout way, to give full rein at last to Miss Ridge's wishes. There's a certain . . . closing of the circle, if you like.'

Arnold nodded. 'Indeed. I wonder . . . may I know how many people there are on the board of the Jersey company?'

David Hall blinked. 'Four.'

'Anyone we know — apart from yourself and Mr Norman?'

'I would hardly think so. They are Jersey residents.'

'Do they know anything about the Mountjoy Survey?'

No one moved in the silence that followed. Arnold's glance was fixed on David Hall. Not a muscle moved in the man's face and his piercing blue eyes were still. It was as though he had been turned to stone, but Arnold guessed behind the facade his mind would be racing. Arnold flickered a glance in Bill Norman's direction: the man's face had darkened, storm clouds of anger staining his features.

Sam Frimley looked up from his minute notes. 'Did you say Mountjoy, Chairman?'

'That's right. The Mountjoy Survey,' Arnold repeated calmly. 'If you don't know about it, Mr Frimley, I'd better explain. Some eighty years ago, Sir John Mountjoy was commissioned by William Ridge to undertake a geological survey of the Ridgeway estates. It was probably connected with anxieties over the building of Ridge Hall — the folly on the crag. But it produced some interesting results. In short, the survey demonstrated that part of the Ridgeway holdings held a stratum of rock known as killas — it's metamorphosed sediments really, thermally metamorphosed mudstone and basic volcanics.'

'Can you go a little more slowly, Chairman?' Frimley pleaded, writing furiously.

'The stratum holds several major vein sets — and each of the veins carry wolframite. That's as far as the survey went. But,' Arnold added mildly, 'such rock formations mean that it could be quite a profitable venture, mining for tungsten on the site.'

'What site?' snapped Sir Jock Hertford. 'What are you talking about here? Where did you get this information from?'

'I used to work in the Planning Department at County Hall. The existence of this survey was drawn to my attention a few days ago.'

'An eighty-year-old survey?' Hall scoffed.

'It was tied in with a planning application.'

A triumphant gleam came into Hertford's eyes. 'I've been involved with Miss Ridge and her estate for years. Knew her well. She never said anything about mining applications at Ridgeway. She never put one in. And neither did we. There's got to be a mistake.'

'No mistake,' Arnold disagreed. The application came in some time ago — three years ago, it seems. But it was never proceeded with. The main reason was that the applicant had no locus standi.'

'What's that mean?' Hertford rasped.

'He didn't own the land.'

'Who was the applicant?' Hertford asked.

'A Mr St Clair.' Arnold paused and looked at David Hall. 'He wouldn't be one of your Jersey residents, would he, Mr Hall?'

David Hall looked relaxed. Deliberately, he leaned back in his chair, shaking his head. 'I really don't know what you're getting at, Chairman.'

'What I'm getting at is this. The map attached to the survey made by Mountjoy covers an area extending over Ridgeway Home Farm — which is owned by the Islands and Mainland Property Company Limited — and the Ridgeway Manor land, which, of course, is owned by the Viking Research Trust, but which is now the subject of a sale to the Jersey company. On the map, it looks like two blocks: a square block designated by the farm area, and an oblong below designated as the manor. The veins of wolframite bearing rock would seem to extend across the two blocks of land in an irregular fashion.' Arnold paused. 'I suppose, what I'm asking is, did any of the trustees know, first, that the survey existed, and second, that an application had been lodged three years ago?'

There was silence around the table.

'And no one knows,' Arnold added, 'who this Mr St Clair might be?'

Again there was silence.

It was broken by David Hall. 'I'm not sure where this is getting us all, Chairman. I know nothing about this survey, or the application, or just what it means. But let's be clear about the implications. Let's assume this survey you mention is correct. The Viking Research Trust is financially unviable. It will go under without a cash injection. The Jersey company has made a fine offer — supported by a charitable donation — which will save the Trust. Now you say there's the chance there's wolframite under the surface of the manor land and the farm land. Is the Viking Research Trust in a position to take advantage of that?'

'It is not,' Arnold said.

'And is the purchase price offered by the Jersey company a fair one?'

'It is.'

'So where's the problem?' Hall asked, spreading his hands wide.

'I didn't say there *was* a problem,' Arnold replied reasonably. 'I merely asked for information — but in fact I've received very little. I've told you all what the situation is. Now, it only remains for me to sign the deed of conveyance — which would seem to be handing over to the Jersey company a piece of land which, possibly, the company could later attempt to use for mining purposes.'

'We don't know that.' Bill Norman said sharply.

'I said it could p*ossibly* use it for mining.'

'So what do you want now?' Hertford asked, shaking his head.

'I want guidance from the trustees,' Arnold said. 'Should I, in the circumstances, sign the deed of conveyance? Or should we make further inquiries? Should we check on who St Clair is? Should we check on the mining possibilities? Should we seek further offers of purchase? I'd like to hear from you, gentlemen.'

'This is nonsense.' Bill Norman argued angrily. 'David and I have stuck our necks out — struggled with the Jersey people to get the best offer on the table. It far exceeds market price; it's a very generous offer. If this is turned down you'll get nothing to match it. The future of the Viking Research Trust project depends on this. I vote that—'

'You're no longer a trustee, Mr Norman,' Arnold said coldly. 'You get no vote.' He turned to Sir Jock Hertford. 'Do you have anything to say, Sir Jock?'

Hertford's features were suffused with anger. 'This is bloody stupid, Landon. We put you in the chair because we thought after your performance in the working group that you had every sympathy with our aims. This is a fine offer negotiated by Bill and David, and just what the hell you're trying to achieve by throwing in these red herrings, I don't understand. You're the new boy here, but you come in throwing your weight around, asking impossible questions, and making implications which I, personally, resent. I'm absolutely certain what is required here. Your damned signature! I vote you sign. Enwright has cleared it. So you should sign.'

'Mr Frimley?' Arnold asked calmly.

Sam Frimley raised his hawk-like face to look around the table. He seemed irresolute. He shook his head. I'm not sure. I'm afraid . . . I'm a bit lost. If what the chairman says is true, maybe we should be thinking a bit more about this. There could be better ways . . . and the last thing we want at the end is to be accused of any . . . well, ill-advised or hasty judgements. We are trustees, after all—'

'And personally liable for breach of faith,' Arnold added. 'So, gentlemen, it really comes down to me. And my own mind is quite clear. We need to make further inquiries.'

'The Jersey company won't wait for ever for a decision.' Bill Norman rasped harshly.

'I'm sure your negotiating and persuasive skills will save us any problems there, Mr Norman,' Arnold replied coolly. 'The fact is, until further inquiries are made, I'm not prepared to sign this deed.'

'And exactly what inquiries would you wish to be made, Mr Landon?' David Hall asked, almost casually.

They're fairly straightforward,' Arnold replied, meeting his gaze levelly. 'But I'd like them to include also the bequests made by Miss Ridge to the Jersey company.'

'And why would you want to bring that in?' Hertford snapped.

'I understand the bequest was made with a half-secret trust attached. I'd like to know what terms were communicated to the board in Jersey. Are you, for instance, able to tell me what the half-secret trust comprised?'

Hertford almost exploded. 'I don't even know what a bloody half-secret trust is!'

David Hall smiled confidently. 'Perhaps I can explain to Mr Landon's satisfaction. The communication made by Miss Ridge to the board, but not detailed in the bequest itself, was quite simple. Basically, the better support of her favourite charity — the Viking Research Trust. And that is precisely what the Jersey company is doing, by offering to purchase Ridgeway Manor at an inflated price.'

'With what was Miss Ridge's own money,' Arnold said quietly.

David Hall stared at him coolly. 'I think you'll find, Mr Landon, that you're barking up the wrong tree, for a quarry that doesn't exist. This is all quite legal — and in line with the wishes of Miss Ridge, both in her original bequest, and the half-secret trust communicated to the Jersey company.'

'That may well be so, Mr Hall, and I'd like to take your word for it,' Arnold replied. 'But I'm sure you'll forgive me, in the circumstances . . . As chairman of this Trust I feel duty bound to make further inquiries.'

'This isn't necessary, Mr Landon,' David Hall warned.

'I feel that it is,' Arnold said, and rose to his feet. 'And now, I have another appointment. And I'm adjourning this meeting.'

* * *

As he left the manor house he was aware of the turmoil he had left behind him. Voices were raised angrily and as he walked to his car he was aware of someone standing in the doorway, glaring in frustration after him. He reached his car, and unlocked it. As he did so he heard someone moving behind him. Skin prickling at the back of his neck he turned, to see a shadowy figure standing there in the fading light.

'Who's that?'

'It's me. Peter Gaul.'

'What do you want?' Arnold asked.

The man stepped forward urgently. 'I heard there was a meeting of the trustees this evening. I knew you'd be discussing the sale of the manor. I wanted to find out whether it's gone through.'

'It's trustee business,' Arnold snapped. 'I really can't discuss it with you.'

'But it's important! You've never given me a hearing, none of you! You don't need to sell.' He grabbed Arnold by the arm, his fingers digging into the muscle, painfully. 'If I was given the right sort of contract I could turn this place around — I could raise money, financial backing that would mean the Trust would have no problems. Why won't you listen to me, Landon? You're the Trust chairman now. You could decide—'

Arnold pulled his arm away angrily. 'I told you. This is Trust business. I'm simply not prepared to discuss it with you at this stage.'

He got into his car and started the engine.

As he pulled away, and headed up into the valley, he was aware of another vehicle flicking on its headlights in the car park at Ridgeway Manor.

3

The road was narrow where it wound through the valley and the trees on either side were dark and menacing. There was the hint of rain in the air, a fine mist blurring his windscreen and Arnold slowed as he switched on his windscreen wipers. He swung left, finally, past the field centre, which was in darkness, and headed for the foot of the crag on which towered the half-finished folly that was to have been Ridge Hall.

He parked the car under the trees, locked it and looked around. If Syl Kirkby was already up at the folly on the crag, he must have parked his car at the other end of the valley.

The evening was dark and the rain had eased but there was a fine, wet mist among the trees. Arnold began to climb the narrow track: it was difficult to make his way in the darkness and once or twice he strayed from the path. It was as though he was not alone on the hill: occasionally he heard crackling sounds behind and around him, nocturnal animals moving through the undergrowth, disturbed by his presence.

Once he reached the plateau, however, it was not so difficult and though his jacket was damp and he felt uncomfortable, breathing heavily after the steep climb, it was not long before he made out the vague shape of the folly ahead of him, looming blackly in the darkness.

It was necessary to move carefully. The structure that had been erected by William Ridge with his dream of a religious foundation in the valley was perched on the edge of the crag, and although Arnold knew it fairly well he was aware that if he strayed too far to the right he would find himself on the edge of the precipice. He clambered over broken stone along the track until he neared the gaping courtyard of Ridge Hall.

On the phone, Kirkby had suggested they met in the ruins but had not specified where. Arnold paused at the entrance, unsure which way to turn.

'Kirkby?'

His voice echoed and skittered among the dark ruins and there was a heavy rush of wings as a large nocturnal bird took flight. Owls would nest here, Arnold guessed, as well as bats. He stepped forward carefully, making his way across the courtyard and the fine damp mist clung to his hair.

'Kirkby? Are you here?'

He had said he would be waiting. He had spent the days since he had left the office in Scotland walking and thinking — but Arnold was not at all sure what was pressing on the man. All he had said was that he could not face the police, he needed time to think, and to talk.

'Over here.'

The voice seemed reedy, thin and attenuated in the darkness. The echo hung among the half-built towering stone walls, and Arnold moved forward, making his way through the broken doorway at the far end of the courtyard until he found himself in the long room beyond. He stood there for a few moments, trying to make out his bearings in the gloom, and then he saw the vague shadowy figure standing in the embrasure, faintly outlined against the dark sky.

'You came, then.'

'You asked me to — and I promised,' Arnold replied.

'You came alone?'

Arnold hesitated. He remembered Jane's insistence that he should alert Culpeper, now he was beginning to think she had been right. He had resisted it, but now that he found himself here on the crag, with a man who he knew very little about, he began to realize he had been foolish.

'I came alone. As you wanted. But I don't know why it had to be up here — and in the darkness.'

'I feel safe here. Isolation . . . They want to talk to me . . . that's what they say, talk. I've had enough talking with them to last a lifetime.'

'I don't understand.'

There was a short silence. The man in the embrasure shifted uneasily. 'What's being said down there about me?' Arnold shook his head. 'I don't know. The police have been to see me, but they've told me very little. Merely that they want to talk to you.'

'And who put them up to that?'

Arnold hesitated. 'I think it was Miss Stannard who started it, in the first place. She had some idea you were under pressure from Alan Crickley. The journalist who was killed.'

'That bitch! She had it in for me, right from the beginning. I didn't fit, you see. She couldn't work me out. And she resented not knowing about me. As for Crickley . . . there was pressure all right! But why do the police want to see me?'

'I told you — I don't know.' Something moved in the darkness behind Arnold, the sound of a rat scurrying among the stones, perhaps. His scalp prickled, and he shook his head. 'I'm sure they discounted Karen Stannard's story. But you didn't help things by disappearing.'

'I had to get away. I needed time to think.' He paused, and the silence grew around them. She thinks I killed Crickley.'

'She didn't convince the police of that.'

'But they came back. They came to see you. They wanted to know where I was.'

Reluctantly, Arnold nodded. 'They did, but your running away will have raised their suspicions—'

'What the hell else would you have expected me to do?' Kirkby's voice thickened with anger. 'You don't understand, Landon.'

'No. I don't,' he replied shortly.

Kirkby began to mutter, almost to himself. 'I've kept my head down, minded my own business, stayed away from people, exercised caution. And people left me alone. They didn't care. You . . . you were different. We spent time together. You accepted me for what I am — you asked no questions. I began to feel I could talk to you. Then Crickley called me.' His voice grew louder. 'I told you he contacted me.'

'Yes.'

'I knew there was a problem, the first time we met — when you introduced us. He thought he knew me . . . I didn't want to talk to him. But it didn't make much difference. I knew in the end he had worked it out for himself. He laughed, when he spoke to me on the phone. If I didn't agree to see him, talk about it all, he'd go ahead anyway. I didn't know what to do.'

'Talk about what?' Arnold asked, puzzled. 'Why did Crickley want to see you? What was he going to go ahead with?'

Kirkby shifted himself away from the embrasure. He stepped forward towards Arnold, and there was an intensity about his movement that caused the skin to prickle on Arnold's neck again. Kirkby sounded odd, almost unbalanced, a tinge of hysteria in his voice. Arnold put one hand out against the wall to his left, almost to brace himself.

'Crickley had recognized me. Maybe from an old photograph — I don't know. They'd covered my tracks, I thought I was safe, but Crickley knew me.'

'Who covered your tracks?' Arnold asked, frowning.

'The police. The Home Office. The faceless mandarins who didn't give a bugger, really, but wanted to save their own reputation, cover their own backs.'

Arnold shook his head. 'You've lost me. Why would the police and the Home Office cover your tracks? What the hell's been going on?'

Suddenly, Kirkby sounded weary. 'It's a long story. But my name isn't really Kirkby. It's Ford.' He paused, as though expecting the name to have significance for Arnold.

'Simon Ford.'

'So?'

Kirkby expelled his breath softly, as though in pain. 'I . . . I was a teacher, in the West Midlands. I was accused of a crime . . . a murder. It was a young girl at the school — Annette Wentbridge. Rape, and murder, they said.'

Arnold's mouth was dry. He had a vague recollection of the case.

'I was charged,' Kirkby went on, 'and the pathologist was a man called O'Connor. He had a mission in life. To root out the guilty, to put them away. Even if it meant manufacturing evidence. His evidence sent me into hell.' His voice took on a harsh, brutal note. 'You don't know what it's like, Landon — you can't imagine what it's like. To be convicted of something you didn't do . . . to be imprisoned. But more than that. Do you know how they treat rapists and killers of young girls in prison? It's not just the prison officers. It's the other inmates. There's a sort of code — and rapists, child killers, don't fall within the pale. I was badly beaten, several times. They had to isolate me, for my own protection. And it wasn't just the beatings . . . they did other things to me.'

Arnold had heard life in prison for a child killer could be the hell that Kirkby described. 'You say you didn't do it,' he said quietly.

'I was innocent. I knew the girl, of course — I taught her. But I swore to them it wasn't me . . . O'Connor's evidence said otherwise. So to prison I went. But then . . . James Thornton started his campaigns, and he finally discredited O'Connor. The cases in which O'Connor had given evidence were overturned on appeal. Unsafe convictions, they said. Not that I was innocent — just that the conviction was unsafe. They released me. They paid me money. They gave me a new identity.'

The room was silent except for the harsh breathing of the two men.

'I went away for some months . . . Southeast Asia,' Kirkby continued. 'But when I came back I had to face life again. I needed a job; I needed to live among people, not in isolation. I had money, but I wanted an . . . identity, you know?'

Arnold nodded. He thought he understood. 'They found you a job in Morpeth?'

The Home Office arranged it. All very secret: they liked that, those faceless men. And I chose Morpeth because it was where James Thornton had lived — in the north-east. I owed my freedom to him, and somehow, I wanted to be close to where he had lived. It sort of gave me a feeling of security. I owed him a lot. I never met him, oddly enough. He died before I came to Morpeth. But it was something . . . I felt safer, you understand, to be close to where he had lived.'

Kirkby suddenly began to laugh. It was a quiet sound at first, then it grew in intensity, became almost hysterical.

'What's the matter?' Arnold asked, stepping nearer in concern.

'It's the irony of it,' Kirkby gasped. 'James Thornton had saved me — and I came north for some stupid reason, some belief I would get peace being where he had been. But in fact it was the least safe place in England. For Crickley was here. And Crickley wanted to destroy me.'

'But why?'

'He realized who I was.'

'But why should he want to expose you?'

'He was a journalist. Maybe that would have been enough. But there was more,' Kirkby giggled unpleasantly. 'He told me, when he said he'd recognized me. He had a reason, all right. His relationship with James Thornton.'

'I don't understand.'

'Crickley was Thornton's adopted son. And he hated Thornton's guts — I don't know why. Thornton was dead, but Crickley still hated him — and anything he could do to damage his reputation, or the good work he had done . . . If he could show that one of Thornton's *monsters* had come to live in the north-east . . . if he could undo Thornton's work . . . As for me, I meant nothing to Crickley, I was just a means to an end, and he was going to tell the world who I really was—'

'So you killed him?' Arnold asked softly.

There was a short silence. 'Is that what you think?'

'I don't know. But the police are looking for you.'

'Give a dog a bad name,' Kirkby snarled. 'That's what it's about. Oh, they paid me compensation, found me a new name, gave me a new identity — but they hated it. It was like admitting their mistake. But if they could pin Crickley's murder on me now — it would be so easy, wouldn't it? It would show they'd been right all along. They'd be able to trumpet it. I always was a killer — if I killed Crickley, I probably really did kill Annette Wentbridge as well, all those years ago! That's the way they'd see it!'

Arnold was silent for a while. Then, in a quiet tone, he said, 'There's no way you can avoid them forever. They're bound to trace you eventually. You asked me to meet you here—'

'To talk. To explain. I feel I can trust you, and you'll understand—'

'*Did* you kill Crickley?'

There was a short silence. Kirkby cleared his throat. 'I swear to you I've never killed anyone.'

'Then speak to the police. Come down with me, we'll go to them, I'll help you all I can. If you didn't kill Crickley—'

'I didn't kill Annette Wentbridge, but they imprisoned me for it!'

'That was because of O'Connor,' Arnold urged. 'It will be different now. Come down with me tonight — we'll go to the police—'

There was the sudden sound of a stone turning underfoot behind him in the darkness. For a brief moment everything seemed to stand still, and the silence swept around them again, but with an added, sharp menace. Next moment Syl Kirkby snarled, leaping forward in a sudden rage. 'You said you'd come alone! You conned me!'

He cannoned into Arnold, knocking him sideways with one wild, sweeping blow, shouting at him. 'You bastard! You brought the police up here with you!'

He had his hands scrabbling at Arnold's throat, tearing crazily at him, and Arnold pushed him away, falling backwards in the process, crashing into a half-sitting position. Kirkby thrust past him, shouting maniacally, and ran towards the broken entrance. As he reached it there was a sudden blur of movement; dragging himself to his feet, Arnold was aware of another man blocking the entrance, arms out to stop Kirkby and then the two men were struggling together in the doorway. Angry that he had been followed by the police Arnold pulled himself upright, and shouted.

'Stop it! Wait!'

The two figures whirled away in the darkness, into the courtyard beyond. Arnold limped awkwardly across the broken floor after them, and heard the sound of running feet, scrambling over the littered steps. He hurried through the entrance, reached the courtyard and gained a brief impression of someone rising from the ground to his left before a heavy blow took him on the side of the head. He went down, senses spinning, and was on his knees when the kick came in, doubling him up, and driving every ounce of breath from his lungs. He knelt on the stone, rubble biting into his knees, unable to move as he struggled for breath, chest heaving, lungs fighting for air. He began to retch and he was dizzy, a violent singing growing louder in his head.

He seemed to be there for an age.

There was a confusion of noise about him, echoing calls and falling stone, the crash of feet, the flailing of arms and legs and the harsh breathing of two men struggling. It seemed to fade away into the distance, only to return again, echoes dancing against the half-built roof, the skittering sound of alarmed night life as two men fought in the darkness.

Still dizzy, Arnold put his hand up to his forehead. He felt the warm stickiness of blood and he rose, standing unsteadily, his stomach heaving, lungs painfully inflating. He reached out with one hand for the wall. He began to walk, staggering forward, his brain spinning, but he had lost his sense of direction. He lurched painfully back into the room he had left, the sickness welling in his throat as his head throbbed madly. He needed air, and he became aware of the embrasure where Kirkby had been standing, when they had talked together in the darkness. He headed for it, his hand groping forward in the dimness but his vision was blurred, his senses awry, and as he reached the embrasure he lost his footing.

There was one heart-stopping moment when his hand touched nothing but air, and then he was falling forward, off balance, outwards through the broken embrasure, down into nothing. He crashed through breaking branches that tore at his face and sent him lurching sideways. He felt a blow on his shoulder and he rolled. Something struck him hard in the chest, and the breath was driven out of his body again. Afterwards, he seemed to be aware of nothing but a vast area of pain until slowly a blackness descended upon him and he lay still, with the fine, damp mist gathering on his face.

The crag was silent.

Gradually, Arnold became aware of his surroundings once more. He opened his eyes but he could see very little in the misty darkness. He explored the ground with hesitant fingers. He seemed to be lying on a hard outcrop of rock: above him he could make out the faint, grim outline of the walls of the folly, the dark snapped branches of the tree that had broken his fall and the gaping window some fifteen feet above him. He tried to move, gingerly, and pain swept through his ribs and stomach, but as far as he was aware there were no broken bones. He had been lucky: his head throbbed unmercifully, but he was alive in spite of the fall. He could easily have received a broken neck, had it not been for the scrawny tree growing from the base of the wall and half shielding him now from the embrasure itself.

But the silence was heavy about him.

Where was Kirkby? Arnold shifted slightly, moaning as he did so. If the police had followed him up here . . . but he hadn't told them he was coming up to Ridge Hall. But there had been sounds among the trees behind him as he climbed — he had thought it was merely the passage of nocturnal animals he had disturbed — now he knew it had been someone following him. But how did the police know where he was going? He lay there, puzzling at it.

Then he thought of Jane. He had told her. She would have been worried about him. She didn't approve of his coming here to meet Kirkby alone. She would have told Culpeper.

That was it. It was typical of her — worried mother hen syndrome. He grimaced, managed a rueful smile. By sending the police up here after him, she had in fact put Arnold in the state he was in.

He became aware of the silence again, and his mind cleared.

If it had been one of Culpeper's men in the folly, he might possibly have attacked Arnold by mistake in the darkness, as Kirkby fled . . . but why the silence now? What had happened to Kirkby . . . and why were the police not looking for Arnold with flashlights?

They knew he was here, if Jane had told them.

There was a movement in the embrasure. Arnold squinted painfully upwards, peering at the darkness of the gaping window, through the broken branches of the tree. He was sure he had seen a movement, and he opened his mouth to call for help, but then his tongue clove to the roof of his mouth. His lips were suddenly dry. There was a man standing in the embrasure, leaning out, staring down over the crag. But there was no flashlight, and there was a stealthiness, a catlike caution, about the man's stance that dried up the words in Arnold's mouth.

It was not one of Culpeper's men.

It could not be. A policeman would have been flashing a light, calling out — not behaving like a thief in the night. The man in the embrasure was looking for something . . . or someone.

Arnold lay still, aware of the thunder in his veins. He recalled the blow he had taken in the courtyard; the vague sounds of shouting, struggling, two men fighting for life. But now, silence, and the head and shoulders of a man watching, searching, quietly and carefully in the darkness. Arnold remained motionless, his fingers gripping the hard stone convulsively, until in a little while the mist became thicker, the dampness turned to a light drizzle and the embrasure and the walls of Ridge Hall faded into a vague, extensive darkness.

* * *

Arnold had no way of knowing how long he lay there.

The drizzle grew heavier and he began to feel wet and cold. A violent, spasmodic shivering struck him. Injured as he was, he could possibly die of exposure if he continued to lie here. But his mind wandered, decision slipped past him, shimmering away in the darkness. At last, after what seemed to be an age, he pulled himself together mentally: he would have to take his chance with the man in the folly above him.

Slowly he rose to his feet, pain tearing at his chest and stomach. He revised his opinion about broken bones: the stabbing pain in his chest suggested otherwise. Breathing was difficult and movement necessarily slow, but carefully, step by agonized step, he negotiated the crag until he reached the wall of the folly itself. The precipice was behind him; he calculated that if he kept moving left he would find himself at the eastern side of the courtyard wall, away from the main entrance, and hidden in the mist from any watcher up above.

If the man was still there.

He moved as silently as possible, careful that no stones were disturbed, moving step by step around the edge of the broken walls of William Ridge's folly. When he reached the end of the courtyard wall he paused, thinking. It was too dangerous to head across past the main entrance: his best chance lay in the woods that cloaked the crag. Painfully he made his way across the narrow clearing until he reached the wet shadow of the trees, and then the water showered down on him from the laden branches, but he pushed through, and down the hill, away from the track, but moving parallel with it over the broken ground, whipped in the face by low, rain-soaked branches.

He was nearing the plateau where he and Kirkby had paused to look at the view and take their breath, ages ago, when he saw the lights.

There were several of them, flickering and dancing among the trees, moving surely up the slope and along the track. He heard the murmur of voices. There was something reassuring about the sound, a lack of menace in the progress the flashlights were making, climbing carefully up the hill towards the folly.

He tried to call out but his voice was a croak. He staggered out of the trees, and fell to his knees. It was there that they found him a few minutes later, kneeling on the track, clutching his ribs. He heard Culpeper's voice, and then there were several burly men around him, lifting him to his feet, assisting him gently down the track, half carrying him as he staggered along over the rough ground.

He could see an assortment of cars parked near his own, at the foot of the hill — some with flashing lights — and he could hear the crackle of police radios. Jane was standing beside one of the cars: she came forward with gentle hands to help him into the back seat, even if her tone lacked sympathy.

'We've got to get you to a hospital,' she said snappishly, 'you stubborn fool!'

He put his head back uncaringly, and as the driver opened the door of the police car parked alongside its interior light came on. Arnold glanced across. Staring at him from the back seat of the police car was a sullen-eyed Bill Norman.

4

'You look an absolute mess,' Jane Wilson announced.

He knew it. Facial lacerations where the branches had broken his fall from the embrasure, a broken rib, and a badly bruised stomach and pelvis made him feel extremely sorry for himself and it was reflected in his face. He glanced sideways: Detective Chief Inspector Culpeper was sitting there, with a quizzical air. 'You feeling all right?'

'I've felt better.'

'You'd have been feeling worse, if it hadn't been for Miss Wilson.'

Arnold scowled at her. 'You told the police about my meeting with Syl Kirkby.'

She nodded firmly. 'It was clear *you* weren't going to tell them. And I thought it unwise for you to meet Kirkby alone.' Arnold frowned and turned his head to stare at Culpeper. 'I saw no sign of the police.'

'Miss Wilson told us you'd arranged to meet Kirkby after the trustee meeting. But you finished earlier than we expected: you'd gone by the time we arrived at Ridgeway Manor. Of course,' he added grimly, 'if she'd told us sooner, or not insisted on showing us personally where the meeting place was . . .'

Jane folded her arms and stared him down. 'I was breaking a confidence; I wasn't easy about it, and I wanted to be there when you faced Arnold.'

'Anyway,' Culpeper continued after a moment, 'when we arrived at the foot of the crag we saw your car, and another. That's when I called for back-up. I assumed the cars were yours and Kirkby's.'

'No,' Arnold said. 'I think he'd come to the crag from the western entrance, and parked somewhere down there.'

Culpeper nodded. 'We've found his car, half hidden among the trees. Anyway, when I saw the two cars I wasn't sure what to do. I called for back-up and then decided to wait till they arrived. We might have missed you both coming down in the darkness. Then, to our surprise a somewhat dishevelled Bill Norman appeared out of the trees, just before the other police vehicles arrived. He wasn't pleased to see us. And he'd clearly been in a fight.'

Arnold's mouth was suddenly dry. There was something they were both skirting around. 'What happened to Syl Kirkby?'

There was a short silence. Jane glanced at Culpeper, who shook his head. 'We found him a little while ago. We'd been searching all night. He was halfway down the crag, among the trees. He'd been beaten . . . and his neck was broken.'

A stab of pain shot through Arnold's chest as he struggled to ease himself upwards. 'How the hell did that happen? What's been going on?'

Culpeper hesitated. 'When you closed the trustee meeting you left some angry men behind you. None more so than a furious Bill Norman. We've heard since that Peter Gaul saw you leave, and saw Norman follow you also.'

'But why would Norman follow me?'

'He was mad as hell, he wanted to have it out with you. You were derailing his future, by refusing to sign that conveyance. Then, I guess, he got curious when you headed for the folly — so he went quietly up behind you.'

Miserably, Arnold nodded. 'I thought I heard sounds behind me — and at the folly itself.'

'He was there all right,' Culpeper said grimly. 'He must have overheard your conversation with Kirkby — and took his chance. He beat Kirkby, threw him off the crag—'

'And would have killed you, too,' Jane said reprovingly.

'But *why?'*

'He realized, from your conversation, that we suspected Kirkby of Crickley's murder. He thought it would be a neat solution — kill Kirkby and hope the police would close the file on Crickley. It could work, he reasoned, if you died too — who would then know what had gone on up on the crag? A clandestine meeting, a fight between you, both of you dying from a fall? But clearly, after he had beaten Kirkby to death, he couldn't find you on the crag. So he thought he'd better get back to his car while he could.'

'But Norman had no reason to kill me!' Arnold argued.

'*He* thought he did.'

'What reason?'

'The same one that motivated him to bash in Alan Crickley's head.'

Arnold felt a throbbing begin in his temples. He was confused. 'I don't understand what the hell's been going on.'

Culpeper grunted. 'And yet you were a catalyst, to some extent. We've interviewed David Hall, and Hertford, as well as Norman and Frimley. I tell you, there's a real panic on now — neither Hall nor Hertford fancy being hauled in on a charge of being accessories to murder. So they're telling the whole story. Frimley's got nothing to give us — he was in the dark, a makeweight. But the other two — they're singing like skylarks on a summer's day.'

'What about?'

Culpeper smiled. 'What's been going on the last few years. Your suspicious solicitor friend, Harcourt-Fanshaw, he got some of it right. It all started when Hertford and David Hall used their influence on a muddled old lady.'

'Amelia Ridge?'

'Ahuh. Hertford swears he didn't really know what was going on, but he certainly went along with it. Hall persuaded Miss Ridge the best way to sort out her affairs would be to transfer a large part of her estate to a Jersey-based company, with the assurance that it would be used to support the Viking Research Trust in due course.'

'The half-secret trust.'

'If you say so.' Culpeper blinked. 'Hall brought Norman into the company as a co-director, with some Jersey nominees. Hall, Hertford and Norman knew the details of the half-secret trust. Hertford . . . he now swears he was bamboozled, but I think he was happy to go along on Hall's coat tails. He admired his financial wheeler-dealing.'

'Sufficient to nominate him for an honour,' Arnold added sourly.

'Well, that's something Hall can kiss goodbye to, that's for sure,' Culpeper said. 'Anyway, that's how it started. But Harcourt-Fanshaw also put us on to something else he'd sniffed out. Hall's company — Wheeler Holdings — went through a rough patch. The shares plunged. Hall needed financial support, so he got Hertford and Norman to buy shares in Wheeler Holdings in an attempt to push up the price.'

'But neither had much money,' Arnold protested. 'Norman, I understand, wasn't rich, and Hertford's wife held their purse strings.'

'But there were assets lying around,' Culpeper said gravely. 'In the Jersey company. They used those assets — Ridgeway land — to raise money to support the Wheeler share price.'

'That's breach of trust,' Jane Wilson suggested.

'Too right. Money that should have been used to support the charitable objectives Amelia Ridge had desired. Of course, the money was paid back in eventually — once the Wheeler shares rose — and our three cavaliers had even made a small profit. But Hall knew that if the dealings were exposed there could be trouble.'

'And they *could* be in trouble,' Arnold agreed thoughtfully, 'with the Viking Research Trust staggering financially and Harcourt-Fanshaw snapping at their heels.'

'But by then, Hall had something else in mind, anyway.' Culpeper glanced at Arnold with a raised eyebrow.

'The mining application,' Arnold said, after a little while.

'Exactly. When Hall got established as chairman of the Viking Research Trust — and was controlling Ridge assets through the Jersey company — he discovered the existence of the old Mountjoy Survey. He got a co-director to put in an application, but then realized the main veins ran through Ridgeway Manor land as well as the land held by the Jersey company. Since the manor was held by the Viking Research Trust, Hall decided to kill two birds with one stone. First, get hold of Ridgeway Manor to link it with the farm property and second, avoid any criticism that might arise if the half-secret trust was exposed, by making sure that the Jersey company made a significant donation to the Viking Research Trust.'

'In other words, he was appearing to fulfil Amelia Ridge's wishes,' Arnold agreed. 'And was Norman in on this?'

'An enthusiastic supporter. Because he was getting cut in. Both he and Hertford paid back the money they'd gained in the Wheeler Holdings support operation, with the promise that there'd be plenty of money to come once they could get the planning application for tungsten mining through, and exploit the whole site. A juicy financial future beckoned.'

Jane Wilson frowned and looked at Culpeper carefully. 'So where did it all start to go wrong?'

Culpeper shrugged. 'The suspicious Harcourt-Fanshaw had always been a thorn in their side. But it was worse when Alan Crickley got involved. Egged on by Harcourt-Fanshaw he did some digging: he had some suspicions about the undue influence, and maybe the share support fraud but, more important, he turned up the Mountjoy Survey.' Ruefully, Culpeper pursed his lips. 'We found his notes — there was a sketch map — two blocks, one designating the farm, the other the manor. And some geological notes. We didn't work out its significance at the time.'

'So what did Crickley do about it?' Arnold asked.

'The gospel according to David Hall,' Culpeper announced sarcastically, 'is that Crickley arranged to meet said Hall at Ridgeway Manor, to discuss things. But he never turned up.'

'And you *believe* that?'

Culpeper shrugged. 'In part. I think the arrangement was made, but Crickley was intercepted, maybe in the car park. The idea was that Norman would try to talk to him first, use the old mates' argument, to persuade him to back off. But, I guess, Crickley wasn't having any — old mates they might have been but this was journalism! And Norman . . . well, he always did have a short fuse. I remember seeing him kick that Aussie in the head at the Northern ground years ago .. .'

'Norman killed Crickley,' Jane said flatly.

'Ahuh. Crickley wouldn't listen to reason, turned his back to walk away, Norman saw red, picked up a handy piece of iron piping, and . . . that was it. End of argument. There was a panic afterwards, of course — Norman bundled the body into Crickley's own car and drove him away from the manor, slewed the car into the hedge, then dragged Crickley's body to the field, hid him in the copse. Then he walked quietly back to Ridgeway Manor.'

'And Hall didn't inquire what had happened?'

Culpeper smiled. 'So he says. His story is that when Crickley didn't turn up, he thought nothing of it. And he swears he'd never linked the killing to Bill Norman. He reckons Norman told him Crickley didn't show. But then, like our friend Sir Jock Hertford, these guys just see and hear what they want to, what suits them. But at least Hertford and Hall have now been panicked into coming clean on the whole financial skulduggery over Amelia Ridge's bequests.'

'So I was right not to sign that conveyance,' Arnold murmured thoughtfully.

'Maybe,' Culpeper conceded. 'Though it triggered Norman to attack you. If that conveyance didn't go through he was back where he was before he killed Crickley. No prospects of a great flush of money coming in, maybe no job with Wheeler Holdings . . . So it depends how you look at things.'

'What will you do about the conveyance now?' Jane asked. Arnold thought about it for a little while. 'I suppose the first thing to do is to reform the board of trustees. Take advice about the Jersey company — because Hall has clearly been in breach of trust, and it seems to me the whole of Amelia Ridge's assets should be made available . . . though it may well take a court action.'

'Somehow, I can't imagine Amelia Ridge would have wanted tungsten mining on the estate,' Jane suggested.

'I'm damn sure she wouldn't,' Arnold agreed. 'Anyway, the Viking Research Trust could be in for a very large windfall, it seems to me. And we'll need to look again at what Miss Ridge originally wanted — the money in Jersey could probably cover all the wishes she expressed in her memorandum . . . Hall's in real trouble, then?' he asked Culpeper.

'No doubt. He's talking freely, to avoid being tied in with Norman. But at the least, we'll get Hall on fraud, breach of trust, unlawfully supporting shares in his own company through nominees . . . yes, he's in trouble, even if we don't make the accessory to murder charge stick. Hertford too . . . though he'll probably get away with most of it by pleading ignorance, and hauling in his upper-crust friends to swear by him.' Culpeper sniffed. 'He can be quite convincing when he explains he's rather . . . thick.'

'And Norman?'

'His world's collapsed. He's confessed to killing Crickley and we had him to rights when he came down from the crag. He'd clearly been in a fight, scratched, bruised . . . Kirkby wasn't a big man, but he must have known he was fighting for his life . . .' Culpeper sighed, and stood up. 'Anyway, I only really called in to see you're all right. I've got work to do: got to tie all these ends up for the chief constable . . . You take care now, Landon — and watch out for Miss Stannard!'

After he had gone, Arnold lay back and closed his eyes. He was silent for a while.

'You'll need to rest for a few weeks, Arnold,' Jane said.

That would leave Karen Stannard happy, he thought. 'I'll take some leave.'

'To take it easy?' she queried suspiciously.

Arnold's words were a little slurred, dreamy. 'Maybe I'll go up and help Dr Williams at the grave site . . . when she opens up the badger setts . . .'

'As long as you don't overdo it,' Jane said severely. She sat watching him for a while, until he began to snore slightly. Only then, when she was certain he had gone to sleep did she quietly leave the room.

5

The stiff breeze sent white and grey clouds scudding over the hills but the workers in the trench were unaffected by it; the intermittent hot sunshine called for shirtsleeves and jeans or shorts as the volunteers patiently scraped and brushed away at the friable earth, painstakingly following the lines of darker soil that denoted the existence of ancient, decayed timber.

Arnold had spent two weeks at the site and he had been proved right: once they had begun removing the topsoil around the old badger setts it was clear his guess had been accurate — the field centre in the valley held a Viking boat burial. Now, small yellow pegs marked the location of the iron rivets that had been collected — two hundred already and the steady curve of the peg line demonstrated the shape of the keel, as it had been laid to rest a thousand years before.

Rena Williams stood with her arms folded across her chest, looking down on the excavation. The badger setts had been demolished during the last few weeks and the earth piled to one side. The badgers had inevitably caused some destruction years before, during their sojourn at the site, but almost two-thirds of the boat had survived in its decayed form.

The boat had been about six metres long, divided into compartments. Arnold had been present when the first signs of the keel had appeared and had shared in the excitement of the whole team when the first significant find was made, a decayed leather quiver full of arrows, which had probably been accompanied originally by a bow. Time, and badger disturbance, had destroyed the remains of the bow, but it was clear that this was a true boat burial and there would be more to find.

It had been an exciting time, and Arnold had been grateful to Dr Williams for the opportunity to be present.

He told her so now, again, as he stood beside her on the lip of the trench.

She shrugged, and smiled. 'If it hadn't been for you, we might not have carried on with the dig at all. The extra commitment of money from the Trust has made all the difference. And certainly we probably wouldn't have bothered with this area, not where the badgers had made their homes. So, as far as gratitude is concerned, well . . . it's why I rang you, to suggest you came up to the site this weekend.'

'You suggested it might be interesting.'

She pointed to the area covered by tarpaulin, silently.

'What have you found there?' Arnold asked.

She led the way around the edge of the boat-trench and crouched above the tarpaulin. She took its corner in one hand and lifted it, exposing the dark earth underneath. But there was more than dark earth.

Arnold felt something move in his throat, a suppressed feeling of excitement. He stared down into the trench. Lying in a somewhat scattered heap was a pile of human bones.

Rena Williams looked at him, unrestrained pleasure in her eyes. 'We uncovered them late last night. I thought you deserved to be here when we progressed. You want to lend a hand this weekend?'

Arnold was quick to agree.

They spent the next two days carefully sifting away the earth. On Sunday, Jane came along also, to enjoy the tremors of excitement that constantly ran around the site.

For it was now obvious that Arnold had not only been right about the boat burial — it was also clear that the site was of some importance. Within hours of starting work around the bones they came across other finds. The original bones were probably those of a male of some status and significance in his community. The remains had been scattered by badgers digging out their home, but alongside them, they quickly discovered another series, lying neatly in place as they had been deposited: the bones of a child.

Further down the site other artefacts were coming to light: an iron sickle, an equal-armed Norwegian brooch, pins and ornaments, a horned axe-blade, the iron boss of a shield. But it was on the Sunday morning, shortly after Jane arrived, that they made a further important discovery.

'I didn't realize you used golf tees to mark the line of the boat,' Jane commented, standing at the lip of the trench.

Rena Williams squinted up to her and smiled. 'And we're running out of our supply. The local golf club is already up in arms. We've taken up all the stock in the shop. But, in my view, it's putting them to a better use than supporting golf balls to be smacked down the fairway.'

'You'll need some to mark that dark area there,' Jane said. Arnold turned and stared at the staining she pointed to. Standing some feet above them on the edge of the trench she had picked it out more easily than they. Arnold leant over it and used a small trowel to dig carefully at the earth. He brushed away the fine soil, rapidly outlining a long, narrowing shape. His breathing grew suddenly ragged, and he straightened to look at Rena Williams.

'It's a wooden scabbard. It's been partly preserved by corrosion.'

'Corrosion?' Jane asked, puzzled.

'Iron corrosion.' Rena Williams explained in a tone overlaid with unprofessional excitement. 'There'll be a sword there . . . look, there's the haft.'

By the late afternoon it lay in their hands, a fine sword, its scabbard only partly preserved, but the iron haft still in sound condition, inset with semi-precious stones, the bone guard still intact. Its long tapering blade was some ninety centimetres in length, the tip rounded, for it was a slashing weapon. Two-edged like most Viking swords, it had been pattern-welded, with the typical shallow, round-bottomed channel running down the middle of the blade on either side, designed to make the sword lighter.

And just below the bone guard there was a runic inscription.

Rena Williams peered at it, ran her fingers lightly over the metal, brushing away remaining fragments of soil. Slowly she spelled out the runes, first in an undertone to herself, and then aloud, wonderingly.

'*Kvernbitr.* '

'Do you know what it means?' Arnold asked, after a short silence.

'*Kvernbitr* . . . '

'Is it important?'

'Important? I can't really believe it . . . it's hardly possible!'

'What are you talking about?'

'A weapon gained in value and virtue as it grew older.' Dr Williams announced, her face radiant with excitement. 'It was often buried with its owner, but if it was of special significance it was sometimes handed on within the family. I'd thought this sword would help us date the burial, maybe even get the name of the man who was buried here . . . Man and child. But *Kvernbitr* . . . it means quern-biter. And there was a legend that the best sword that ever came to Norway was one that cut a quern stone to its centre. *Kvernbitr* . . . the sword given by King Athelstan of England to Hakon Haraldsson, King of Norway!'

'Are you suggesting -?'

'No, no,' she interrupted fussily, 'this isn't Hakon's grave, but his sword would have been passed on and whoever was buried here, with this weapon, was an important man, of royal blood, perhaps the last of his line with his young son! Do you understand, Arnold? This is a marvellous find, and it'll give rise to a hundred academic theses, as to how the sword came here, and who the man and child might be — and it'll be the making of this site in terms of historical significance . . .'

The light was dying as they clambered out of the trench.

Mugs of coffee were waiting for them in the hut, and they stood there silently for a while — Dr Williams, Arnold and Jane.

'This is quite a coup for you, Arnold.' Dr Williams said quietly, staring at the sword as it lay on the table in front of them.

'I don't see it that way. I just made a guess about the boat burial. It was luck—'

'Maybe. But that's something Karen Stannard argued you possess a great deal of,' Rena Williams replied, smiling. 'And it makes me wonder . . .'

'About what?'

'I get the impression she . . . is not too happy having you working with her.'

Arnold shrugged, noncommittally. Annoyed at his lack of response, Jane dug him painfully with her elbow.

'She might be prepared to second you.' Rena Williams suggested thoughtfully, 'for a little while, at least. Not to this site, because the main work has been done. From now on, it will be collating, identifying — lab work, really. But you seem to have a flair, and I . . . I have a site.'

'You're suggesting I work with you?' Arnold asked doubtfully.

'There are signs it could be a Celtic, Iron Age site of some importance. You could be of real assistance.'

'Miss Stannard would never agree.'

'I'm not so sure.' Rena Williams eyed him, ironically. 'You must surely have noticed how her personality . . . changes, when she talks to me? I'm afraid she is in awe of . . . ah . . . my reputation. Anyway, we'll see. Leave it to me.' Her mouth lifted at the corners. 'I presume you would like to do some more intensive field work?'

'Do you really need me to answer that?' Arnold replied, grinning.

They finished their coffee, and went back in the gathering gloom to look down at the open boat site, where a warrior, and perhaps his son, had been laid to rest together, with the arms he had used with distinction during his life. But Arnold's thoughts drifted after a while, away from the long-buried bones, and the mystery of the Viking warrior interred here with his weapons in the valley. Jane, always conscious of his moods, glanced at him.

'What are you thinking about?' she asked.

It was not something he could really put into words, even to her.

He was thinking not about a long-dead Viking chieftain but about the man who had died on the crag above. The man in the boat grave had been a warrior, a man of violence in a violent world, but Simon Ford — the man Arnold had known as Syl Kirkby — had never done anyone any harm. Yet his life had been destroyed, first by the pathologist O'Connor in the West Midlands and then by the journalist Crickley. His new identity had not saved him, and had even contributed in a way to his death at the hands of Bill Norman.

The Viking warrior had died in his prime and had slumbered for a thousand years. Now he would come alive again, in a sense — his life, his identity, discussed and debated and pondered over. But for Syl Kirkby, it would be different. Arnold could now guess what Kirkby had meant when he had described himself as a ghost, that evening he had got drunk at the King's Head. Insubstantial, unimportant, without roots, in limbo without a real identity — an unreal person in almost every way . . . a ghost.

And he had even been prophetic in what he'd said. A short-lived ghost.

THE END

ALSO BY ROY LEWIS

ERIC WARD MYSTERIES

Book 1: THE SEDLEIGH HALL MURDER
Book 2: THE FARMING MURDER
Book 3: THE QUAYSIDE MURDER
Book 4: THE DIAMOND MURDER
Book 5: THE GEORDIE MURDER
Book 6: THE SHIPPING MURDER
Book 7: THE CITY OF LONDON MURDER
Book 8: THE APARTMENT MURDER
Book 9: THE SPANISH VILLA MURDER
Book 10: THE MARRIAGE MURDER
Book 11: THE WASTEFUL MURDER
Book 12: THE PHANTOM MURDER
Book 13: THE SLAUGHTERHOUSE MURDER
Book 14: THE TATTOO MURDER
Book 15: THE FOOTBALL MURDER
Book 16: THE TUTANKHAMUN MURDER
Book 17: THE ZODIAC MURDER

INSPECTOR JOHN CROW

Book 1: A LOVER TOO MANY
Book 2: ERROR OF JUDGMENT
Book 3: THE WOODS MURDER
Book 4: MURDER FOR MONEY
Book 5: MURDER IN THE MINE
Book 6: A COTSWOLDS MURDER
Book 7: A FOX HUNTING MURDER
Book 8: A DARTMOOR MURDER

ARNOLD LANDON MYSTERIES

Book 1: MURDER IN THE BARN
Book 2: MURDER IN THE MANOR
Book 3: MURDER IN THE FARMHOUSE

Book 4: MURDER IN THE STABLE YARD
Book 5: MURDER IN THE CHURCH
Book 6: MURDER IN THE HOUSE
Book 7: MURDER IN THE TOWER
Book 8: MURDER UNDER THE BRIDGE
Book 9: MURDER BY THE QUAY
Book 10: MURDER AT THE FOLLY

Thank you for reading this book.

If you enjoyed it please leave feedback on Amazon or Goodreads, and if there is anything we missed or you have a question about, then please get in touch. We appreciate you choosing our book.

Founded in 2014 in Shoreditch, London, we at Joffe Books pride ourselves on our history of innovative publishing. We were thrilled to be shortlisted for Independent Publisher of the Year at the British Book Awards.

www.joffebooks.com

We're very grateful to eagle-eyed readers who take the time to contact us. Please send any errors you find to corrections@joffebooks.com. We'll get them fixed ASAP.

Printed in Great Britain
by Amazon

44499422R00142